Lock Down Publications and Ca$h Presents

DYIN' TO GET RICH

BY ANY MEANS

Written By
CHRISTOPHER "DIESEL" HORNEZES

First Edition 2026

Printed in the United States of America

This is a work of fiction. Names, characters, places, and incidents either are products of the author's imagination or are used fictitiously. Any similarity to actual events or locales or persons, living or dead, is entirely coincidental.

Lock Down Publications
P.O. Box 944
Stockbridge, GA 30281
www.lockdownpublications.com

Like our page on Facebook: Lock Down Publications
www.facebook.com/lockdownpublications.ldp

Stay Connected with Us!

Text **LOCKDOWN** to 22828 to stay up-to-date with new releases, sneak peaks, contests and more…

Like our page on Facebook:
Lock Down Publications

Join Lock Down Publications/The New Era Reading Group

Visit our website:
www.lockdownpublications.com

Follow us on Instagram:
Lock Down Publications

Email Us: We want to hear from you!

ACKNOWLEDGEMENTS

What's good, all? Please allow me to speak real to you all real quick. I struggled so incredibly hard during the creation of this novel. Ca$h told me that "the strength of a man is how he reacts during adversity. Things aren't always going to go your way or go as planned. You can't let it derail you." I do agree, but sometimes, I ask myself, how much adversity am I supposed to endure? So, I channel my frustrations into these books, and I turn negatives into positives. At the end of the day, I am providing entertainment for people all around the world that want it. I have to look at the good things, not the bad.

I thank the man above for blessing me like he has been. I thank Ca$h for taking the time to talk to me as a person, not just an author. I thank ALL of you who are buying my books and enjoy them then anxious to see what else I got.

To my homies Chino, Snoop, Dre, Lil' Tony, I thank y'all from the bottom of my heart for all the selfless help you all contributed to help me keep it together while I'm writing.

To Mattie. Yo, you drive me insane. But I love and admire your aspirations, and how you are building your life, all on your own. To my fans, and new readers, I'm open if you want to reach out for whatever reason. You can write to me by letter, or via Text Behind app, of which you will have to download and ask me to rap.

Christopher Hornezes# 7049756

Racine Correctional Institution

P.O. box 189

Phoenix, MD 21131

God bless you all, and keep reading, 'cause I'ma keep writing.

ACKNOWLEDGEMENTS PT.2

Blessings to you all and mad gratitude for the support. I only hope to keep on being able to entertain you all so that one day, your boy Diesel becomes your favorite writer, or one of your top favorites. Shout outs to the greats of LDP! Ghost, J Blunt, Meesha, Aryanna, DG Santana, Molotti, Say no More, Jelissa, T.J. Edwards, Askari, Nikki Tee, Destiny Skai, Mimi, and everyone else that has come together with hits to make LDP what it is today . . . **THE SHIT!** And of course, I cannot forget the big homie Ca$h!

To my family. Steve, Stephaine, Braylan, Ray Ray, my barber Twan, mad love, yo, I appreciate everything y'all are doing to help me hold it down. It will not be forgotten.

PITTSBURGH! CHICAGO! WAUK-TOWN! ZION! NOGO! TURN UP!

To the real niggaz here in this clown-ass prison!

And now, everybody . . . ENJOY!

Diesel

Prologue

Brrrrr! Brrrr! Brrrrr!

"Shit!" Araña cursed, as bullets flew at the Cadillac Escalade he was in the rear seat of. The driver's head and that of the man next to him exploded, brains flying all over the interior, courtesy of a hailstorm of 7.62 mm rounds coming from out of the ratty little motel's window.

The other SUV, which had more of Araña's goons inside, took fire as well. The shooter inside the motel wasn't going without a fight.

"Boss!" shouted Reynaldo after jumping out of the other Escalade and running to get his boss out of the line of fire, while eight of the men they had come with began shooting back at the room.

"Stop. Cease fire. Cease fire!" he yelled to them all. "The boss wants her alive, idiotas."

They obeyed Araña's command, stopped firing their military-grade assault rifles and machine guns, and now, out of the Cadillac truck, ducked down behind it. Araña's was covered by Reynaldo. They saw other people who were temporarily residing at the motel running out of their rooms, hauling ass to get to safety, screaming and crying in fear.

"Send them in, Reynaldo. She's trapped, and we need to get her and go before the cops get here!"

Reynaldo ordered the goons inside, remaining at Araña's side to keep him safe. Araña stood, looking through the Caddy truck, through the blown-out windows, watching them run into the room.

His heart pounded in his chest. The target had to be retrieved in order to find the merch she had stolen. The boss of the Espinoza Cartel, of which Araña was his right-hand man, demanded she be brought back alive. Giovanni would rather just kill the bitch and be down with it, but he couldn't go against Marcello. That would be suicide.

Boom!

A devastating explosion suddenly rocked the property the entire motel sat on. Flames flew up out of the room Araña's men ran into. A few of them were hurled out, looking like balls of flying fire.

"Que chingao," Araña cursed, shocked beyond belief.

Reynaldo stood all the way up, dumbfounded. The explosion had completely destroyed the room—and the two others on its sides.

"The bitch blew herself up?" Araña questioned, bewildered, standing next to his lieutenant.

Reynaldo was about to respond when, in his left peripheral, he caught the sight of movement. He turned his head and saw her, running through the lot, pulling her 4-year-old daughter with her right hand, a large duffel bag strap over her shoulder, and in her left hand, a mini AK-47 pistol.

"Alla! Boss!" Reynaldo yelled, pointing his AR-15 in her direction.

But before he could get a shot off, she started firing the Draco while still running with her daughter.

Brrrrrrrrrrrrrrrr!

Reynaldo grabbed Araña and pushed him out of the line of fire, but unfortunately for him, he could not escape the swarm of hot ones flying at him like killer bees in full metal jackets.

Araña caught a face full of bloody chunks of flesh as Reynaldo was chopped up to pieces. Stupefied, Araña was paralyzed with disbelief as the girl, her daughter, and the bag that he just knew contained the life-changing amount of merchandise she had stolen from the cartel's boss, made it to the shiny new black S680 Maybach Benz that she had also stolen from the Espinoza estate.

Becoming blinded by rage, Araña crawled to the seat he had been sitting in and grabbed the Glock 21 he had tucked in between. He hurried and cocked it, pointed it at the rear of the car as she hurried to back out of where she had parked, and started dumping.

Boc! Boc! Boc! Boc! Boc! Boc! Boc! Boc!

Each bullet he fired pinged off the car as she burned rubber, peeling off like a bat out of hell. Araña cursed angrily, remembering that all of Marcello's cars were armored with the finest ballistics protection money could buy.

He watched the equivalent of a luxurious turn-turbo V12-powered tank smash up out of the motel's parking lot, with the boss's priceless belongings inside.

Araña dragged himself out of the Escalade right as the sirens from multiple emergency response vehicles en route filled the air.

Seeing cops leading the convoy of fire trucks and ambulances, Araña quick-stepped away from the bloody scene. He ran to the lot past the office building, reaching the open dirt field. Using the cover of night and the lack of street lights anywhere in the field, Araña escaped the heavy police presence that was getting even heavier by the second.

Far enough away from the chaotic scene, he pulled his untraceable smartphone from his Armani pants pocket, making a call to deliver the bad news.

"Did you get her?" Marcello asked the second he answered.

"No, patron. That puta set off a bomb or something in her motel room. All my men are dead."

"And you aren't?"

"Boss. I sent them in together. How was I supposed to know that would happen? The bitch managed to escape. With your shit, too."

"Find her, or I will find you," Marcello threatened, then ended the call, leaving Araña boiling with anger and plotting death on the girl and her daughter.

***

Leticia cried her eyes out, scared to death. Strapped into the back seat of the Mercedes, the gunshots and the sound of her mother panicking had the 4-year-old so scared that she wet herself.

"Lety. Don't cry, mi amor. Everything's gonna be okay, mamas. I promise," Cynthia told her, as she kept her gas pedal to the floor, using every bit of power the engine under the Benz's hood had.

"I'm scared, Mommie!" Leticia told her.

"I know, baby, but I swear we'll be fine. You see I got us out of there. He will never hurt you or me again. I swear it, baby."

Leticia wiped her eyes then.

"Where are we going?"

Cynthia took a deep breath, then sighed.

"I don't know right now, Lety. But as long as we get out of Texas, far, far away from it, we'll be okay. Trust me, okay?"

"Okay, Mommie. I love you."

"I love you, too, baby. Close your eyes and get to sleep. When you wake up, we'll be safe."

She glanced up and saw her precious little girl yawn. Leticia nodded, then closed her eyes, falling right to sleep from straight exhaustion.

Cynthia wiped the tears that threatened to fall. She had never pictured herself being in such a fucked-up situation. Since coming to the States, life had been hell for her and her daughter. She was repulsed by some of the things she had to do in order to survive and protect her daughter. She was alone in the world.

Feuding between cartels in her hometown of Reynosa, down in Mexico's northeastern regions, had been how her mother, father, her two sisters, three uncles, and one brother had all been killed. Fighting over the drug route from southern cartel-controlled states to the U.S. had people in Reynosa and Matamoros dropping like flies. Cynthia had been at school, and her daughter was at home with her family. By the grace of the man above, Leticia had hidden in a closet, under a pile of clothes, when vicious men from one of the cartels ran into the house and began shooting at anyone inside. They had come for Cynthia's father, who had owned an auto shop. They had wanted him to put traps in their vehicles, but he refused, wanting to fly straight.

But it was the wrong answer.

Cynthia got a call from one of her friends while she was in class and ended up running all the way home, sick with grief and terrified. Cops were everywhere on her street. Other families had been murdered in surrounding houses. Bodies were laid out in the street in pools of blood.

She found her daughter with her friend, across the bloody street from her family's house, and thanked God. Leticia was petrified, but unharmed.

Cynthia decided it was time to leave Mexico. She got connected with a guy who smuggled immigrants across the border a day later. Using what little money she had, she paid for her and her daughter to get snuck into the U.S. She had Leticia make it into Laredo successfully, and just two days later, after sleeping in a homeless camp under an old bridge, Cynthia found work at a beer factory, which provided daycare for employees with kids, limited funds, and/or no family or trusted friends to care for them during work hours.

She worked hard to make a living for her and her daughter. Her work ethic was recognized by not the manager, but by the factory's owner, who had taken a personal interest in the 5'3" tall Mexican beauty. She was blessed with radiant brown skin, her long jet-black silky hair, her round face with plumpish cheeks, and a curvy physique that came with a round ass, wide hips, thick thighs, and runner's legs. She had the looks of a true *paisana*, with the body of a model. He wanted her the minute he saw her, packaging a box of beer.

Marcello Espinoza came in that day to give word to all his employees. Donald punk-ass Trump had turned Immigration and Customs Enforcement agents into mobsters, and they were coming for anyone that wasn't a natural citizen, not caring if they committed a crime or not.

For days, he had come in and treated Cynthia to lunch. The other female workers grew envious of her, wishing the wealthy and powerful man had noticed them. Cynthia let Marcello down, though, the first few times he had asked her to dinner. She told him that she only wanted to work and provide for her daughter, who had no father now. He had been arrested for drug dealing, then killed in prison by a rival dealer.

One day, Marcello pulled up in a limo filled with roses and gifts, all for Cynthia. A few of the friends that she made at the factory told her to give the man a chance. So, she accepted his invitation to dinner.

Dinner turned into dating, and dating turned into Cynthia and her daughter moving into Marcello's gargantuan mansion. One week later, she found out that Marcello was not who he had been while dating her. It was too late by then, though. Cynthia and her daughter were his, and he did not allow anyone to come into his world, then let them leave . . . alive.

She tried to escape with her daughter. Leticia was taken from her and placed with the other little girls that belonged to the other women Cynthia later discovered were also captives. Cynthia was then forced to prostitute for one of Marcello's brothels. She was told that if she didn't satisfy every customer, every day of the week, Marcello would send her daughter to one of his clients who felt that age was nothing but a number.

Having no choice, for two long dark years, Cynthia worked as the brothel's slave, serving everyone that came into her room, whether it was one, two, three, four, or five, all at once. While she lost her soul, she did learn a lot about Marcello's operation, his dealings, stash houses, and his estate's weak points. The day came that she put her escape plan into play, and moved swiftly and quickly.

She dipped off from the brothel, finessed her way into one of Marcello's dope houses, and shot the man running it in his face. She took enough merch to fund a small gang, bagged it, then hurried to where her daughter was being held.

With no hesitation, she caught the old woman that kept all of the kids in locked rooms and slit her throat. She released all of the children, and even found where their mothers were being held, freeing them as well.

Lastly, Cynthia got to one of Marcello's garages, got the key to one of his armored Benzes, got her daughter and the merch inside, then she dipped out of there like a bat out of hell, commencing what was either going to be the start of a new life, or the countdown to the end of her life . . .

Chapter 1

2 Months Later…

"Yes, it'll be here in a week. I've already ordered it," Quinton told his client. "When it gets here, I'll give you a call, okay?"

"A'ight, fam. Lemme' know asap," the client again requested, anxious to get his hands on the custom diamond chain he paid an arm and a leg for to shit on everyone else in his circle.

"No doubt, bruh. Be safe."

Quinton ended the call and chuckled. "These niggas and their damn diamond jewelry," he said to himself, shaking his head. "Guess they don't know diamonds don't actually mean as much as original vintage pieces."

He looked at the vintage 1970 white-gold Presidential Rolex on his wrist as an example for real value that would continuously grow. He had plenty of vintage timepieces secured in special glass watch storage safes, and he did have some new-age watches that had jaw-dropping price tags.

As the owner of a prestigious diamond jewelry store, Quinton had access to any and everything shiny, flawless, and high-priced in his store. He established himself in an outlet mall shopping plaza in Pleasant Prairie, Wisconsin, where the stores and restaurants around catered to folks with the same money, as compared to discount store shoppers.

Drug dealers, gangsters, crooked business men/women, politicians, celebrities, and athletes chose '*Q Diamonds & Co.*' as their preference to get drippy, or to have *anything* custom designed.

***

After a long day of clocking hours in, raking in tens of thousands of dollars from all the sales and pieces being displayed in the store, and for the elite that came in to pick up their specially ordered drip, Quinton was ready to call it a day. But before he could leave, there was one more thing that he had to do.

He reached for the phone on his desk and pressed the intercom call button.

"Janelle?"

He waited a second, then her voice came back through the speaker.

"Yes, Q?"

"Is everyone gone for the evening?" Quinton asked.

"Yes, they are. I'm getting ready to go, too."

"Hold on. Before you go, can you come to my office? I need to see you."

It was a whole five seconds before she replied with a "Be right there."

Quinton grinned to himself. The dirty thoughts that were in his mind about his assistant had been having his dick throbbing all day, especially because of the way the vivacious spitfire always dressed for work. Earlier that morning, when he arrived at the store in his new Rolls-Royce Ghost, the second he laid eyes on her, he made a promise to himself that before the day was over, he was bringing her to his office and bending her over.

***

A minute or so later came a knocking at the door. Quinton quickly put on some mood music, choosing some Sade to serenade his seductive moves. Then he looked into the full-length mirror at himself. His beard was thick and perfectly lined. His head was cleanly shaved and glossed like a polished bowling ball. He had smooth mocha-brown skin and stood an athletic six-foot-one. The tailored Brooks Brothers suit he wore with Prada dress shoes fit him perfectly. In his ears were big, flawless diamond studs that flickered like the rocks in his wedding band.

Smiling at himself, he went to the door and opened it. Her perfume wafted right into his nostrils from the gust of wind made by the door opening up. Amazed by the sight of the curvaceous dark-chocolate drop, Quinton could do nothing more at the moment but gaze at her, loving how her long, rust-colored hair flowed down her back.

She stood 5'4" without the shiny, dark-red leather, pointed-toe stiletto pumps she had on her little feet, which matched the form-fitting, long-sleeved, open-back and low-cleavage-lined dress she flaunted. The dress's hem went down to the middle of her thick thighs, allowing the black fishnet pantyhose she had on to spice up her DKNY ensemble with to enhance the look of her sexy legs.

She wore minimal makeup, consisting of only dark-red eye shadow and dark-red glossy lipstick. Silver hoop earrings in her ears with the necklace to match, a silver Movado on her wrist, a tennis bracelet, and silver rings on her fingers were all she could afford, but she made it all work for her. She was a bad bitch, and she knew it, all at just 22 years of age.

***

"Come on in, Janelle. I been waitin' for you," Quinton told her in a low and deep tone that worked on every chick he was trying to charm out of their panties.

Stepping aside, Quinton invited her in. She smiled up at him with a sensually mischievous smirk that made his dick twitch. After she passed him, he got an eyeful of her ridiculously fat 48" ass that looked like it was full of Jell-O.

Her booty cheeks bounced up and down with every step that she took, and it made him yearn for it to be bouncing up and down on his dick.

He closed the door and watched her turn to face him once she reached his desk. She leaned against it and put her hands on her wide hips.

"Somethin' I can do for you, boss?" she asked in such a flirtatious way.

"Yes, Janelle." He walked right up to her and looked down into her beautiful hazel-brown eyes. "You can drop the act and let a nigga do what you been wantin' me to do for a long time."

She giggled. "Oh really? What might that be, Quinton?" she asked, then licked her lips.

"You've been wantin' me to hit the pussy like yo' so-called boyfriend can't be doin' the right way, and I'm dying to do that right now," he told her, feeling his dick pulsating inside of his Tom Ford boxer briefs.

"Hmmm. Let's say I do want that. I'm in a relationship, and you're married. It wouldn't be right."

"But it would feel right," he countered.

Then, without waiting another second, he took off his suit jacket, undid his belt, and undid his pants. He took her hands and made her grab the bulge that he caught her looking at as he walked up to her.

"Let's not pretend anymore, Janelle. I want you, and you obviously want me," he knowingly stated, since she was still gripping him. "Pull this dick out and show me how those lips feel around it."

She again giggled at him. "Okay, boss."

Quinton grew even more excited as she pulled his thick nine-inch dick out. She wrapped her hand around it, licked her lips, then moved her hand down and cupped his balls.

"Come on, Janelle. Lemme see how that mouth feels, baby," Quinton nearly begged.

Sinking down to her knees before him, she put her glossy lips to the bulbous tip of his dick and kissed it. She opened her mouth, then and ran her tongue around the head while still cupping his nuts. Continuing to tease him, she ran her tongue down the side of the shaft, down to his balls, and lifting his balls up, she sucked them into her mouth. She began jerking his dick while sucking his balls. Quinton groaned gutturally, pleased with how she was working with him.

"Yeeaah, baby. This shit feels too good. Fuck!"

She pleasured his nuts for a minute, then releasing them, she went back to the tip of his dick, opened wide, and engulfed all of him with the ease of a porn star that was born to suck on dick.

With her right hand, she cupped and massaged his balls while using her left hand to stroke him as her mouth made his head spin in circles.

"Ooohhh shit. Oh shit. Goddammit. Fuuuuck." Quinton could barely contain himself from the triple sensation of pleasure that she was fucking his head up with. "Goddamn, Janelle, baby! You're so good at suckin' dick, but damn, I want some of that pussy!"

He took his dick out of her mouth, pulled her up from her knees, and made her turn around.

"Grab that desk!" he demanded.

She obeyed, then leaned over, tooting her bubble booty up for him. He rubbed on her ass through her dress, then he raised it up, exposing chocolate cheeks in fishnets.

"No panties, huh?" he noticed. "Nor a thong?"

She looked back at him and grinned. "Like you said, I've been wantin' you to hit this pussy, because my man ain't doin' it right. I was just wonderin' what took so long."

"Never mind all that, baby," Quinton told her, then he ripped her pantyhose open at the crack of her ass, making a big hole in them. "We are here now, and this pussy is mine now."

He grabbed his cock with his right hand, her ass cheek with his left. Sliding into her wetness from behind, Quinton's eyes rolled to the back of his head as her super wet warmth enveloped him like it was made just for him.

She moaned as he filled her up, stretching her tight walls out like he was trying to park a jet plane inside a little garage. She called out his name and met his strokes by throwing her ass back at him. Quinton was so overwhelmed by how good the pussy was that he could already feel his nuts tingling from his impending release. Cursing that he was going to cum way sooner than he wanted, he decided to get his nut how he really wanted it.

Quinton pulled his dick out of her pussy, not even caring that she hadn't reached her climax. He grabbed her booty cheeks, spread them, and opened her up. Then he spit a wad of saliva down into the crack and on his dick; he rubbed his spit all around her asshole, getting it all wet and slippery. He was glad that she hadn't tried to stop him, because he had no plans to obey if she told him, "Not there."

"Go ahead, big daddy," she purred, looking back at him with a desperately sexy fuck face. "Put that big black dick in my big fat black ass."

He eased the tip in, then the rest of him. He nearly lost his head from her heated tunnel swallowing him up so good. As he slowly began stroking her ass, she moaned out his name, then he exploded, drenching his thighs with her hot sweet juice.

Quinton continued on, grabbing her ass cheeks and pounding her ass. She cried out in bliss, screaming how much she loved it, begging him to not stop. A few minutes later, he felt his nuts tingling again. His back muscles tightened up, and he started grunting, coming so close.

Another five seconds later, he pulled his dick out of her and made her drop back down onto her knees in front of him. She parted her shiny lips and all-too-willingly let him stuff his cock back into her mouth and fuck her face until he reached his nut.

"Aaghhhh ssshhheeeeiiiit. Fuck!" he howled as she gripped him with both hands and sucked him while twist-stroking his cock.

Quinton exploded in her mouth, filling it up with hot globs that trickled out and splattered down on her chest. She swallowed it all with no problem. Using a finger, she scooped the cum that dripped onto her chest and slurped it up. Quinton was breathing hard, heart beating fast, body feeling like it was literally vibrating.

"Oh my God! That shit was bomb as fuck!" he then exclaimed, truly astounded by how she had just allowed him to dominate her.

"Uh-huh. Now yo' ass gon' be thinkin' every day that we gon' be in here gettin' it before we go home to our lovers," she chuckled.

Quinton stuffed his limpness back into his pants after pulling them and his boxer briefs up. He fixed his belt, ignoring that she was still on her knees. She ended up picking herself up off of the floor.

"Maybe," he finally replied, giving her a devilish smirk. "I will admit: it was everything I had hoped for and more . . . but now, I gotta get home. Are you ready?"

"Are you?" she countered snidely.

"Uh . . . Yes," he told her, hearing it in her tone. "You okay?"

"Yep. Got me a nut off at work with my sexy boss and I made me some money today. It will get better from here. Let's go 'n get home and act like we had a plain-ass day."

"Sounds good to me, sexy chocolate drop."

***

Quinton followed her out of his office into the hall that led to various doors. They both headed towards the rear exit, where the store's parking section was. Her phone rang as she reached the door first. She got it out of her leather tote bag and answered while entering the code to arm the store's security system.

"Hey, baby! I'm literally just 'bout to leave work and come home," Quinton listened to her say as she opened the door while the countdown beeps blared until the alarm was actually on. "Where are you . . . Aaahhh!"

Quinton suddenly saw a masked man with two semi-automatic pistols in his hands, a hood over his head, and a ski mask on. He ran inside and put one pistol to his assistant's head and pointed the other at him.

"Turn the alarm off! Now! Or die, bitch!" the gunman demanded.

"Okay, okay, okay! Please don't kill me!"

Quinton immediately raised his hands up. He stayed silent, cursing mentally, wondering how the hell he could have gotten caught up so easily. The alarm was shut off before it activated. The gunman ordered her to lock the door next. After she did, he looked at them both.

"I'm sure I don't need to say it, but just in case y'all are slow . . . hand it over to the jack boy. This is a robbery. Now let's go back into the boss man's office and see those goodies that my nigga Jayson said you keep in the safe," the gunman suggested, non-negotiable.

Quinton cursed under his breath when he heard his store manager's name. *Fucking snake! Wait 'til I get my hands on Jayson!*

"Okay, man! Just don't shoot," Quinton's assistant pleaded. "We'll give you whatever you want. We just wanna get home."

"Then shut up and move."

***

Quinton stood nervously with a gun to the back of his head while he entered the code to the six-foot-tall safe he had next to a cherry-wood credenza. The sound of the lock disengaging came. Quinton's heart dropped as he opened the thick steel door, unveiling stacks of cash, custom cases containing pricey jewelry, and a kilo of cocaine.

"Oh yeah! Yessuh! That's what I like right there, joe. Aye, lil' moma, find me a bag and empty that whole safe," the gunman ordered.

"Janelle!" Quinton panicked, knowing that some of the jewelry inside was already paid for by some seriously wealthy people. "I will hunt you the fuck down," Quinton told the gunman, trying to scare him.

Wham!

His attempt earned him a gash in the back of his shiny head that gushed blood profusely on the money-green carpet that covered the office's floor.

"Fuck!" he cursed as his head pounded. "What the hell, man!"

"Shut cho' bitch ass up, clown!" the gunman barked. "Next word to come up outta yo' mouth, I'ma put a bullet in it, pussy! Try me!"

Quinton laid where he fell and didn't say shit else.

"Okay! Here! It's all in there!"

With double vision, Quinton saw his assistant wheel the luggage over to the jack boy. "Now please go!"

"As soon as you get in front, we'll go. Yo' ass comin' wit' me 'til I get to my whip, so yo' boss don't get no funny ideas."

"Wait! No, hold up! Wait!" she pleaded as he forced her at gunpoint towards the doorway.

"Hey! Oh shit! Hey! Leave her alone!" Quinton shouted.

He gathered all of his strength. Woozily, he rushed towards the man as his assistant pleaded for him to let her go.

"Hey! Stop, mothafucka!" Quinton yelled when he got to the hallway.

Then he froze. The gunman was pointing both pistols right at him.

"Quintoooon!"

Bocka! Bocka! Bocka! Bocka! Bocka! Bocka! Bocka! Bocka!

Both Glock 9s spit hot ones at Quinton, smacking him up and putting him onto the ground.

"Nooooooo!" his assistant screamed.

The gunman took off and pushed his way out the door with hundreds of thousands of dollars worth of merch.

"Quinton! Oh my God! Nooo!"

He felt searingly hot stinging all over his body. He was wet and getting weak.

"H-H-Help! Help me!" he cried.

He felt her take his hand then. He looked up into her eyes, and he saw them go from terrified to sinister. Her lips curled up into a smirk, and she squeezed his hand tightly.

"There's no help for you, Quinton. Just let go, and it'll be all over."

Quinton's heart dropped despite his body being riddled with bullets. He tried to talk, but he started choking on his own blood. His vision got blurrier, the light fading fast. He tried to hold on, but in a matter of seconds, everything went dark . . .

***

Inez let go of his hand and felt for a pulse. It was gone. Quinton was dead.

"Rest in piss, bitch ass nigga," she said to the corpse.

Hurrying then to find her phone, she found his name and quickly typed a text message:

Bae! We did it! WE fucking did it! Ha! OMG I love you so much! I can't wait to get home! I'm about to finish this, then I'll be there! Love you!

She sent the text, then turning her phone off, she went to Quinton's desk and used his desk phone to make the call that she had been practicing for the last few months.

"9-1-1, what's your emergency?"

"Help! We've been r-robbed! He shot my boss! Please! Help!"

***

"Yeah! Yeah! Yes!" Marcus was geeked! Months of planning had finally paid off. "I can't believe it worked! On Black Stone we really did it! Ohh shit!"

Excited beyond like ever before, Marcus hauled ass from the rear of the jewelry store, passing Inez's white 2003 Lexus GS 430 and Quinton's Rolls-Royce Ghost, heading towards where the getaway car was.

He felt his phone buzzing in his pocket as he cut down a dark side street that led out to Highway 160 and pulled it out. He saw it was a text from Inez and opened it while still running with the Louis Vuitton luggage bag rolling right along with him.

"Love you, too, baby. This what we've been waitin' for; we've been dyin' to get rich, and that's gon' happen finally," he said to himself.

Tucking his phone back into his pocket, he kept on running, going in the opposite direction of the plaza's main parking and shopping area, hidden by the darkness of the side road.

The dark-colored Dodge Charger SRT8 sat where it had been parked when he had hopped out. He quickly hopped up front and was ready to get up out of there.

"You get it, joe?" asked his homie Block, a dark heavyset nigga with dreads that resembled the rapper Tee Grizzley, in a very anxious manner.

"Yeah, nigga! Fuck you think, I stole just this Louis joint?"

Block smiled then. "Cool, fam. We are all good, joe."

Click-Clack!

Marcus heard the sound that was the most recognizable to any nigga or chick from the hood. Then he felt something hard press to the back of his head.

"Good job, Marcus. Now give my baby yo' gun. Do it real slow, or I will knock yo' shit back. I am not gonna' say it again, nigga. You know how I get down."

Marcus was stuck damn near. He couldn't believe it. After so many months of planning this, getting Inez hired under a fake alias, having her flirt with the freaky-ass jeweler to get his guard down and allow her to go in on his ass just once, his own homies were now robbing him.

"Tashira. This really what y'all on, joe? On the five this shit's grimey as fuck!" Marcus snapped as he reluctantly gave his gun to Block.

Crack!

Block cocked back and hit Marcus dead in his jaw, rattling him.

"I just saved yo' ass, Marcus. She ain't playin', fam. Now get the fuck out, joe, and if you even think about comin' for me, you will lose. On the G, nigga!"

Marcus opened the door and got out. The Charger sped off, disappearing around a bend. Marcus could only hear the Hemi engine roaring as Block stomped it. The sounds of the monster V8 faded and, in a matter of seconds, were replaced by the police sirens.

"Fuck," he panicked.

With no wheels and no money, Marcus had no choice but to run for it and trudge his way all the way back to Zion, and on the way, hope to God that Inez didn't go ballistic on him when she got to their apartment after having to deal with cops and explaining the robbery as if she had really just been an innocent employee, and not the slimeball bitch that set the whole thing up.

Chapter 2

The detective handed her a tissue as she cried her eyes out. She was so distraught and broken over the death of her boyfriend, such a brutal murder right in front of her eyes. His blood was all over her hands and the towel she had used to try to stop the bleeding. But her efforts to save him had not been enough.

"It's going to be okay, Miss Vance. Thank you for your cooperation," he told her. "Will you need help getting home?"

She shook her head. "No. I drove to work."

"Okay, ma'am. I'm sorry for your loss. You can go now."

***

Inez kept up her act until she was inside the brown leather interior of her bubble-body Lexus. She started the V8 engine under the hood, put it in drive, and pulled off—away from the store—for the last time. She only wished that she could've had Marcus take more, but what he had made of it was more than what he made selling the little bits of weed he had connections on.

Only when she turned onto Highway 160 did she scream out excitedly, super geeked! She grabbed her phone out and turned it on, immediately sending a text message to an unsaved number. Then she called Marcus.

No answer.

She tried again. The voicemail came again.

Twice more, Inez got the same results.

Giving up, she hit the gas and hurried to get to Zion.

***

Inez made a pit stop at a gas station on 21st and Lewis to get gas. It was nearly empty. An older Impala sat parked at the building's side. The second she turned her engine off, she saw a Hispanic chick get out from behind the wheel, and a man from the passenger's side. He was wiping his nose, and she was stuffing money into her pocket. Noticing the girl had a *BP* work shirt on as she headed toward the store's entrance, and the guy heading off into the alley that ran between Lewis Ave and Joppa, flaming up a cigarette, Inez shook her head.

"Could she be any more obvious?" she asked herself.

Inez made her way inside to pay for her gas. The Hispanic chick was just re-entering the bulletproof-glass-enclosed cashier section. Inez heard music coming from inside there. Looking toward the end of the protected area, she saw a little girl watching the new movie *Wicked* on an iPod.

Inez shook her head once again when she realized that the cashier was really selling drugs out of the gas station, dipping in and out to do so, and all the while leaving the little girl by herself.

Talking about bad parenting, she thought to herself.

The girl came up to her register a second later, smiling at Inez. Inez twisted her lips up out here, giving her a look of disapproval.

"Sorry for your wait, ma'am. I was—"

"Sellin' dope outside when that lil' girl was in hea' by herself? Yeah. I know. Check it out. I'm in a rush," Inez told her, pulling her wallet out of her tote bag and fishing out a $20. "All of that on pump three," she concluded. Then she marched out of the store as three people that looked like fiends waited by the store's corner, where the cashier's car was.

***

After she pumped her gas, Inez pulled off and hopped back onto 21st, shooting east. Cruising out the speed limit so as to not attract the plentiful amounts of Zion police that cruised around the suburban town—bored and just looking for someone to fuck with.

Two minutes later, she came up on the notorious apartment buildings that were the wildest and livest ones in the Z.

The Hebrons was home to the hood niggas and hood bitches, robbers, hustlers, and gangsters. It was a big part of why Zion was now called *The Zoo*. Lions, tigers, and bears ruled the Hebrons, preying upon other folks from other housing complexes—or other parts of Zion—that came through, thinking shit was sweet.

Most people that came for more than to buy drugs found that the Hebrons were not sweet.

***

Parking next to Marcus' run-down '87 Oldsmobile Cutlass G-Body, Inez grabbed her bag and hopped out of her Lexus.

"Aye, shortie? What up, joe? Come blow this stick wit' me. This fi' right *hea*!" said the old man that stayed two doors away from her and Marcus' apartment.

"No, thanks," she replied, knowing the old-ass nigga laced his weed with crack.

Passing him, Inez made her way to the door of their two-level apartment. She unlocked the door and stepped into the dark living room. She called out his name but heard nothing. Reaching blindly for the light switch on the wall, Inez saw him sitting on the longer of the two couches in the room. His head was bowed, and his foot tapped repeatedly.

“Marcus?” she walked up to him, dropping her bag on the love seat. “Hey? Bae? What's up wit’ chu’?”

He didn’t respond, so she reached a hand under where his chin was and lifted his head up. The first thing she noticed was the bruise on his left cheek. Then, she saw the fire in his eyes.

“What the hell happened? I been callin’ you, and I been callin’ Block and ‘Shira. Where the hell are they at?”

“Gone,” Marcus told her.

“Gone?” she asked, with a raised eyebrow. “Gone where, Marcus?”

“Gone, Inez! They flew the coop on a nigga! They robbed me of the merch as soon as I got in the fuckin’ car!” Marcus exploded, jumping up from the couch, so heated he could punch through a wall.

Inez stood where she was and looked at him, breathing angrily, shoulders rising and falling as he fumed. Even heated, she had to admit to herself that Marcus was a handsome-ass nigga. Yeah, he was young—five years younger than her 28 years of life—but he could become the man, if guided by the right person.

He kept a fresh bald-fade haircut, with curls-for-the-girls up top, a neat and low beard/goatee, and his gray eyes hypnotized women that looked into them. His athletically muscular 5’8” frame was tatted up all over, which included a red five-point star on his right pec, with **BPSN** in black letters inside of it. And under the five, he had a tattoo of a pyramid with a crescent moon over it.

Marcus’ light caramel-toned skin was compliments of his Puerto Rican mother, while his hard-body physique and his deep, soulful, and fearless personality had been bestowed upon him by his African-American father—both of whom were from the gutters of Chicago.

Marcus grew up in Moe Town, out South, with his mother, who was a fearless lady Black Stone, while his New Breed father was from K-Town. He was the product of a killer and a gangstress that went hard for each other, and for their only child. At 23 years of age, Marcus still had a lot to learn, and his father and mother had taught him what they could. But like all young niggas, Marcus wanted to carve out his own path instead of following those that had come before him and had the means to show him a better way to move.

***

"Marcus. Bae, try to relax," Inez said, walking up to him, and looking up at him. "Can you look at me?"

He did.

"Are you okay?"

"How could I be okay? I just got stained for all that shit, Inez! I know that Hublot I saw wit' the diamonds all over it had to be worth a buck by itself!"

"Okay, okay, Marcus! I get it! I'm mad, too, but you could've died! Look at Quinton's bitch ass! He outta *thea*! Gone! That coulda' been you, nigga!

Marcus inhaled a deep breath, then he exhaled.

"Please. Relax, baby." Inez cupped his face in her hands and made him look at her. "We'll get them two pussy muthafuckas, Marcus. You know Block is dumb as fuck, and Tashira's messy. As for you, though, I'ma need you to smile for me."

"As beautiful and as thick as you are, nothin' can make me smile right now."

"Oh, is that right? Nothing, you say?" Inez grabbed his crotch then and squeezed his dick. "Still nothin'?"

He raised an eyebrow up at her. His phone started ringing suddenly, catching Inez's attention.

"It's my O.G.—her ass has been callin' me for the past hour," he told her.

"Uh . . . Yo' momma gon' kick yo' ass. That lady cray-cray, always shoutin' *On Stone, On Stone!* Just like yo' ass."

Marcus stared at her. "Okay, I so do *not* wanna discuss my momma while you grippin' my dick, Inez."

"Oh! Yeah! My bad! Where was I?"

"Thinkin' you could make me smile."

"Mhmmm! Oh yeah!" She remembered, then she added her other hand and undid his jeans. She started backing him up, towards the couch, stopping before he could sit. "I'm 'bout to give you a Viagra man smile, you sexy gray-eyed niggarican mothafucka."

Inez dropped his pants and his Tru Religion boxers, feeling his hard 9" cock. She wrapped her hand around it, marveling at his two-tone pussy-whipper.

She then pulled off his hoodie, pussy dripping down her thighs. Pushing him back until she sat his ass on the couch. Inez grabbed the hem of her dress and pulled it up, over her head, and tossed it away.

No bra, no panties, she stood in front of him, looking like a thick ebony BET award in her ripped fishnets, and her stilettos. She saw the hungry look in his eyes as they roamed all over her body.

Inez stepped forward. Lifting his head up with her hand, she leaned down and pressed her lips to his, and kissed him wildly for a minute. After she lip-boxed him and won, she dropped to her knees, scooted in between his legs, and gripped his dick at the base. Looking at him, she lowered her head, and started kissing and licking all over his hardness. She sucked his balls into her mouth and pleasured them, while she slowly jerked his shaft with a firm grip.

Marcus groaned. She could feel him tremble. She loved it when she reacted to her oral skills.

Releasing his nuts from her mouth, Inez licked her way up to the tip of his dick, and took it into her mouth, sucking on it, swirling her tongue around it.

"Shit, baby. Damn . . . that feels good," he told her.

Inez deep-throated him then, going balls deep. She hummed when she felt the tip touch the back of her throat.

Marcus jumped in shock. The vibration in his balls tickled him down to his toes.

She went crazy on him a second later. She sucked his cock like a pro, spit a wad of saliva and pre-cum out on it, then with two hands she jerked him with twisting motions and sucked him at the same time.

"Oohhh sshhhiiiiit! Gooooddamn! Ohh f-f-fuuuck, I finna' buuuss!" he hollered, feeling his nut rising so fast.

Inez went a porn-star crazy on him until Marcus exploded in her mouth. She kept sucking and jerking until he was completely empty, and her mouth was full. She opened her mouth up for him to see his jizz, moving her tongue around, which made someone spill out and dribble down her chin.

"Swallow that shit," he told her.

Inez obeyed, then licked her lips, smiling afterwards.

Then Marcus smiled.

"See! Told yo' ass I can make you smile, nigga! Ha!"

"Yeah, uh huh," he replied, playfully waving her off.

Inez stood up. "Now it's time to go upstairs and make each other smile, until the sun comes up. Think you can handle that, baby?"

"On Stone I can."

She busted out laughing. "See!" she exclaimed, taking his hands and pulling him up. "Wit' cho' gang-banging' ass!"

"I took an oath, baby. Real niggas live by it 'til death comes for them, you dig I'm sayin'?"

"Mhmmmmmm. I hear you, but really, I'm tryna feel you all up in this juicy pussy, and all up in my fat juicy ass. So hush it up and let's go."

Marcus yanked his boxers and pants up, then allowed her to pull him along, following her *Oh My God-sized* ass, loving how her fishnets made it look twice as good, even with the big hole in them at her ass crack.

I'm finna beat this pussy up sooo muthafuckin' good, then I swear on God, I'ma find that bitch ass nigga and his dick-

eater bitch and knock both their tops off, joe, Marcus thought, as they reached the stairs.

Following Inez up, forty-eight inches of ass was just a whisker away from his face, causing his dick to get so hard that it hurt from throbbing like a rapidly beating heart.

But for now . . . Fuck Block and that bitch . . . I got all that ass to satisfy, and it needs my full attention, he then added to his thoughts, and got ready to go so hard on the thick chocolate drop.

***

"Yeah, I got you. Gimme ten minutes," Cynthia told the girl, as she locked the gas station door after closing up for the night.

"Okay. I'm already here," the guy replied, then ended the call.

"Mommy? Are we going home?" Leticia asked, sleepy and ready for bed.

"Not yet, sweetheart. Mommy has to make a few stops before we go home."

Cynthia had gotten the job at the gas station under a fake name. The owner wasn't dumb. He could easily figure out that she and her daughter were not legal citizens. He didn't care, though. Hiring her, he could get away with paying her less than minimum wage while he faked some W-2 paperwork to make it look like he hired a chick that was born in Chicago.

For the last month and a half, Cynthia had been working at different spots and getting a little money on the side. Selling the hot Maybach Benz to a scrapyard owner for less than half of its worth, she had gotten enough to get an apartment for her and her daughters, then bought herself a 2001 Chevy Impala, which used to be a police car. It even had the high-performance chip in the engine still, with darkly tinted windows and black wheels. She bought it for $5,500, hoping people thought it was still a cop car and shied away from it. With her apartment and her car in a different name, Cynthia was content that Marcello nor his minion couldn't track her with their complex connections.

***

Cynthia got her daughter into the back seat and strapped her into the seat belt. Hopping behind the wheel, she started her engine, put it in drive, and pulled off, leaving the gas station and taking 21st Street east towards Zion-Benton High School.

She hit a right onto Kenosha Road and headed to the massive Horizon Village apartments. Seconds later, she came to the intersection of Kenosha Road and Route 173. She rolled through the green light and came up to the left turn lane to the big Walmart there. Turning in, Cynthia hit a right and rolled towards the store's Tire & Lube Express car service garage. She saw her customer's old Chevy Astro van parked next to a shopping cart corral.

A few other vehicles were scattered around the lot—the Walmart was a 24-hour location. Cynthia thought nothing of them.

She pulled up next to the van, parking her window next to the driver's side of the Astro.

Right away, she saw Giuseppe's smiling face when he rolled his window down.

"Hey, bonita! ¿Qué pasó can I get a ball?"

"I got you. It's $100."

"Can I get a ball?"

"Yup," Cynthia replied, with a 3.5-gram bag already made for him. She tossed the coke to him and watched his eyes light up with excitement.

"Enjoy!" she told him, then pulled off to her next drop.

Cynthia shot up 173 to a bar at the corner of it and Green Bay Road. Three people that were in the bar came out and bought 8-balls as well, adding $750 to her pocket.

She made four more stops around Zion, selling the last of the two ounces she had brought out with her that morning.

Leticia was fast asleep in the back as Cynthia headed south on Green Bay Road from off of 9th Street. It had been a long day, and she was ready to get home, tuck her daughter in, and lay herself down. She was off work tomorrow. Plans to really think about her life, and her daughter's, were all she had planned, because living paycheck to paycheck, selling bits of coke every so often, was not going to cut it. She had to do something. Her daughter deserved more.

***

Cynthia came up to Green Bay Road and 173, getting over into the left turn lane, pausing at the red light. She leaned back in her seat, nodding to Doja Cat's "97" as it bumped from her radio.

A pickup truck pulled up next to her and stopped for the red light. Cynthia caught movement in her right peripheral. She looked and could see through her tinted window—the driver of the pickup was trying to get her attention. The horn beeped a second later, and she rolled the window down, seeing a big Latino bent wheel, wearing a cowboy hat and a denim jacket.

"Oh, damn, my bad. I thought you were a cop. I needed directions," he told her.

"Naw, not a cop. But maybe I can help? Where are you tryin' to go?"

"To 21st and Lewis."

"Oh! I work at the gas station there. Yeah, so just go up to the next street, make a left at the light. You'll pass Kenosha Road, a high school, then the next light is 21st and Lewis."

"Okay. Sounds simple. Thanks a lot for your help . . . Cynthia."

The second her name left his lips, she heard tapping on her window. Jumping with fright, she saw another man standing outside her window, and in his hand was a big .44 Magnum, pointing right at her.

***

Araña chuckled from the passenger's seat of the Range Rover Supercharged that was right behind the Impala, after sneaking up on it without the headlights on while the girl was distracted by his men.

"Got chu' now, you little puta," he said to himself, as he watched Gerardo tap on the window with his bulky revolver.

In the pickup, it was Alex, pointing an Uzi at her.

"Bad girl, bad girl, whatcha' gonna' do? Whatcha' gonna' do when I come for you?" he said to himself.

"She's probably gonna pee on herself, jefe," said Pote, sitting behind the wheel of the Range.

"Yeah, I bet she—"

Brrrrrr!

Skuuuuuurrrrr!

Araña's words were halted when bullets flew out of the car, pushing Gerardo back and laying him out—then the car peeled off. Alex opened fire at the rear, blowing its back window out.

"Pendejo! Marcello wants her alive!"

"Sorry, boss!" Alex apologized, then he mashed the gas and took off to catch up with the fleeing Impala.

"Vámonos!" Araña yelled out.

Pote hit the gas and peeled off, rushing past the dead man that had a pool of blood already forming around him.

Araña reached down and grabbed the Russian AK-47 he had at his side, equipped with a custom double-stack clip, filled with fifty 7.62 mm rounds.

Araña chambered a round and got ready to complete his mission. This time, he wasn't letting her get away.

***

"Mommy!" Leticia cried, terrified from the glass shattering and the sounds of bullets hitting the car.

"Stay down!" Cynthia yelled to her, with her foot on the gas, pushing past ninety miles an hour.

Speeding her ass off down Green Bay Road, she saw the pickup behind her, but also an SUV. Gripping her Glock 9mm, fitted with a switch that she bought from a young goon-turned-cokehead, Cynthia waited for her chance to get them off her ass without her daughter getting hurt.

She made it to the light at Green Bay Road and 21st Street. Cutting a hard left, she floored it, heading in the direction of her job. She glanced in her rearview mirror and saw that both vehicles were far enough back for her to pull a move.

¡Pinches cabrones! You shoot at me and my fucking daughter? Okay! I got cha'll! Let's go! she thought to herself, after a glance to her left gave her a view of the Horizon Village through the acres of open residential land in between her and it—this giving Cynthia the perfect plan of escape.

"Lety! Baby! Listen to me, okay! It's about to get really scary, but don't worry! We're gonna' be fine!" she hollered.

"Okay!" Leticia shouted back.

Cynthia made it to the stop sign at 21st and Kenosha Road. Still with a wide gap between her and her pursuers, she yanked left onto Kenosha Road and reached the entrance to Horizon Village. The second she reached it, she swerved in and flew down the curved asphalt entryway, and hurried to get into position—so she could show the pussy motherfuckers what one little Mexican chick with a daughter to protect would do to survive an attack by anyone meaning them harm.

***

“¡Pinche estúpida! She trapped herself! Go! Go! Go! Catch the little bitch!” Araña shouted to Pote as he flew down the exit way, next to Alex, flying down the entryway.

They got to the bottom of the entrance road. Araña shouted to Alex to split up. He and Pote zipped in and out of each parking lot, which each had two big apartment buildings in them. They searched each lot, coming up empty each time, until they reached the last building where the road ended.

They saw the Impala on fire, burning brightly in the middle of the parking lot. Pote and Alex screeched to a halt a few hundred feet away. Araña looked around the dimly-lit area, knowing it was a ploy for her to get away.

“Find her. Now.”

Pote got out with his AK-47. Alex got out with his Uzi. They both looked around for any signs of movement, when, from out of nowhere, gunshots rang out.

Brrrrrrrrrrrrrrrr!

Araña gasped when Alex’s upper chest opened up, then his head exploded.

Pote quickly looked to where he saw muzzle flashes coming from in between a group of bushy trees by the rear apartment building.

He fired at the bits of light. Araña jumped out and yelled for him to stop shooting.

“We can’t kill her, idiota, or Marcello will kill us!”

Brrrrrrrrrrr!

More gunshots came flying and hit Pote in his back, slamming into him so hard that he fell into Araña, sandwiching him between himself and the Range Rover.

"B-B-Boss! H-Help me!" Pote stammered, as blood trickled down from the sides of his mouth.

Araña pushed Pote off him. Pote hit the ground, twitching and gasping, unable to move. Looking around, Araña saw nobody, but could hear people that lived in the buildings in front and in back of him. Sirens of police cars and other emergency vehicles filled the air.

"Fuck! Goddammit!" he cursed.

Boom!

The Impala exploded as the flames reached the gas tank, sending a big fireball and thick plumes of smoke up into the sky.

Araña jumped into the Range Rover and peeled off, whipping a 180-degree turn, then raced to get up out of the complex before the cops got there.

"Son of a bitch! Fuck . . . fuck . . . fuck . . . fuuuuuuck!" he yelled irately.

He swore he had her. How did he fuck up? How did she beat him? Again?

He didn't get it. Locked in on the GPS tracker that her phone had was how he located her general area of travel, but now, he knew she would be even harder to find.

And when Marcello found out that his top enforcer had once again been given the slip by a plain-ass chick with a fucking four-year-old, something bad was going to happen . . . to somebody.

He has all the cocaine he could want! Why the fuck does this little bitch matter so much? Araña wondered, right as he got up to Kenosha Road.

Flashing lights flickered to the right as Zion PD cars came down 21st. Araña banged a left onto Kenosha Road and put the supercharged V8 engine under the hood to work, dipping away from the screw-up before the first cop could get there.

***

Cynthia watched from a pair of bushes next to where she had been. After the second guy fired in her direction, before she witnessed who she knew was Araña jump out of the SUV and stop him, she had seized the opportunity and emptied her clip, hitting the man in his back from just over one hundred feet away.

Then her car that she set on fire exploded in a big ball of fire.

As soon as the sounds of residents panicking and sirens wailed from somewhere close, Cynthia saw Araña hop back into the SUV and rush off before the first cop could pull up.

"Come on, baby! Hurry!" Cynthia urged her daughter, trying not to run too fast, but fast enough to get the hell out of the apartment complex before the cops swarmed it.

Holding onto Leticia's hand, Cynthia hurried through and opened at the side of the complex, cutting through a grassy pathway between two ponds. She and Leticia came out of the marsh and were now in the parking lot of a swim gear business. With Route 173 just a few hundred feet away. Across the major road were the Water Fort apartment buildings, where they lived in a one-bedroom apartment.

Cynthia kept on running, crossing the street with her daughter doing her best to keep up. They cut over a grassy hill, bypassing a man-made pond and hurrying through the parking lot at the very front of the complex.

Minutes later, Cynthia got her daughter to their building, all the way in the back, close to the Walmart that sat right next to the Waterfront. The second she got her and Leticia into their second-floor apartment and locked the door, Cynthia grabbed her daughter, sank down to the floor, and burst into tears—completely bewildered by how the hell Giovanni had found her, and pissed that she had run out of bullets before she could blow his ass down with his other three shooters that thought, because she was a chick with a kid, it was going to be easy.

Now look at them . . .

Chapter 3

A day later . . .

"Mmmm, Marcus! Oohhh, baby! Oohhh!" Inez cried out, as Marcus hit it hard from the back in their quaint little kitchen.

Her hands on the table littered with boxes of cereal, snacks, and spices, bent over in front of him, Inez was seeing stars from the savage pounding he was putting on her. The ensemble she had chosen to wear for the plans they had made the prior day—Inez just knew his ass was going to turn into a hornball, fiending for her body like an addict. She loved teasing his fetish and making him go nuts for her.

She had dressed so provocatively in a very tight, white, long-sleeved top which had a very low cleavage line, with a super short pink and white plaid schoolgirl-style miniskirt with a pleated hem. He had the biggest fetish for thick chicks in pantyhose, so she wore them every time she wore a dress or a skirt. With her seductive outfit, Inez wore white fishnet stockings that had roses and stars woven into them, and on her feet, she had on beige-suede high-heeled boots that went up to just under her knees.

Her hair had been flat-ironed and combed down, left to hang down her shoulders. Glossy pink lip gloss on her lips with pink eyeshadow on her lids, silver hoop earrings dangling from her ears with a silver necklace around her neck, all had her looking so sophisticated and sexy as fuck to Marcus that he had to get him some before they left. And him rocking his typical T-shirt, jeans, and Air Force 1s always had her ready for a little thug lovin' from the young hood nigga version of the singer Ginuwine.

***

Inez exploded all over his dick a minute later, drenching him. He pulled his dick out of the wet-wet and slipped it right into her asshole, then kept on stroking until he got to his nut. Roaring animalistically, Marcus pulled out and jerked his dick until he skeeted all in her crack, coating her asshole with globs of semen.

"Wooooo! Shit!" he shouted, once he was completely empty.

Inez stood upright and turned to face him. She wore a devious smile on her face as he reached a hand behind her and scooped some of his cum from out of her ass. Marcus' jaw dropped when she brought her hand to her mouth, then licked it clear of his sperm, moaning as if it tasted like Skittles.

"Wow," Marcus chuckled. "When we get rich, baby, I'm puttin' a big dumbass rock on yo' finger."

She licked her glossy lips and smiled. "Then I guess we should get on our way then, huh? 'Cause I'm definitely ready to be wifey."

Grabbing her matching plaid-print tote bag, phone, and keys, Inez led Marcus out of the apartment to the parking area. Marcus paused and looked at his run-down Cutty. Seeing it look so . . . bogus . . . Marcus' desire to make their next move count grew tenfold. He was tired of ratty apartments and cars with no engines and flat tires. Being broke should be against the law. He had to get rich. Glad that he had him a down-ass bitch that stayed ready for action, Marcus felt that his moment was coming very soon.

***

Waiting for him to drive, Inez gave him the keys to her Lexus GS. He helped her into the passenger’s seat then hopped behind the wheel. Starting the V8 engine, he backed out of her spot, then headed down the alley towards 21st. The second he turned out to head west, Inez reached over and started undoing his jeans. Marcus chuckled as she freed him, while getting up on her knees in her seat.

This girl really loves suckin’ dick! Yeah, I got to wife her! he thought to himself, cruising with his left hand on the wheel.

The second she lowered her head down into his lap, he turned on the music. As GloRilla’s “I LUV HER” bumped from the stock audio system, he reached behind her, lifted her skirt, and caressed her plump ass, rubbing and smacking on it while she deep-throated him like a pro.

***

“Hey, hey, hey! Look at you!” exclaimed Percy, with an ear-to-ear grin.

The second she walked through the entrance door to his pawn shop, he felt his dick begin to get hard. She was just so damn bad! And thick as fuck! She was always dressed to impress. On that day, she was looking like a freaky-ass schoolgirl in her naughty little outfit. His mouth watered up at the very sight of her and that big round ass. He wanted sooo badly to see up her skirt, then put his face there.

***

“Hey, Percy! Lookin’ good today, big daddy!” she replied with a flirtatious tone and smile.

“Why, thank you. Armani’s best only. So what brings the sexy, beautiful Milena by?”

She held up her tote bag. “I need these thangs in here disappeared, and I was wonderin’ if you were able to get yo’ hands on that new Snow Whizzle that's been comin' in lately?"

"Hmm," Percy looked at her bosom and licked his lips. "I think I can maybe find some in my office. If you really want some of it?"

"Mmmm," she purred seductively. "I definitely do want some. You got me, baby?"

Percy made his way around his little merchant station and went to the entrance door. He locked it, then he closed all the blinds. Turning towards her with a slick smile, he started walking.

"Follow me, Milena. I got what you need in my office," he told her, then he led the way towards the hallway that went to his rear area.

Hearing her high heels tapping on the floor, Percy's smile got ten times bigger as he prepared to finally be able to get some ass from the thick chocolate drop.

"Hey. Take my bag, Percy. I'ma use yo' bathroom real quick," he heard her say, as they neared the door to his office.

"Sure. I'll get started while you go."

He took the bag from her and opened the door to his office. Stepping into the dim and stale-smelling confines of where he conducted his off-the-books business, Percy went to his desk and sat her bag on it. Opening it, he saw the FN Five-seveNs, a Glock 19X, and a Glock 21. He took them out and laid them on his desk. He saw the rolls of cash that had been under them. Pulling them out, he saw big faces as he popped both rubber bands.

Percy nearly jumped out of his skin when he heard her voice. He looked up and saw her, surprised that he hadn't even heard her coming.

"Okay, I'm good now," she said, giving him a seductive smile.

He smiled at her with lust in his eyes. "Uh, you know, my offer still stands. It'll be worth it for you. Believe me."

She stepped towards him, matching his smiling gaze. Coming to his desk, she placed her hands on the surface, then looked up into his eyes.

"You've been dyin' for some of this for a long time. A man that wants it, he has to show me how bad. I'm waitin' on you, Percy baby."

Without words he moved from around his desk, went to the painting he had hanging on the wall behind the desk, and revealed to her the old-school combination safe that was built into the wall.

"What you want is behind that steel door," he told her.

"And what you want is behind me," she countered, then she bit her bottom lip and leaned down on his desk, tooting her ass up.

Needing not another invite, Percy flew around to get behind her. He stood inches back from so much ass that he could bust a nut without even touching it. Percy scooted closer, lifted her skirt up over her ridiculous rear end. He grabbed a cheek and rubbed on it, giving it a light smack.

"God, this is the fattest ass I have ever seen!"

"You doin' a whole lotta talkin' right now, Percy. You're supposed to be showin' me, not tellin' me."

"You want a show, don't tell? All right then!" he readily replied and sank down to his knees, coming to eye-level with her ass crack, pulling her pantyhose down with him to her knees.

He placed his hands on her cheeks and opened her up. He marveled at her for a second. Then he put his face in between and ran his tongue up her crack, slurping her like she was some ice cream.

"What is that taste? It's like . . ." he licked his lips and smacked them, trying to figure out what it was.

"Somethin' sweet?" she asked, giggling.

"Well, yeah, I guess."

"Good, lick it all up then, big daddy. Lemme see how nasty you can be for Milena."

Percy went crazy on her. He held her ass cheeks open and he licked, slurped, and tongued her ass like he was eating pussy. The random taste that was there at first no longer bothered him. His dick was throbbing so hard that it hurt. He couldn't wait to stick it inside of her ass.

"Oohhh, Percy! This feels sooo good, big daddy!" she moaned out, as her pussy dripped down her inner thighs. "I wish we could finish, but, ooo, time's up!"

Hearing the second sentence made him pause, with his tongue still inside of her asshole. And then . . .

Wham!

A surprise blow to the back of his head sent him sideways to the floor with a splitting headache. He groaned, rolling onto his back. Wincing from his brain pulsating inside of his skull like it was a Rockford Fosgate P3 Punch subwoofer, Percy opened his eyes and saw her standing over him, with a man wearing a sheisty standing next to her.

***

"Aye, Percy. Just so you know, before we came here, my man's dick was all up in my ass, then I let him buss' his nut in it. So that sweet taste you was wonderin' about, yeah, that was all him, nigga," Inez said, then started laughing.

"You're a nasty nigga, fam," Marcus then spoke, wrinkling his nose up at Percy. "It's all good, though. To each their own. What I give a fuck about is you gettin' yo' nasty-mouth ass up and openin' up the safe that you got, without actin' like you forgot the combination. You try me, and I'ma shoot cho' ass in yo' dick."

Marcus gave Inez his gun, then he grabbed Percy by his button-up shirt. Hoisting the heavy man up off the floor, he pushed him towards the safe. Inez positioned herself at Percy's right, putting the cannon to his temple. Percy nervously spun the dial to enter the combination. The safe unlocked when he hit the last one.

Marcus pulled Percy away then, in case there was a loaded gun inside. And there was, along with five kilos of an unknown drug, two stacked-up piles of cash, and a clear ziplock bag filled with pills.

“Oh shit! BINGO!” Marcus shouted, eyes wide with excitement, shaking, looking at the life he craved sitting in front of him. “Bae! We on, joe! Let’s bag this shit and get up outta here!”

“Say less, baby! Hold up, though,” Inez replied, then without warning, she swung the pistol at Percy’s head.

He screamed a millisecond before it cracked his skull. He flew sideways, falling to the floor, crying and screaming in pain.

“Well, damn!” exclaimed Marcus, when Inez jumped on the man and began viciously pistol-whipping him in his head and his face.

Crack! Crack! Crack! Crack!

Marcus heard the sound of a skull cracking every time she hit him. Blood flew all over her. He saw the demonic look in her eyes and took a step back. After one last hit, Inez stopped the brutal attack. She looked up at Marcus with blood splattered all over her face.

“Uh . . . whaat is you waitin’ for?” she asked him.

“Right . . . um . . . yeah,” he replied, then hurried to find a bag to stuff all the shit in.

He found one in the corner and started emptying the safe. Inez got up off of Percy after making sure he was dead. She told Marcus she was going to clean the blood off her in the bathroom, then hurried off, leaving him gathering the merch.

“What the hell.” He got the loaded pistol and saw distinct markings all over it, similar to seeing car engine oil on the ground, then being soaked with water.

He heard Inez’s heels clacking just then. Looking up, he saw her re-enter the office—face and hands clean of blood, though there were still spots on her shirt and skirt.

"Bae, look at this muhfucka, joe! I ain't never seen a thumper like this befo'." Marcus held it up for her to see.

"Oh shit! Do you know what that is?"

"It's a fo-five," he answered.

"Yeah, but that's the one made of Damascus steel! Them thangs like forty thousand dollars, baby! I seen 'em in a *DuPont Registry* magazine! Eeeee, we just hit a stupid lick!"

"Maaaan! A'ight! Let's pack up! Burn this bitch to the ground too—no evidence!" Marcus demanded, having watched a lot of crime scene investigation shows and knew how easily crime scene techs could find traces of DNA, linking people to murders in the most unimaginable ways.

***

Flames instantly overtook the pawn shop within minutes of Marcus introducing a lit Zippo lighter to a bunch of cleaning chemicals that Inez poured over Percy's body and whatever else she could. Running out of the shop before they got burned up, Marcus—with the bag full of goodies—and Inez, with his gun, got caught in a storm that was drenching Antioch, Illinois.

Hopping back into Inez's Lexus, Marcus stomped it back east to Zion, making it away from the fiery murder scene. The rain continued to pour the whole way back to the Z.

Beyond incited and eager to see how much they came up, Marcus could barely keep still. Inez Google-searched the gun they got from the safe, then showed Marcus at a red light, which sent his excitement through the roof!

***

Kendrick Lamar's *"Not Like Us"* bumped as Marcus came up on their alley. He turned in and rolled towards their building. Parking in front of his Cutty, Marcus killed the engine and reached in the back to get those bags.

"MARCUS!" Inez suddenly screamed.

Before he had time to reach, his door was yanked open. He tried to grab his gun as he turned to see who had just ran up on him.

WHAM! CRACK! CRACK! CRACK!

A blow to his temple, then three more to his jaw, shook his whole world up.

"MAARCUUUS!" he heard Inez scream again.

Her door was open, and she had been yanked out of the car.

"Inez!" he struggled to shout, dazed with double vision.

"Shut cho' bitch-ass up, nigga!" he heard a man say, right before he was yanked out of the car into the rain.

Marcus recognized the voice right away. He didn't even have to see his face.

On his back, the side of his face swollen and beating, Marcus looked up into the rain, seeing him standing right at his side with a Glock in his hand.

"Twice in twenty-four hours, Moe?" Block chuckled. "Maaan, yo' ass ain't cut out for this, fam. It's cool, though. I'ma—"

"Marcus! Marcus!"

He heard Inez screaming again. He could hear what sounded like a struggle. Managing to turn his head and look towards the rear of the Lexus, he saw a guy just as big as Block—big enough to be a linebacker in the NFL—holding Inez, while he saw who he knew was Tashira opening the Lexus's trunk.

"Hey. Marcus. Focus, Moe man," Block said.

Marcus tried to get up.

Wham!

Block's size 13 Nike ACG boot put him back down on his back.

"Maarcuuus! Help m—"

The sound of her last word being cut off by a loud crack made him look back to where Inez was.

She was unconscious now. The big dude tossed her into the trunk. Tashira closed it, then joined Block at his side.

"Marcus, good lookin' out on another one!" she teased, quoting DJ Khaled's famous words. "We'll make sure yo' time and effort was worth it, boo-boo."

"You bitch! I swear to—"

Bocka!

"Aaaaahhhh!" Marcus screamed in pain as Block fired a round and hit him in his right thigh. Block crouched down next to him then and put the barrel to Marcus' jaw.

"Sshhhh. Someone's likely calling the cops right now to report the gunshot. When they get here, you can give me up. I will find you, and so will they. Now, as I was sayin', I'ma take all the merch off yo' hands—and yo' bitch—'cause she probably tired of broke-nigga dick and need that boss nigga shit."

He stood back up then.

"I'll see you around, my nig'. Anytime you are ready, I'm ready."

Block, his homie, and Tashira jumped into the Lexus and peeled off, leaving Marcus on the soaked ground, bleeding in the rain, stained . . . again . . .

Chapter 4

The rain poured so hard and fast that Cynthia could barely see out of the windshield of the used 2005 Pontiac Bonneville GXP, which she had literally just brought two hours prior, for just over five stacks. The windshield wipers were going as fast they could, but could barely keep the glass clear enough for her to see.

Riding West up 23rd Street in Zion, she was taking all back roads to get home. In the back seat, Leticia was strapped in by her seat belt, and had a worried look on her face.

Cynthia was afraid. Even though the Impala had not been in her name, Marcello's blood hound now knew she was in the area, and was likely looking for her at that very moment.

She had to get out of Zion. Fast. She bought a new whip, registering it with a fake I.D.

Happy that the whip had dark tinted windows, she was heading to her apartment to load up her and her daughter's things and get the hell up out of Zion. She still had Marcello's valuable merchandise, and once she popped it all off, she would be set for a long time, if she ever got the chance to do it.

***

"Goddammit," she said when her window fogged up suddenly.

She reached out to turn on the defroster, when a flash of movement in front of her caught her eyes. She screamed, slammed on her brakes. But her tires slid on the wet asphalt.

Boomp!

Cynthia gasped when a person came flying up her hood and hit the windshield, cracking it, before rolling it off and hitting the ground.

"Oh my God! Oh my God! Oh my God!"

"Mommy!" Leticia cried from the rear.

"It's okay, baby! Hold on! Mommy will be right back," Cynthia told her, putting it in *park*, then jumped out of the car to go see who the hell she had just hit, and if they were alive.

Immediately pelted by the heavy rain, Cynthia ran around the front of her car. She saw the guy, on the ground, holding his side where his ribs were, trying to get up.

"Hey! Wait! Don't move! You just got hit by a car!" she informed him, in case he had hit his head, and wasn't aware of what had just happened to him, "I can call an ambulance if you—"

"No!"

His eyes went wide suddenly. His outburst startled her. She looked at him, puzzled by his refusal of medical treatment. He then drew strength from somewhere within himself, and frantically looked around.

"Inez!" he whimpered.

"What's your name?" asked Cynthia.

His eyes rolled to hers. "Marcus," he said weakly.

"Marcus, my name is . . . Evanna," she replied, keeping her real name a secret.

"Marcus, you need a doctor! You just got hit by a car, and . . ." She then noticed bleeding coming from his right thigh. "You're bleeding! Really badly! I can put you in my car and take you! But I can't just leave you in the street!"

Marcus shook his head. "No hospital . . . Shot . . . Just . . . Take me . . . Home . . . Please!"

“Okay! Okay! I’m gonna help you up now! If it hurts, I’m so sorry!”

Cynthia grabbed his arm as gently as she could and used all of her muscle to hoist him up. He wasn't that tall, but she noticed how built he was, like he worked out for a living.

She helped him to the passenger door, opened it, and as she carefully put him inside, she told her daughter not to be afraid.

***

Marcus heard the girl speak to a child in the backseat, before closing the door. He managed to turn his head and look back. He saw a very young little girl in the back seat. She looked scared.

“D-Don’t worry . . . I’m M-Mar . . .”

The driver's door opened up, and the girl named Evanna got in the car. Before she even got a chance to sit in her seat, Marcus’ vision blurred, then not even a second later, everything went dark as he slipped into unconsciousness.

***

Days Later . . .

Light turned the insides of his eyelids red. Even with them closed, he squinted from how much his head hurt. Then, it all came back to him.

Marcus’ eyes popped open and he shot straight up, immediately feeling the sharpest pain in his ribs, chest, and legs. The foreign bedroom that he was in kept him from shouting in agony. He had no clue where he was, nor how he got here. He just remembered Inez being taken by Block and his bitch.

The door to the bedroom suddenly opened up. Marcus jumped, surprised by it. A woman entered—a Hispanic chick. He saw her and remembered getting hit by a car. Her car had nearly taken him out as he tried running to the house where Block and Tashira stayed. He'd thought they may be just dumb enough to go back there. Block had always been a cocky dude, thinking he was untouchable.

***

"Hey? Marcus?" the girl walked towards him, with heavy concern etched all over her face.

A beautiful face. Extraordinarily beautiful, he noticed. Round, with plump cheeks and slanted eyes, with perky lips. She had a nose ring in her right nostril as well. She wore leggings that fit her tightly, emphasizing her shapely bottom half that amazed Marcus. The short-sleeved T-shirt she had on also fit snugly and showed that she was blessed with big, succulent breasts. She was barefoot, Marcus saw. Pretty toes, nice feet. A perfect package had just walked in the room, but the biggest question he could ask was: where the hell was he?

***

"Where . . ." he spoke one word, then winced from how much his throat hurt. He cleared his throat, then tried again. "Where am I?"

She came up alongside the bed and looked into his eyes. Something about hers soothed him, as they both shared gazes that were full of questions.

***

Oh, my God . . . His eyes . . . Wow!

Cynthia couldn't make herself look away from him. She hadn't noticed how unbelievably handsome he was until that exact moment, even in his current state of injury. He had curls; his face was strong, angular, with high cheekbones.

His lips put things in her head that made her nipples hard, and his gorgeous gray eyes were so deep; they gave her a sense of peace, all the while giving her butterflies in her stomach.

"You're at my apartment," Cynthia told him. "I was gonna take you to the E.R., but I noticed how bad you were bleeding from your leg. I checked it when you were passed out. You've been shot, Marcus!"

Weakly, he nodded. He winced as he swallowed what felt like sand.

Cynthia hopped up and ran out of the room in a slight panic. Marcus' eyebrows furrowed at her sudden departure until she returned less than a minute later. In her hand, she had a bottle of water and an orange pill bottle. Coming to the edge of the bed, she sat at his side and showed him the pill prescription label. He saw Oxycodone on them, at a very high milligram dosage per pill.

"Water to quench your thirst, but do you want one of those for the pain?"

He nodded.

She popped the top and took one out, then gave him the water bottle. Marcus took the pill and washed it down with a whole bottle of water. In all of a second, he felt refreshed but was still ridiculously thirsty.

"How did you get shot? Who is after you?" she asked.

***

Marcus cleared his throat a couple of times, then he looked her in her eyes, studying them. He saw sincerity and genuine concern in them.

"Me and my chick went to make a move. Shit went left. All the way left."

Her eyebrows furrowed, as if she understood but was still confused. Marcus' mind went to Inez, his eyes beginning to well up with tears.

Fuck type of nigga lets his girl get snatched up from right in front of him and doesn't do shit about it? he asked himself, mentally beating his own ass for just standing there, pistols pointed at him or not.

"Hey? Marcus?" she called his name, then gently took his hand into hers.

He looked at her, seeing such worry in her eyes.

"At some point, whatever's going on, it will be okay."

The sound of his phone ringing interrupted her before she could say more. Marcus looked and saw his phone on a long dresser, connected to a charger. She got up off the bed and went to get it for him.

"It's been ringing for three days. It's all good."

"Three days?" Marcus gasped, cutting her off with sheer shock. "I've been out for three days?"

"Yeah. You passed out in my car. I brought you here and did what I could to patch you up. You got shot. I was sure that you didn't need cops all on you, since the E.R.s have to report gunshot-wounded people to them. I'll go get you more water. You hungry?"

Marcus' stomach felt so empty that it was like it didn't even exist. He nodded, dying for something to eat.

"You said yo' name's . . . Evanna?" he asked, as she turned to head out.

She paused. He heard her take a deep breath, then she turned back around to face him.

"I lied. I didn't know if you were trustworthy when I did that, but my name's Cynthia. I'll be right back."

She left the bedroom then. Marcus looked at the screen of his Samsung Galaxy S6 and saw he had a video message from an unknown number. Then he saw he had three of them. He clicked on the first one and saw a hefty dark-skinned man wearing a mask, with no shirt on. The tattoo of pitchforks on his right pec Marcus knew very well.

It was Block.

The video started once Marcus hit play.

"What up fam? How yo' thigh doin'? I meant to hit the ground next to you. Sorry. Anyways, aye, my nigga, yo' bitch got a *bomb* on the *head*, joe! I see why yo' lame-ass sprung on her. Check it out, though!"

The camera zoomed out then. It kept going until Marcus saw Block was standing in a bedroom, and on her knees in front of him was Inez, ass naked, as was Block. Rage filled Marcus as he watched Block grab Inez's head and force his dick into her mouth. He fucked her face like it was a pussy while he held onto her head. Marcus then saw that Inez's hands were tied behind her back. Whoever was holding the camera began moving to the side, giving a much more graphic view of Block's dick going down Inez's throat while he forcefully held her head. Hearing her gagging and choking had Marcus blind with fury.

"Yeeaah! That's a good bitch! Suck this dick so yo' lame-ass boyfriend can see! Mhmmm! Shit!"

The video continued until *Block* started groaning and grunting. He pulled his dick out of Inez's mouth, then stroking himself, he held her by her hair and skeeted all over her face.

"Wooo! Aye, Moe Man! Stay tuned, my nigga! This is Pornhub in the Hood, fam! Slut bitch gone wild, joe!"

The video ended a second later. The second one Marcus saw was of Block fucking Inez from the back while she was tied to a corner bedpost. She screamed and cried for Marcus. Block smacked her ass hard and yelled for her to shut the fuck up.

Unable to watch any further, Marcus clicked out of the video and hesitated when he looked at the third one, hoping and praying that it wasn't a recording of his chick's final moments in life. He opened it and saw, now, another masked man in the picture, fucking Inez from the back while Block again forced her to suck his dick while he sat on a chair in front of her.

The camera suddenly rotated away from the grotesque sight. Another masked figure was up close—likely the one holding the camera. Marcus saw the lips. They were female lips with red lipstick on them. They curled up into a smirk as dark eyes glared at Marcus.

"Heeey, Marcus!"

Immediately, Marcus recognized Tashira's voice. He got even angrier at the moment.

"Nigga, yo' girl got all the dick right now wit' her stingy ass. I finna go get me some, too. Just wanted to say hi, and thanks for makin' gettin' rich so easy for us! Deuces, dummy!"

The video ended with laughter. Marcus felt paralyzed with grief. He had just witnessed his chick being gang-banged. To him, that was worse than catching her cheating on him with a purpose.

***

The door creaked open, interrupting Marcus' thoughts. He thought Cynthia was coming back in, but it wasn't her. It was the little girl he had seen in the backseat. She peeked around the corner, looking at Marcus. He looked back in her direction, and with a warm smile on his face, he waved at her.

"Don't be shy, baby," he heard Cynthia say just then. "Go ahead inside. Marcus is mommy's friend."

"*Ven aquí*," she then said in Spanish, telling her daughter to "come here."

Cynthia entered with a covered plate, then her daughter stepped in behind her carrying a big bottle of cranberry juice.

"Say hi, Mr. Marcus," Cynthia told the little girl.

Shyly, she did as her mother told her to. Her tiny little voice was angelic, sweet enough to put Marcus' heart at ease. She represented new life, full of sinless happiness while living in a cold, cold world.

“You okay?” Cynthia asked him, setting the plate down on his lap.

“To be honest . . . far from it. I gotta go find my girl, Cynthia. She really needs me,” he told her, unable to push the images he had seen out of his head.

“I understand. I just want to say this. You are in very bad shape, Marcus. You are shot, and you are bruised and battered from getting hit by a car *after* you got shot. I’m gonna assume that the people the cops are looking for, which is all over the news, is you and those that double-crossed you. There are no suspects, but still. For now, maybe you should just lay low.”

Marcus knew she was right. He knew it wholeheartedly, but the fact remained that his chick was being gang-raped by two guys, and it was being filmed by someone that was allegedly her homie.

“Mr. Marcus?”

Her daughter’s little voice brought Marcus back from the dark tunnels he had been in once again. He looked at her and saw that she had come closer to him.

“My mommy made you some food.”

Cynthia smiled adoringly at her daughter. Marcus felt his heart warm up.

“I see. It smells good, too,” he replied.

“Leticia, why don’t you grab a cup for Mr. Marcus? Mommy forgot to bring one.”

She nodded, then leaving the cranberry juice jug, Leticia ran off to do as her mother said.

“I can’t wait to have kids,” Marcus spoke when she had left.

“You don’t have any?”

Marcus shook his head. “Not yet. Haven’t been livin’ the type of life to where I should bring a child into the world. Too many kids out there are already fucked up.”

Cynthia chuckled. “No lie. And as hell, too. That’s noble of you, but the world is gonna’ be fucked up until the end of time. Snakes, haters, punk-ass bitches and snitches, rapists, and just plain ol' crazy people are going to increase in number. Look at how everybody hates fucking Donald Trump's bitch-ass, but they voted for him. And now look what's going on!"

Marcus shook his head.

"Dude a muhfuckin' trip. Fuck him. I hope next time it's his head, not his ear."

Cynthia laughed.

"That shit was fake as hell. It was a sympathy play so he wouldn't lose to Kamala, which he was definitely about to."

She reached over and took the top off the plate. Marcus saw scrambled cheese eggs, bacon, and four silver dollar pancakes there.

"Damn. You bring a nigga back to life, and you cooked him breakfast?" he asked, right as Leticia returned with a big cup. "Are you married? Or you got a man?"

Cynthia started laughing.

"Naw. None of that shit. Men are booty holes, no offense. All I need in my life is my baby girl, and maybe, a good friend. Me, myself, and I."

"Oh." Marcus nodded. "Well, I've been told I'm a good dude to have around. Soon as I can get up outta this bed, maybe you'll let me show you?"

She smiled at him, bashfully turning her head to hide her face.

"Um . . . let's just get you back on your feet for now, Marcus. One thing at a time, okay?"

Sensing that there was way more woven between their words than what the average person could pick up, Marcus could tell that Cynthia had a story—and he found himself really wanting to hear it. All of it.

Chapter 5

“On the G, folks! Aye! You see this shit, joe? On God, we came up! Thank you, Marcus!” Block shouted at the top of his lungs.

On the table in the kitchen of Block’s crib, the results of both licks on Marcus had the surface looking like Block was about to open up his own jewelry store. Watches, chains, rings, bracelets. White gold, yellow gold, rose gold. Plain or diamond-encrusted. New-age and vintage. There were watches ranging from simple $500 G-Shocks to $30,000 Cartiers.

Aside from the icy drip, bricks of heroin, cocaine, bottles of pills, stacks of cash, and a few guns were laid out. It looked like it was all ready to be photographed by an evidence technician after a major police raid.

***

“I can’t believe we actually robbed that nigga twice! In twenty-fo’ hours, G!” Block once again exclaimed.

“On what, though!” laughed Cam, Block’s GD homie from up in Milwaukee.“Dog a muhfuckin’ clown! How you get hit up two times in a row—and got cho’ bitch snatched up!”

“Never seen it befo’, fam. But fuck that nigga. joe, you see this thumpa’ right here?” Block grabbed the distinctive-looking 1911 .45. “Aye, Google this muhfucka, G. On ‘erythang, I swear I seen this gun in a magazine befo’, and it cost a bag!”

Cam got right on it. He took a flick of the gun with his smartphone, then transferred the image to be searched. The results popped up with the gun-maker's name and the significance of the gun's creation.

"Goddamn! Fam, this bitch cost forty grand!" Cam exclaimed, then showed a picture of the gun and its eye-catching swirls.

"Nigga . . . on *God*, we up now, joe! It might be time to head back down to 107th and State after this," Block thought out loud, thinking of where he grew up and how he could return and take some shit over with his newfound wealth.

Cam looked at Block.

"I thought you hated Chicago?"

"I did—'cause I was broke, starvin', and gang-bangin'. Now, this shit here, joe? This shit here! This shit finna have me ridin' Bentleys 'n livin' in condos! All the hoes gon' jock a nigga 'cause I'ma be made of money, joe! Matter of fact . . . why not Miami?"

"Oh God, nigga! Aye! Do you realize how good we could live down there?"

"Hell yeah! These bitches out here broke as fuck and dick-ride like they think they got bus fare. I finna elevate myself, my nigga. I will never go broke again! On GD muthafuckin' N, nigga!"

Just as Cam was about to speak, the clacking of high heels got their attention. They looked toward the entryway that adjoined the kitchen to the living room—and saw Tashira appear, looking like she was about to pop out and catch every baller she came across.

The 5'6" tall beauty, blessed with flawless cinnamon-colored skin, arms tatted up, with a flying heart over the center of her chest, and the word *Blessed* tatted above her left eyebrow, was jaw-droppingly gorgeous and had the body of a goddess. Her long, lustrous hair was dark at the roots but flowed out into a reddish hue at the ends. She had walnut-shaped eyes under perfectly arched eyebrows. A small nose, and perky lips glossed with the same color lipstick that matched her tinted hair ends.

Tashira was looking so damn good in the tight orange long-sleeved dress that clung to her voluptuous frame. Its low-cleavage line let her chest ink show, and it stopped at mid-thigh. She wore sheer brown pantyhose with it, brown leather calf-high stiletto boots, and a brown leather mini biker jacket with gold earrings, a gold necklace, and a gold Gucci watch on her wrist.

Block's jaw dropped as he looked at his bad-ass gangster bitch, eyes filled with lust—and anger—for the 23-year-old belle.

Cam's jaw also dropped as he gazed at Tashira with awe-struck eyes. His dick grew hard instantly, and he wished she had been in the gangbang video he and Block made of Inez.

"Aye, nigga!" Block barked at Cam, seeing him ogling his girl.

Cam immediately turned away and looked at him.

" 'Sup?"

"Fuck you mean 'sup?' You see somethin' you like?"

Block heard Tashira giggle while Cam scratched his head.

"Bae, relax. I'm a sexy-ass woman. Niggas gon' be lookin' and tryna touch all night long," Tashira told him.

He looked at her.

"And where the fuck you think you goin', lookin' like that?"

She smacked her lips and rolled her eyes.

"Out," she sassed, placing her hands on her hips.

Instantly infuriated, Block shot up out of his chair and rushed her—so fast that Tashira's brain couldn't register the menacing move fast enough to send signals to her legs to RUN!

"Bitch!" Block snapped, grabbing her by the throat. "Out where?"

"To a club, Block! Lemme' go!" Tashira demanded.

Block contemplated choking her ass out, but ended up falling back when he thought about how he needed her. Releasing his grip, he took a step back, raising his head with a silent 'pardon-me' look.

"Joe! Yo' ass tweakin' wit' that possessive-ass shit, nigga! Calm the fuck down!" she growled angrily.

"Yeah, Block. You just went—"

Cam had started talking, but a deadly look from Block shut him right the fuck up before he could finish his sentence.

"You two muhfuckas had y'all fun!" Tashira continued. "Makin' porn videos in shit. Now we finna go have us some fun, pig-ass niggas!"

"Hold up . . . *We*?" Block questioned, as he sat back down, looking puzzled.

They all heard more high-heels clacking right then. Seconds later, Block and Cam went wide-eyed, when they saw Inez walk right up to Tashira, cup her cheek with one hand; then turning her face towards her, she pressed her lips to hers, and kissed her. And Inez kept kissing her, slipping her tongue into Tashira's mouth. She yanked Tashira close up on her, and with both of her hands, she grabbed her plump 44" ass, squeezing her cheeks while they both moaned from heating each other up like an oven turned all the way up in a little-ass house with no heat in the freezing winter.

"What the fuuuuck?" Block was dumbfounded by what he was seeing, but even more so, when Tashira actually kissed her back.

"Woooooow!" Cam was just stuck in disbelief.

Inez continued kissing Tashira like she was ready to strip her naked and get to try right in front of them.

The curvaceous chocolate drop was dressed to kill as well that evening. She wore a ridiculously tight two-piece outfit that was beige, tan, white, and brown, with snake-print all-over the long-sleeved cropped top belly shirt and leggings. Down on her feet, she wore shiny white six-inch pointed toe pumps. Her rusty-brown hair was pulled up into a high ponytail, and her baby hair edges were gelled down and told to emphasize her stunning face.

She put on matte-brown eyeshadow, black eye liner, gold lipstick, and was flossing huge gold hoop earrings, two gold chains around her neck, her nails painted gold, with white air brushed designs on them.

Block was truly astounded by how bad Inez was. He thought to himself, *Maaaan, if the bitch didn't suck so much dick, I'd wife the hoe. Wit' her Naturi Naughton-lookin' ass....*

***

"Well, damn! That's how y'all feel?" Cam asked with surprise.

"What the hell? Tashira? . . . What the hell?" Block added, lost for any more words than that.

The ladies broke away from their hot and steamy embrace and looked at Block and Cam. With sheepish smiles on their faces, they grinned broadly, looking like horny-ass college girls that just fucked their professor for a passing grade.

The biggest shock was more from Inez. She was just a complete mystery. She was a freak that knew no boundaries, and she was a down-ass bitch that was down to ride. The thing was, nobody knew where her loyalty would ever lie. The way she got down on Marcus actually shocked Block. He really did think that she had loved the little nigga, but she was just that good of an actress. To Block, nothing was more unnerving than a drop-dead gorgeous snake-ass bitch that had no limits on who she would get down on, for whatever reason.

"Okay, then . . . sooo . . . um . . ." Block was nearly speechless, as was Cam.

"Pick yo' jaw up, Bae," Tashira spoke. "We'll be back later, a'ight?"

"Um . . . yeah," he nodded, then his eyes went to Inez, seeing a smirk on her lips.

"Looks like you and Cam have a lot of work to do, Block," she said. "This means I get my cut some time soon, right? All the shit I had to do to get it?"

"Duh, muhfucka," Block chuckled. "You deserve an award for all that dick yo' swallowed, shortie. On the G, you got that lil' nigga sprung!"

"Nigga, what?" Inez snapped angrily.

Cam laughed.

Tashira grabbed Inez before she could run up on Block. He smirked at her, finding her anger hilarious.

Bitch, yo' thot ass let us run a train on you on camera, just to keep a lie goin' to Marcus' lame ass! Cam thought to himself.

"Block, come on now wit' that extra shit," Tashira scolded, standing in front of Inez to keep her back. "We dun' hit that hood lottery because of how much dick she sucked!"

"Shira!" Inez yelled, now at her.

"Well, bitch, it's true! Stop gettin' mad, 'cause if it wasn't for you, that shit wouldn't be sittin' on the table! Ain't that right, Block?" Tashira cut her eyes towards her dude.

"Yep. It is true." Block looked at Inez and smiled. "We couldn't have done it without you and yo' . . . skills."

Cam was rolling with laughter, tears filling his eyes and damn near choking from how hard he was laughing. Then he heard Tashira shout, "Inez!" a second before he opened his eyes and saw her coming.

Wham!

Her fist flew and sailed into his nose, hard enough to knock the 240-pound goon and his chair backwards.

"Daayuum, Joe!" Block shouted, then he started laughing at his homie who was laid out on the floor with a bloody nose.

Tashira grabbed Inez and pulled her back before she jumped on Cam and went apeshit on him.

"Better control yo' lil' bitch, Tashira," Block told her, wiping his tears of laughter from his face.

"Shut up, Block!" Tashira snapped as she finally got Inez out of the kitchen. "Just for that, I'm stayin' out all night, nigga!"

He heard the two stomp through the living room, then seconds later, the sound of the front door opening, then slamming shut came.

"Why do bitches think that they can't be replaced?" he asked aloud to himself, shaking his head afterwards. He looked over at where Cam still was laid out on his back, eyes closed. "Damn. She fucked that nigga up! Aye! Cam?"

Cam didn't respond.

"Okay, then. Holla when you wake up. I'll be here, joe," Block clowned, then he grabbed his iPhone, went to his music, and put on some EST Gee before getting started on going through all the merch to calculate the worth of it all, and then to plan his next big move that was going to turn him into a hood star.

***

"Damn, that shit was fi', Cynthia. Thank you," Marcus said to her, grateful for the home-cooked breakfast and her hospitality.

"You're welcome. Is there anything else you need?" she asked him.

"Yeah. Money, a life . . . revenge. Right now, though, I'll settle for leavin' outta Lake County before I go insane."

"Well, where do you wanna go? We could get an Uber. My car needs a windshield."

Marcus looked at her. She looked away, towards the window. He knew that he was *why* she needed a windshield.

"Cyn', I promise you, I will pay you for messin' yo' car up."

"Pay me? For hitting you with my car? Now that isn't somethin' you hear too often," Cynthia couldn't help but chuckle.

"I told you. I'm a good dude to have around," he told her, right as his phone dinged from a text message. He asked her to hold up a second, then seeing that it was Inez texting him, Marcus' eyes bugged wide in shock. "Oh shit! This is my woman!" he exclaimed, opening the text right away.

Marcus. I am okay. I managed to get away from Block when they let me take a shower. I am going to my mom's down in Alabama for a while. Please rest your mind. I know you've been worried about me. I need you to give me some time to heal. I am broken. I will call you when I can function. Please don't call, nor text. Just let me be. I love you.

"What the fuck," he said.

"Is she okay?" Cynthia asked, looking at him with concern.

"No. She isn't."

Marcus tried to call her. It went right to voicemail. It did for all four times he tried to call her. Cursing, he gave up.

"I'm sorry, Marcus," Cynthia told him. "Do you want some alone time?"

"Naw, I'm . . . she said she's cool, but . . ."

His phone started ringing, interrupting what he was about to say. He saw who was calling and groaned, really wanting to not answer her call. But if he didn't . . . she would find him and put her foot up his ass.

"Hello?"

"Fuck you mean *hello*?" he heard his mother snap. "Nigga! *¡Tú me tienes jodia! ¿Crees que 'stoy jugando contigo?* Huh? You think I'm fucking playing wit' you?"

Marcus sighed. "No, ma, I don't think you're fucking playing wit' me, and I do not have you fucked up," he said, addressing the first thing she said in Spanish. "Why is you yellin' at me? What happened to 'Hi, mijo! How are you, my handsome sexy baby boy?'"

Cynthia had gone from having furrowed eyebrows to snickering at Marcus.

“Where are you, Marcus?” his mother asked.

“Well, in a bedroom wit’ a gorgeous Latina that saved my life. Other than that, I do not know.”

“*¡Cabrón!* Keep fucking playing! *¡Te lo juro por Dios!* I will kick your motherfucking ass! On *Stone*!”

“Hold, please.” Marcus muted the phone and asked Cynthia where they were. “Cynthia, check it out. My O.G. *loves* to fight. If I don’t tell her what she wants to know, great bodily harm will come to me.”

“Oh my,” Cynthia replied back, with a look of disbelief on her face.

She gave him the address and he gave it to his mother.

“I’ll be pulling up in a minute. Marcus, I swear to you, if you leave before I get here, it ain’t gon’ be me that you gotta worry about.”

The call ended. Marcus’ furrowed brows had Cynthia wondering what was just said.

“Wow. She’s really bringin’ him here?” he said to himself, perplexed by his mother’s threat, which shook him to the core.

The man was a beast, in the truest form.

“She’s coming here now?” Cynthia asked, bringing Marcus out of his stroll down memory lane to the days he split living in Moe Town with his mother, and in K-Town with his pops.

“Yeah. Do me a favor,” Marcus requested.

“Sure. You want me to be at your side when she gets here?”

“I was thinkin’ more on the lines of wrap me up in bubble wrap, gimme a helmet, and stand by wit’ a bucket of ice water.”

Cynthia busted out laughing. “Marcus. Come on, now. She can’t be *that* bad.”

While she was laughing, Marcus looked at Cynthia with a serious expression that put her laughter away.

"Cyn' . . . my momma is from Chicago. *Southside*," he told her. "The blanks that remain, I will let you figure it all out. I warn you. If you make eye contact, she might turn yo' ass to stone."

***

"All you have to do is call that number. The second you see her, don't hesitate," Araña said to the group of youngsters posted up in the lot outside of Salem, a small convenience store in Zion, on the corner of Salem and Galilee. "Whoever does right, you'll get $10,000 in cash."

"Ten bandz?" one of the youngsters replied, with his eyes bugged wide.

"Just to call you if we see the bitch?" another asked.

"Yup. That's all," Araña confirmed, while one of his men continued holding her picture up for them to get a good look at. "But do not touch her or the little girl! Only call!"

"Who is she to you? Wifey on the run?" one more asked with a chuckle, which made his guys laugh.

Araña faked his own laugh. "No. She just lost her way, and I need to help her find it."

Just then, his phone vibrated in his pocket. He excused himself while his crew answered the young dudes' questions. Pulling his phone out, Araña's eyes went wide when he saw the notification on his screen. Then his lips curled into a smirk.

"*¡Vamos*"*!*" he hollered to his men, after turning back towards them.

Without question, the ten goons that he was with—all armed and ready to shoot at their boss's command—left the young guys and headed back to the two black GMC Denali XLs, hopped in, and peeled off like the store had a nuclear bomb inside of it about to go off and vaporize everyone close to the blast.

Chapter 6

Cynthia heard the doorbell ring as she finished up the dishes. Turning off the water, she grabbed her phone from off of the counter.

"Who you got coming to see you? I thought you were out there laying low, Cynthia," Carmela, from back in Reynosa, asked her.

"I am," Cynthia told her. "It's my new friend's mom. She's coming to see him . . . or beat him up. He swears she's crazy."

Carmela laughed.

"Lemme call you back, though, chica."

"Yup. Talk to you later. Be safe, mami."

Cynthia ended the call as she got to her door. She reached for the button to buzz the door dam at the main entrance door.

Less than a minute later, Cynthia heard the sounds of stamping coming from inside the hallway. Standing up on her tippy toes, she looked out of the peephole in the door.

Oh wow . . . she thought to herself when she saw the statuesque Latina appear at her door.

Incredibly voluptuous, like a strip-club dancer, the woman was stacked with an hourglass-shaped frame, and she was tall as hell, with fiery red hair and oh-so-delectable Puerto Rican caramel-browned skin.

Cynthia unlocked the chain and doorknob locks. She opened the door and was wowed by the 5'10" tall woman. Her stature alone was intimidating, and her beauty was alluring.

She was dressed in a red sports-bra neck-strapped top that let her inked-up arms, neck, and back show, along with a flat and toned stomach. The red leggings accentuated her runner's legs, thick thighs, and an ass so fat that it could be seen from the front. Down on the woman's feet, she had on all-red Air Force 1 low-tops.

Cynthia looked at the woman's remarkably gorgeous face and thought to herself that she kind of favored the wild-ass tattoo show chick, Sky, from *Black Ink.*

***

"Hi. Are you Alondra?" Cynthia asked her in a pleasant tone.

"*Sí,*" she nodded, looking Cynthia up and down. "And you are?"

"I'm Cynthia. Please come in."

Stepping aside, Cynthia invited Alondra in. As the tall vixen entered, Cynthia just could not help but look at the lady's ass. It was so perfectly round and plump. The leggings she had on looked like they had their own thong built into them.

She closed and locked her door as the woman paused, looking over at where Leticia was in the living room, watching a movie through a pair of virtual reality goggles, laughing and giggling.

"Your daughter?" the woman asked, which made Cynthia relax. She turned and looked at her.

Cynthia nodded with a proud smile. She looked over at their angel and saw Leticia was now looking their way, with her goggles lifted up from her eyes.

"*Mi amor. Vente y conocer esta señora.*" Speaking in Spanish, she called her daughter and told her to come here and meet the woman.

Leticia got up and ran to her mother, hugging her while shyly looking up at the Boricua.

“*Hola, mamita,*” Alondra cooed softly, crouching down to get eye level with the toddler. “*Soy Alondra. ¿Cómo te llamas?*” she then said, introducing herself, then asking what her name was.

“Leticia,” she said shyly.

Alondra smiled. “I’m Marcus’ mother. He’s my baby boy, and I love him so much, I came to see him really quickly and to tell him how happy I am for him bein’ such a good boy. Do you know where he is?”

Cynthia stifled a laugh. It was clear as day in the woman’s tone that Marcus was in deep shit.

“Um . . . no.” Leticia shook her head and then turned her head away.

Alondra chuckled. Standing up, she smiled at Cynthia. “She’s a soldier.”

Cynthia nodded. “She learns quickly, but this isn’t that type of situation, baby,” she told her daughter. Then to Alondra, “Marcus is in my bedroom . . . um . . .”

“Hiding?” Alondra cut in.

“Um . . . no,” Cynthia replied, with absolutely no conviction in her voice.

Alondra chuckled. “Good job. I’ll assume the bedroom is down the hall and happen to find my son.”

Cynthia watched Alondra walk off, ass bouncing and jiggling with every step she took. She got to the bedroom and walked in, disappearing from her line of sight.

***

“Marcus Velez.” Alondra saw a human-shaped bump under the blanket on the bed trying to keep still. “Get your ass up, or I will rock bottom yo’ ass! On Stone!”

The blanket slid down. She saw his handsome young playboy face. Her anger started to subside when she saw her son. She loved him so much. She would kill for him. She *had* killed for him, but receiving a random text about him in "deep trouble" had her ready to strangle his ass.

"Why you dressed like that?" he asked, frowning at her.

Alondra furrowed her brows. "What's wrong wit' my clothes? This that new *Fabletics* shit that Khloé Kardashian put out. You seen the commercial? Where she showin' all that ass in them baby blue leggings wit' a built-in thong?"

Marcus stared at her. "Why are we havin' this type of conversation?"

"Marcus, get your ass up! You're comin' with me to my crib, so stop worryin' about how I'm dressed and come on!"

"Ma! Why is you so fired up right now?"

Alondra marched towards him. He slid back towards the opposite end of the bed when she plopped down close to where he had just been.

"Negro, stop actin' all scary 'n shit, joe. On the Five, I raised yo' ass to be way tougher than to be scared of a girl."

"Ma . . . when I was nine, you beat a chick up in the grocery store wit' a can of baked beans, and you bought them afterwards to make pork 'n beans for me."

Alondra laughed. "And yo' ass ate 'em all up, too."

"When I was eleven, you beat up my teacher in the parkin' lot and took her car."

"She gave you an F on your report card, papa, so I F'd her stupid ass."

"When I was thirteen, you put a man's face on the corner of a curb after dad beat him up and stomped his face literally in! You are not a regular girl."

"Hey! I ride wit' my nigga, okay? Me and Bae made you, so don't be questionin' how we regulate on bitch-ass niggas."

Marcus laughed. "Yo' ass wild, ma, real talk."

"Mhmm, whatever, little nigga." Alondra stood up then. "All that is besides the point, Marcus. You out here robbing mothafuckas 'n shit when you supposed to be staying outta trouble, yet you fucking wit' bum-bitch-ass niggas' shit."

"Who told you that?" Marcus looked at her peculiarly, feeling his heart rate speed up.

Alondra took her phone out of a pocket on the side of her leggings. She went into her texts and brought up the random number with a disturbing message. Handing it over to him, Alondra watched his facial expression go from curious to pissed as he read it.

"Bitch-ass nigga," Marcus muttered.

"Kind of sound like what a nigga that's supposed to be yo' guy, but is really a back-doorin' snake, would say."

Marcus shook his head. "This nigga Block," he said to himself, astounded by the text telling his mother that he was out here robbing people and was going to end up getting killed to go save his life right away. "I'ma kill that hoe-ass nigga, on Stone that nigga foul as hell!"

"He *been* foul, Marcus. You just found out firsthand. Now get up so we can get goin'."

She then heard what sounded like weird skidding outside. As Marcus got up, Alondra went to the window. She saw two black SUVs in the middle of the apartment complex's parking lot with a mob of men hopping out of them.

"The hell?" she spoke out loud.

"What's wrong?" he heard Marcus ask.

"There's a gang of Hispanic dudes out in the lot. They just hopped out of two black trucks like they were twelve."

She saw one man in a suit, seeming to be giving orders to others, then they all split up: five running towards the entrance of the building across from where Cynthia's was, the other five heading towards Cynthia's apartment, while the man in the suit stayed by the SUV.

"Them niggas is not the cops," she heard Marcus say, discovering that he had come up alongside her.

"Lemme find out they're here for you, Marcus!" Alondra snapped with panic.

"Hell naw. That's a fact. On Stone, ma."

The bedroom door flew open just then. Cynthia rushed in with Leticia. Cynthia looked terrified, and so did her daughter.

"Hey? What's wrong, Cyn?" Marcus asked her as she hurried to her closet and started pulling out bags that looked filled and heavy.

"I have to go! Right now!" Cynthia replied, truly sounding scared to death.

It suddenly hit Alondra. Seeing Cynthia scared shitless and her daughter in tears, she surmised that the men outside had to be there for her. Marcus had hobbled over to where she frantically got bags of luggage out of her closet, trying to find out what was wrong.

"Those men outside are here for me, Marcus! They work for a cartel leader in Texas! He's been after me since I escaped him! I need to go now!"

"Cynthia," Alondra called to her.

She and Marcus turned towards her.

"Do you have a gun? Mine is in my car," Alondra told her, already gearing up to go crazy on anyone threatening her son or who her son happened to be very fond of.

Cynthia nodded, then pointing to a suitcase with wheels on it, Alondra scrambled over to it, unzipping it.

"Ol' school." Alondra nodded in approval of the O.G. assault rifle that was stashed inside. "Listen up. This shit is about to get hectic. Follow my lead, and we all live. Got it?"

"Yeah! What's the plan, ma?" Marcus eagerly asked, with Cynthia and Leticia by his side.

"The plan is to stay Stone to the Bone and get Cynthia and Leticia outta here, baby boy. No fuck-ups! Now listen to me really good . . ." Alondra instructed, then ran it all down for them with a backup plan to follow in case shit went to the left.

***

Araña listened to his goons with the two-way radio earpiece in his ear. He could hear Team One, sent to the two-story building that sat with its back to the big Walmart behind it, announcing to him that they were coming up empty. He heard doors being kicked in, residents yelling, screaming, cursing, and in some cases, he heard assault rifle gunfire that he knew came from his guys.

The Water Fort apartment complex he had been drawn to—when his I.T. technician sent him a notification of Cynthia's phone being turned on and a call being placed on it, enabling it to be tracked—was filled with folks from other suburban areas and those from the trenches. He knew there were going to be hustlers and gangsters living there that would shoot to defend themselves, and he knew they would regret it.

Hearing Camino, leader of Team Two sent into the building that sat off to the middle of the complex's rear, Araña listened to the man question a resident about Cynthia, after it sounded like the person knew of her.

"Yes! She stays two doors down! Please! Don't hurt us! We're just—"

—Brrrrr!—

"Oh my god! Geraldo!" a woman screamed.

—Brrrrrrr!—

Araña heard silence then.

"Boss, we have her location. We're going in right now," Camino told Giovanni.

"Hurry up! *¡Agarra a esa puta!"* he ordered Camino, telling him in Spanish to "get that bitch!"

He then called to Team One, demanding they get over to assist Team Two. Anxiously, he waited, hoping and praying that the goose chase would end so he could get back to Texas. He hated the Midwest with a passion.

***

Camino and his four shooters huddled up at the door that the girl was said to be at. Standing back, he silently counted down with his fingers, then gave the command to the first man to move.

—Boom!—

With his Mossberg pump shotgun, he blew the door out, then the second man kicked the door in like he was the police. The third and fourth man ran inside with their AK-47s up and ready to blast. The second they stepped in . . .

"Aaaaaahhhhh!"

The two dropped to the floor, screaming and crying in pain, while the second and the first ran in, with Camino behind them.

—Brrrrrrr! Brrrrrrr!—

Camino flew to his left, just in the nick of time. He had seen a woman in all-red with red hair jump up from behind the dining room table at the immediate right upon entering the apartment. She blew at his first two guys with an SKS, taking them by surprise and laying them out with chest and face shots.

"*¡Vamos, Mamabichos!* Let's go!" he heard her yell as he crawled behind a couch in the living room to take cover.

"Team Two! My men are down! *¡Ayúdame!*" Camino urgently requested through his earpiece.

"We're coming, Camino!" he heard Edgar tell him.

—Brrrrrrr! Brrrr! Brrrrr!—

More bullets flew. Camino braced himself as they came so close to hitting him through the couch.

"Fuck is you hidin' for, puta! Get cho' bitch-ass up and fight like a man!"

The woman's words made Camino's gangster feel challenged. In a fit of rage, Camino gathered himself and jumped up with his chopper, ready to blast the bitch. But before he could look in on her . . . he heard a whistle right next to him.

***

The second the cartel goon turned his head toward him, Marcus pulled the trigger and put a .40 caliber slug right through the center of his forehead, blowing his brains out through the gaping hole in the back of his head.

The man fell dead to the carpeted floor, and blood oozed out, pooling around his head.

Brrrr! Brrrr! Brrrrr!

The chopper's loud blasts got Marcus' attention. He looked up and saw his O.G. put the two guys who'd been burned by Cynthia's boiling salt water out of their misery.

"Come on!" Alondra shouted, dumping the spent clip and slapping in another one.

Cynthia, with two duffel bags strapped over both shoulders and holding Leticia's hand, hurried out behind Alondra. Marcus caught up and held down the rear, refusing to let anyone catch them slipping.

***

Alondra crept low and fast toward the stairs, gripping the SKS like she was in a war zone, about to run into an enemy stronghold. She heard yelling and shouting coming from below the stairwell.

Holding up a hand, she halted Cynthia and Marcus, then waved her hand to signal them to get back. Seeing men running up the stairs, she got ready to empty another clip.

***

Araña ran towards the building with his modified SIG Sauer MPX submachine gun, locked and loaded with a forty-round clip filled with 9mm rounds. Hearing Camino's plea for help—then nothing—told him Cynthia had help.

As he got there, Team One had just run in through the main entrance door. Hurrying to catch up, he heard assault rifle fire inside. He reached the doorway and saw three of Edgar's men tumbling down the stairs and landing on the main floor's landing, all of them with bullet holes in their faces and heads.

"¡Patrón, boss!" Edgar called out from the side of the stairwell.

Araña saw him and his last two guys ducked off to the side, out of the line of fire. Grinding his teeth in anger, he marched toward the steps, raised his machine gun up, and started firing upward as he climbed the stairs.

Boooom!

An explosion suddenly went off right behind him. The blast was powerful enough to knock him forward to the floor, dropping his gun in the process.

Extreme heat came from below him. He managed to roll onto his back, ears ringing from the loud blast. Flames roared where he had just been. Edgar and the other two were laid out, their charred bodies burning like charcoal in a grill.

He then saw a tall and wide figure, dressed in all-black, step into the entryway area with a huge gun. Unaffected by the burning hallway, the figure walked nonchalantly toward the flames.

Seconds later, he saw a woman in the sexiest red workout outfit, running toward the exit with a chopper aimed forward. She'd come from the opposite end of the hall where emergency stairs provided another way down from second-floor tenants. Right behind her, Araña saw Cynthia with two big duffel bags—and her daughter.

Araña immediately went to grab his gun, when a young dude came behind the chicana and the little girl, gripping a pistol in his hand. They all ran out of the building together, unaware of his presence.

Araña got up and, through pain, grabbed his street sweeper, then limped down the stairs, through the fire, and out of the building. Outside, huge crowds of people who lived there gathered at the far end of the lot, while the sirens of emergency vehicles wailed from very close by.

"Fuck!" he cursed out loud, unable to see where they'd gone.

Someone screamed just then.

"He has a gun!"

Araña looked in the direction it came from. He saw a group of women with a few men. They all backed away—then turned and ran.

The sound of engines starting up got his attention as the sirens grew louder. He saw two vehicles peel off from the middle of the parking lot, heading toward the path road that exited the complex.

"Fuck no!" Araña cursed.

He pointed his machine gun at them and pulled the trigger, refusing to give up without at least making someone bleed.

***

"Shit!" Marcus cursed as bullets flew at his mother's red 2018 Dodge Charger Hellcat, blowing out the front and rear passenger windows.

"Cyn! Stay down!" he hollered to the back seat, staying low himself, as did his O.G., while racing for the exit.

Suddenly, a big bulky H2 Hummer SUT pickup truck sped up alongside them and stayed there, purposely getting in the line of fire.

Marcus looked over at the Hummer. The windows were limo-tinted. He couldn't see the man behind the wheel—but he knew who it was. Seeing his face when they had escaped the flaming hallway had dumbfounded Marcus. He couldn't believe it. He just couldn't.

***

"Ma! what is he doin'?" Marcus shouted, hearing gunfire hitting the other side of the H2.

"Saving our asses! Again!" Alondra yelled, seconds before they were both out of the line of fire.

"You better thank him when we get to Chicago, Marcus! Then hope he doesn't put his foot in yo' ass!"

She reached Loreli Drive and swerved a hard left, with the H2 right behind. Racing to Route 173—just as fire trucks and ambulances came flying around the corner to get to the scene—Alondra banged a right onto 173 and put the pedal to the metal.

Marcus looked back and saw the H2 still behind them. Looking into the back seat, he saw Cynthia and Leticia still lying low.

"It's okay now. We good, Cyn. Lety," he told them. "I promise. Where we goin' now, dude gotta bring an army if he wanna get at y'all."

"Straight up," Alondra cosigned. "No me importa un carajo qué hiciste, mami," she added, telling Cynthia she didn't give a fuck what she did. "On Stone, you wit' us now, so relax. You and Lety are safe."

Marcus saw Cynthia nod. She picked up her daughter and pulled her onto her lap, holding her tightly.

"Thank you," Cynthia wept, grateful for him, his mother, and even the unknown savior that had aided their escape from sure death. "Thank you so much."

Marcus nodded to her, then gave her a warm smile.

"I told you, my O.G. a muhfuckin' goon. Just wait 'til you meet the nigga that's in the Hummer."

"Haa!" Alondra laughed out loud. "Straight up, baby girl! On the *Five*, my baby is the epitome of a Black Gangster! ¡Tú vas a ver, mamita!"

***

“Motherfuuuckeerr!” Araña cursed angrily as the two vehicles got away. Watching them swerve up out of the Water Fort Apartments and race toward Zion’s Route 173, he boiled with rage at his own failure.

Fire trucks and ambulances turned onto Loreli Drive. As they turned onto 173 and sped west, the vehicles disappeared from his view.

He turned around to get back to his vehicle—when he heard:

“Police! don’t move!”

Araña complied and dropped his machine gun.

“Hands up!”

He raised his hands and waited. Hearing the crackling of radios behind him, he could tell more cops were en route. Desperation and fear of being locked up when he had a mission to complete set in.

The second he felt a hand grab his left wrist, Araña made his move.

Years of hand-to-hand combat training had made him a very skilled fighter. He had no intention of going to jail that night.

Like a lightning strike, Araña spun to his right, fast, and grabbed the cop’s wrist.

“Freeze! Stop!” another officer yelled, pointing his gun at Araña.

Quickly, forcing the cop to be his human shield, Araña disarmed him and put the cop’s gun to his head. The four uniformed Zion police officers there, all aiming at him, demanded he drop the weapon.

“Shoot him!” the cop he held at gunpoint shouted.

“Put your guns down, or this motherfucker gon’ be the next one on the news!” Araña threatened.

“Okay. Okay. Don’t do anything you gonna regret, man!” a female cop said, releasing her grip on her gun. “We’re gonna put our guns down, all right? Take it easy.”

Araña waited for the others to lower their weapons.

"What the fuck are y'all doin'? Shoot this son of a bitch!" the cop he had hemmed up shouted again.

"Put your guns on the ground and walk away!" Araña barked, pressing the Glock's barrel harder to the cop's head.

They complied, then began to back away.

Araña heard more sirens blaring. He saw a wave of cop cars flying into the Water Fort's parking lot entrance.

The second the other cops got within ten feet, Araña let go of the cop and bashed him in the head with the gun, then pointed it at another officer.

Pow! Zzzzzzzzzzzzzzzzzz!

Before he could fire, a loud pop sounded—and a searing, hot, shocking sensation surged through him.

He immediately lost his grip on the gun, seizing up, and dropped to the grass, shaking and convulsing as the cop who'd snuck up behind him tased the shit out of him.

Araña thrashed and kicked like he was possessed by a demon trying to stay inside him during an exorcism. The cop tased him for a grueling ten seconds, then let go of the trigger, leaving Araña immobilized and twitching.

"You're under arrest, you stupid cocksucker!" the cop yelled as the others ran up and roughly cuffed him. "Fuck your rights too! Trump says we can do as we please, so we'll be making a pit stop in a dark tunnel before you go to lovely Lake County Jail."

Chapter 7

Kendrick Lamar's "Not Like Us" blared from the club's speakers. The massive crowd inside was turnt up! They rapped along with the gigantic middle finger to the wannabe American-but-Canadian non-hood rapper, sipping drinks, ballers throwing big faces at the thick-ass dancers shaking their asses to make it rain on them. Voluptuous bottle girls moved about, delivering high-priced liquor to those that could afford it.

Lights up in the ceiling flashed different colors every few seconds. Fog machines poured down thick clouds of mist from the ceiling. It was lit the fuck up in Club T'D Up. Gangsters, hustlers, ballers, dancers, sluts, classy ladies, and hood bitches had the place nearly filled to capacity. Zion, Waukegan, and North Chicago were all there, partying their asses off, and had no plans of leaving until six in the morning.

***

Tashira sipped her *Sex on the Beach*, then continued tapping her foot on the ground. Still pissed at how Block had gripped her up in front of Cam, she was trying hard to think of a way to get back at him. He was so abusive mentally, emotionally, and physically. As much as she did for him, he should be treating her like everything she touched turned into gold.

"Shira!" Inez yelled, which made her jump.

Tashira looked at Inez like she was crazy. "What the hell are you yellin' for?"

"'Cause, bitch! Yo' ass been in some other world since we got hea'. Fuck is wrong with you?"

"Block. He be really tweakin', and it be havin' me wantin' to . . ."

Tashira paused before the words could come out of her mouth.

"Wantin' to what?" Inez looked at her with confusion, then her eyes went wide with realization. "Oh! You wanna fuck you one of these niggas up in here!"

"N-no! I . . . no!" Tashira capped, then took another gulp. Inez burst out laughing at her.

"Tashira, see! That's why yo' ass needs to be single. Number one, that pussy is mine and always will be. But I know you like dark dick more than pussy, so I don't mind lettin' you do you. But that bitch-ass fake-ass Tee Grizzley-lookin'-ass nigga ain't for you. Ain't nothin' wrong wit' havin' a thug-nigga in yo' life, but he needs to be more than just capable of pullin' grimeys on his own homies because his ass scared to go at real killas. You need a nigga that gets the bag, one with good dick, who actually cares for you."

Tashira snorted a laugh. "You mean like how Marcus was? To you?" she asked back with a raised eyebrow.

Inez waved her off. "Girl, we ain't talkin' about mine. We talkin' about yo' nunnish-ass."

"Nunnish? Bitch, you forgot that I used to be wilder than you?"

"Sheeeeit, ain't nobody ever been like me. When's the last time you sucked a random nigga's dick?"

"Uh . . . never!" Tashira swore, as Future's "Move Too Fast" came on.

"That's gon' change tonight, joe. On the Fin!" Inez swore, looking around the club for potential hookup-worthy dudes.

Tashira smacked her lips, rolling her eyes. "Here you go wit' that gang-bangin' shit. You're a whole female, like, chill out."

"Hoe, I grew up wit' them Mafia Insanes. I'm forever Vice Lord, biiiiitch! Now shut cho' ass up so I can find you a dick to suck."

Unable to help it, Tashira busted out laughing at her. Inez started pointing out a bunch of dudes around them.

"Nope. Fat and clowned out," Tashira said of a chunky nigga trying way too hard to impress a dancer with jokes, when everybody know that bands will make her fuck.

Inez showed her a light-skinned guy, flossing in jewelry, rocking designer. "How 'bout him?"

Tashira shook her head.

Inez laughed. "Okay. Ummm . . . ooooo! How 'bout him? And he's comin' this way!"

Tashira looked where Inez was pointing and saw a muscular dark-skinned man rocking all-white, diamond chains around his neck, a diamond watch, long dreadlocks that were freshly twisted to the roots then put into two-strand twists, and a razor-sharp low-trimmed beard.

Next to him was a man with a neat bald fade and a sharp goatee, with skin the color of Nutella. He, too, was dripping in icy jewelry, rocking designer, looking fresh.

Tashira's eyes went back to the muscle-bound man with dreads. His eyes seemed to be locked right on her, and as he got closer, she could see how white his teeth were from his million-dollar smile.

***

"Ladies, ladies, what up, though? How y'all doin' tonight?" the man with dreads asked pleasantly, with a voice made for being a radio show DJ.

Tashira found herself to be lost for words; the very sight of them had her nipples getting hard. The man was tall, dark, and handsome, like a GQ model.

"We good. How you doin'?" Inez asked, speaking up for the both of them.

"Now that we finally found the sexiest girls in the entire club, and they look like they need some company, me and my nigga C-Note are super good," said Dreads, smiling at Inez for a second, then to Tashira. "I'm Dollaz . . . what's your name?"

"Um . . . um . . ."

"Monica! Girl, stop actin' shy like that!" Inez scolded, giving Tashira a look that told her to get it together!

"Right . . . my bad. India," she then played along, putting on a smile for Dollaz. "It's nice to meet you. You and yo' guy tryna' join us?"

"Only if ya' boyfriend won't care. It's our last night out here in Illinois. We head back to Cleveland tomorrow."

"Oh, okay. Y'all from outta town," Tashira restated, glancing at Inez.

"Well, I think we should give you two handsome 'n fly-ass niggas a farewell that you can be proud to tell yo' people back home about," Inez said to C-Note.

He smiled with eagerness in his eyes. "Sounds like we gon' need us a bottle."

He and Dollaz both pulled out wads of cash so thick that they looked like pages from a Bible ripped out and rubber-banded.

"Your choice, ladies," Dollaz told them, popping the rubber band on his cash. "Anything y'all want, it's on us."

Inez and Tashira exchanged looks with each other, then they looked back at their two handsome licks with phony smiles on their faces, as they both plotted evil things in their heads.

***

Block pulled up to the candy-painted Box Chevy sitting on big chromed Forgiato sixes, parked in a dark parking lot of a pawn shop out in the Winthrop Harbor area.

"Be right back," he told Cam, putting his Tahoe in park and popping out with a half-brick of coke tucked in his jeans.

He made his way around the Chevy to the passenger's door and opened it up. He struggled to climb his big-body frame inside the donk but made it inside, hearing the sexy giggles of the chick pushing the banana-yellow Caprice.

"Don't be laughin' at me, Nikki," he said, closing the door. "This muhfucka too damn high off the ground."

She laughed again. "You lucky I ain't got the thirties on it no more. Yo' ass would really struggle. You need to get all that extra shit together, nigga."

"Shorty, I don't need to lift any weights. I'm liftin' bricks," he flaunted, pulling out the halfie for her.

"Mhmm. I hear that. Yo' ass better be careful wit' gettin' them bricks, Block."

He turned and looked at the chick. She was the same color as brown sugar, with dark brown dreads that hung down her back. She was 5'9", a tomboy lesbian that wore baggy clothes, sneakers, and Timbs. Diamonds flickered in her ears like the one in her right nostril. On her wrist was a white-gold Versace watch. She was tatted up and thuggin', but Block swore that if he ever got the chance, he would fuck the dog-shit out of the sexy-ass stud. He knew a thing or two about ladies that licked ladies but still got it in with niggas from time to time, thinking nobody could tell that they still like dick.

"Shortie, I buy my work, just like every other real nigga," Block capped, handing her the coke.

She laughed. "Uh-uh. I hear you, my nigga."

Block's phone rang just as he tucked the coke in a trap spot in a custom woodgrain dash, after pulling out two stacks of cash.

"What up, joe?" Block answered, taking the eight thousand Nikki handed him.

He could barely hear the guy talking. The music in the background was way too loud. Block hollered for him to text him, then ended the call.

"What chu' on for the night, though?" he asked Nikki.

"Home, chop up and bag up, then pump this shit out."

When you goin' lemme' pump that tight ass pussy out? he thought, then glanced at her lips and felt his dick twitch.

"A'ight, then. I'ma slide on you when I get a chance. Have that thang ready for me when I get there."

"That thang?" she asked him, knowing that he meant that pussy.

"Yeah. That money," he replied, though he was definitely thinking about that wet ass pussy.

"Oh." Nikki chuckled. "Thought cho' ass was tryna' flirt again wit' me, knowin' I like pussy."

"Me too! Let's go get some together!"

"Nigga, get cho' ass outta my car," Nikki laughed. "Tee Grizzley-lookin'-ass nigga."

Block waved her off, then got out with her money. The big monstrous 502 under the box's hood roared as Nikki pulled off, gangsta leaning with her sexy ass.

Hopping back behind the wheel of his Tahoe, Block was about to put it in drive and ride out when his guy sent him a link on Instagram.

Cam heard the music from Block's phone and looked over to see what it was.

"What the fuck!" Block roared.

"Oh, damn!" Cam gasped, then looked at Block. "Come on, fam. She just—"

"Finna get beat the fuck up!" Block cut in, slamming it in drive.

He mashed the gas and about-faced, shooting out of the parking lot and rolling like he wasn't riding dirty. Cam put his seat belt on and held on for dear life as Block raced towards Waukegan.

***

"Oooo, yeah, baby! Yeah! Suck this muhfucka!" Dollaz groaned, eyes rolling to the back of his head as the feeling of her warm, wet mouth swallowing his nine-inch tool made him repeatedly feel it in his spine.

On her knees in the bathroom, Tashira shamelessly deep-throated the man's dick while he held onto her head, thrusting in and out of her mouth like he was fucking some pussy.

She let him have his way with her. The *1738* she had drank after her *Sex on the Beach* had her so lit that she didn't give a fuck about anything but getting her freak on.

In the last stall with a sit-down toilet, she had Dollaz against the wall, sucking him like she was trying to earn a new car.

Out in the main area of the bathroom, Inez was pleasuring C-Note, swallowing ten inches of cock while on her knees. She moaned as she sucked, drunk as hell, worry-free, thinking about getting her cut from setting Marcus up twice, then shooting down to Chicago with exactly what she had left the West Side for in the first place: a real come-up.

***

Tashira spit his dick out of her mouth and gripped it at the base. Looking up at him, she stuck her tongue out, then she flicked it along the slit of the tip. She felt him shudder as she made circles around the head with her tongue, then licked down to his balls.

"Oh, fuck!" Dollaz groaned the second she took his hairy nuts into her mouth and sucked on them like they were made of candy.

She sucked them while using her tongue to massage them. He cursed up a storm. His pleasure had her pussy dripping with anticipation of having his Mandingo buss' her open.

"Goddamn, you're a freak! Shit!"

Tashira let go of his nuts and looked up at him with lust in her eyes and a seductive smile.

"You like that, Dollaz?" she purred.

"Hell yeah, but fuck all that, Monica! I need some pussy!" he told her, then he pulled her up and made her turn away from him. "Grab the rail!" he demanded of her.

She obeyed. Placing her hands on the metal rail that was there for handicapped people to use, Tashira widened her stance, then she bent over, letting him see sooo much ass.

"Mm! Look at that ass! Shit, Wooo!" Dollaz was super geeked. Eagerly, he ripped a big hole in her pantyhose, exposing her ass.

Dollaz leaned down, and as he licked his lips like he was about to feast on a juicy steak, he ran his tongue up from her goodie box.

"Oh yeah. It's that type of time with my girl," he declared, then he ripped a hole in her pantyhose, exposing her crack and her wet-ass pussy.

Dollaz ran his tongue up from her goodie box, slurping her juices, drinking her, then he ran up through her ass crack, swirling it around her booty hole.

She squealed in delight when she felt his tongue go inside of her asshole. It turned her on to no end for a man to be that freaky. Never had Block eaten her ass. He barely ate her pussy.

"Mmmm, Dollaz! That shit feel sooo good! Oh, my God!"

He licked and slurped her ass for a minute longer, then he stood back upright. Tashira could hear Inez getting fucked wildly. The sound of skin smacking sounding like clapping. She moaned and repeatedly cried out C-Note's name. She felt Dollaz slide up inside of her from back, filling her tight, wet pussy up with all of him. He groaned from how good she felt around him. It was better than snacking on some honey-barbecue wings.

“Goddammit, goddammit, goddammit! This pussy is so good, baby!”

“Oooo, it is, daddy!” Tashira cried out as he went savage on her as fast as a Lamborghini Aventador hits 60 from zero. “Oohh! Oohh! Oooohhhh yeeess! Fuck me, Dollaz! Get all this pussy, baby!”

Tashira closed her eyes and reveled in the feeling of him pounding her. He was working it.

He smacked her ass cheek so hard that it made her explode all over him. She drenched his dick and his thighs from one of the most intense orgasms she remembered ever having.

The next thing Tashira knew, Dollaz pulled out of her. She looked back at him and saw a wickedly sexy smile stretch across his face.

“I hope you ready for this, baby. All that ass you got. I gots to see how it feels,” he told her.

Tashira didn’t even dispute his desire to put his dick in her ass. She had never before let a man fuck her booty hole, but then again, she had never sucked and fucked a random nigga in a club bathroom before.

YOLO! she told herself, then toasted her ass up higher for him to do what he wanted.

Dollaz grabbed her plump ass cheeks and opened her up, exposing that puckered brown eye. He spit down a wad of saliva on it, then used the tip of his dick to rub his spit all over it. Still gripping her ass cheeks, Dollaz slid his dick in, working himself up her ass. She could feel his dick spasm inside of her walls. He cussed and groaned gutturally, while demanding him to keep going.

Obliging her, Dollaz started stroking, holding onto her ass while he watched his dark dick go in and out of her honey buns. She went from clenching and hurting to opening up and begging. She could tell that he was on the verge of cumming, and then he let out a beastly growl that barely covered up loud sucking and moaning. He heard C-Note holler out that he was cumming, then heard the sound of sucking and moaning.

"Shit! I'm 'bout to buss!" Dollaz groaned and yanked his cock out of her, forcing her back down onto her knees in front of him. "Put this dick back in ya' mouth, baby!"

Tashira opened up wide and let him stuff his dick back in. He grabbed her head and fucked her face while she used one hand to tickle his balls.

"Oh sh-sh-sheeeeeiiit! Ohh fuuuuck!" Dollaz roared as he busted his nut all in her mouth.

Tashira grabbed his pipe with both hands and pretended she was playing a skin flute. She twist-stroked and sucked all of his cum out, filling her mouth up with his globby sperm.

She put on a grand finale show for him next. Spitting it all back up, then she swallowed it all, moaning from his taste.

"Oh my God, baby, I think I'ma need you to come back to Ohio wit' me," Dollaz said, breathing heavily as he leaned up against the wall, watching her lick him completely clean.

She giggled. "If you be givin' it up like that, then I might just end up over there one day."

—Bang!—

The sound of the door smacking so suddenly made Tashira shriek and Dollaz jump.

"Oh shit! Aye!"

"Aahh!"

Tashira heard C-Note shout in panic, then Inez scream, right before . . .

—Bocka! Bocka! Bocka! Bocka! Bocka!—

Five gunshots filled the bathroom with eardrum-splitting sounds. Tashira's heart dropped out of her ass when she didn't hear Inez nor C-Note anymore. Dollaz stood frozen in place, pants still down around his ankles, dick hanging, terror in his eyes.

Footsteps came. They sounded so loud. They got even louder as whoever came towards the stall where there was no escape.

Oh my God, oh my God! Tashira panicked.

Then, the shooter appeared, and Tashira screamed in fear. He pointed a big gold Desert Eagle at them and smirked.

"Block! Baby, Wait!"

He looked to his right and saw the dreadhead with his dick out. They both saw his jaw muscles flexing as his eyes went demon-red.

"You dirty-ass bitch!" he snapped, then pulled the trigger.

—Bocka!—

"Aahh!" she screamed when a .357 slug exploded Dollaz' head.

Tashira was smacked with blood, brains, and skull fragments. His headless body dropped to the floor and blood squirted out of the stump.

Tashira was so scared that her bladder released and pee ran down her legs, into her booties.

"Block! Please . . . baby! Please!" she begged.

He turned the big cannon on her next, finger still wrapped around the trigger.

"Fuck you, bitch! Suck on this!" he shouted.

—Bocka! Bocka! Bocka! Bocka! Bocka!—

***

Riding along 51st Street in Moe Town, Alondra skipped past Paulina, where her house sat, and made her way to the alleyway that ran in between Paulina and Marshfield. The big Hummer SUV was right behind her still, never having lagged behind the whole way down to Chicago's south side.

Halfway down, she arrived at her two-car wide garage that sat behind her two-story house and her fenced-in backyard. Coming to a stop once she hit the button on the remote up in her overhead visor, Alondra sighed to herself. She was beyond happy that Marcus was finally back. She had been pissed when he left with Block, Tashira, and Inez to go "*do him.*" She had always had a bad feeling about the three of them, but her baby boy was too trusting. Now he knew what it was, and she only hoped that he could wise up. Until he did, Alondra had no intentions of letting her only child go astray again, until she knew he was capable of making boss moves, like his father was, and like she was.

***

The garage door rolled up a second later. Alondra pulled her car inside, parking it there to hide the shot-up Hellcat from prying eyes until it could be swapped out. The Hummer parked in front of the garage and stayed there.

"Go. Talk to him, Marcus," Alondra told her son, killing the engine.

"Hmmm. How about I just go inside and talk to him next year?" Marcus renegotiated, wanting so badly to not have to face the man, especially in front of Cynthia and Leticia.

"How 'bout he comes to holla at you?" Alondra turned and gave him a look that dared him to debate any further.

He sighed to himself, then without arguing anymore, he opened the door and got out.

Alondra looked in her rearview mirror. Cynthia, still holding her daughter, was looking back to see where Marcus was going.

"*¿Listo?*" she asked if she was ready.

Cynthia turned her head back and looked at her in the mirror. She nodded, with a worried look etched in her face.

"Don't worry. He'll be okay. Let's go inside. I'll cook us dinner and we can all kick back and relax."

Cynthia nodded, then glancing back once more, not seeing Marcus anymore, she opened the door and moved with her daughter to get out.

Alondra got out and went to help her with one of her bags.

"It's okay! I got them!" Cynthia quickly said, gasping at her own reaction. "Sorry. I mean . . . I can carry them."

Taken aback by Cynthia's mood, Alondra stepped back, hands raised in surrender.

"Okie dokie. Follow me," Alondra told her, then turned on her heels to head to the door that led out of the garage, to the fenced-in backyard, and to the back of her house.

***

Marcus rounded the front of the big-ass Hummer, heart racing in his chest as he got closer to the beast that awaited next to the monster. Then he saw the man that had come to his mother's aid, his aid, and to Cynthia's and Leticia's aid.

Six feet tall, 240 pounds, long dreadlocks with grays infused in them from fifty years of life in hell on earth. His brown skin was a little deeper than Marcus' skin tone. Their faces were almost identical: same nose, bushy eyebrows, and strong jawlines.

No longer wearing his hoodie, the black tank top displayed his muscular shoulders, bulky tatted-up arms, and his wide barrel chest that had the letters *B* and *G* inked across it. That ink had been there since he had pledged himself to the Black Gangster Nation in his teen years, telling the story of a true Chicago born-and-raised O.G.

Just short of two decades in prison out in Wisconsin had hardened him even more than the streets did. He had been out for a few months and had slowly reintegrated himself back into his son's life, but as he looked at Marcus, the call he got from his baby mama to help her get their son told the O.G. that he had a lot of work to do to get Marcus on real business.

***

"Care to tell me why yo' momma callin' me and tellin' me you throwin' pebbles at the pen?" Snoop asked his son in a deep baritone that always sounded menacing when he was upset.

"Dad, I'm just tryna get money, man."

"Wit' Block's snake-ass, right?"

"If it matters, I didn't know he was a snake 'til a couple of days ago."

"If I'm right, back when I was still locked up, yo' momma told me that dude left you to get caught by the cops wit' a dirty gun. You got up outta that jam because they ain't physically catch you with it before they kicked in the door."

Marcus shook his head. "It was a crazy day, Pop. On Stone, nothin' became obvious 'til the other night."

Snoop stared at his son for a minute. Marcus faltered. His father's glare had always made him want to run for the hills.

"Who's the girl you was shacked up with?" he then asked, changing topics.

Marcus explained how he met Cynthia, leaving out no details. Snoop just shook his head, then he chuckled.

"Only my son gets hit by a car after his snake-ass homie shoots him, then shacks up wit' the chick and falls for her."

"Oh, whoa, whoa, whoa. Fall for her? Yo' ass tweakin' now, Dad."

"Nigga, I'll punch yo' ass in the jaw if you lie. You and yo' momma did all that to save lil' momma and her daughter. You can act all you want, but I ain't new to this, lil' nigga."

Marcus didn't know what to say to that. Truth be told, he was most definitely feeling Cynthia, but to him, it was more so due to her kindness and hospitality; also, he adored Leticia. He somehow developed a soft spot for the two in the short time he had been in their presence.

“The fact that yo’ ass just flew off while I was talkin’ about her tells me exactly what I thought,” Snoop again chuckled. “Yo’ momma tamed me when we was young. That’s why you exist. Just know, if muhfuckas is after her and you protect her, her problems are yours.” Snoop paused and looked at his son, studying his reaction. He did not see an ounce of fear in Marcus afterwards, and it brought an admirable smile to his face.

“I know this gon’ sound crazy, Pop, but I don’t care. She could’ve left me for dead and she brought me into her crib where she was already in danger wit’ her shortie. Ridin’ wit’ her just . . . feels right.”

Snoop nodded in understanding. “See you tomorrow, lil’ nigga.”

Marcus raised an eyebrow as he watched his father make his way towards the driver’s door of his whip.

“That’s it?” he asked.

Snoop opened his door, got one foot up on the step bar, and looked back at his son.

“For now,” he told him.

Getting in, Snoop started his engine, then putting it in drive, he pulled off, heading towards 52nd. Marcus stood where he was until the H2 turned out of his line of sight.

Closing the garage, Marcus made his way through the backyard and entered his mother’s house through the rear.

Immediately upon entering the enclosed back porch section, Marcus was hit with the aroma of his mother’s cooking. Realizing it had been almost the entire day since he ate, his stomach started growling with hunger.

Stepping out of the back porch into the luxurious chef-style kitchen that looked like it belongs inside of a condo, Marcus saw Cynthia and Leticia sitting at the table in the dining room, looking at Chicago’s WGN news station on Alondra’s wall-mounted 55” HDTV. The beloved actor from the Cosby show had lost his life in a tragic drowning out in

Costa Rica. Celebrities he had worked with were shouting out to him, saddened by his sudden passing.

Marcus saw his mother was at the stove, frying up chicken and crinkle-cut French fries. She looked over at him and gave him a warm smile. She nodded in Cynthia's direction, gesturing him over to her.

Taking the hint, he went and took a seat next to her.

"You two okay?" he asked.

Leticia surprised the hell out of him when she got off of her mother's lap and walked up to Marcus. She leaned in and hugged him, laying her head against him.

Cynthia gasped, then smiled adoringly at her daughter. Marcus was beyond shocked by Leticia. He hugged her back, and as he did, he peeped his mother looking over at them, awestruck by the gesture. Marcus even swore her eyes glistened from welling up with tears.

Leticia pulled back a second later. She looked up at him and started smiling.

"Well, I can't say that your hug didn't just make me feel really happy, Lety. Thank you so much for it," he told her.

"Mommy gives me hugs when I don't feel good, so I hugged you so you can be better, Mr. Marcus."

"And it definitely worked. I feel a whole lot better now."

"You'll feel even better after you get some sleep," Cynthia chimed in. "How about we eat, then go to bed? Tomorrow's a new day, and we could all use a much better one."

"True," Marcus agreed, then he yawned, exhausted.

"Papi, I put Cynthia up in your room, okay?" Alondra informed him.

"A'ight. I can sleep on the couch," Marcus replied.

"Mommy, mommy! Can Mr. Marcus sleep with us?" Leticia suddenly asked, excitedly hopping up and down at her mother's side.

Surprised once again by how her daughter was taking such a liking to him, Marcus looked over at Cynthia. She looked shocked as well.

"Um . . . well . . . that's fine with me if he wants to keep us company. It is his room, so I couldn't tell him no."

"I don't mind, Cyn," he told her, looking her right in her eyes, seeing that twinkle that said a whole lot more back to him.

"Aww!"

Marcus looked over at his mother. She stood by the stove, looking like she was going to cry.

"Ma!"

"Negro, 'Ma' me again and I swear to God you won't get no chicken and no fries!"

"Well, damn!" Marcus held up his hands in surrender. "I do *not* want no smoke, but I *do* want some food."

"Then hush all that noise up and be happy. Today, you gonna be eatin' at my table wit' two real-ass chicks and a beautiful little angel, all of whom obviously really care for you, papi. *¿Me entiendes?"*

Marcus nodded. "I understand, crazy lady." Marcus then looked at Cynthia, who was holding her daughter now, smiling at him, with not only her lips but with her eyes as well.

Chapter 8

"Noooo! Nooo! Nooooo!"

"Aye! Monica! Hey!"

"Monica! Moooniicaaa!"

Tashira snapped out of it after nearly a minute of being shaken and yelled at. Her eyes laid upon Inez, with Dollaz at the side and C-Note standing in the entryway to the stall. All three of them were looking at her like she had gone mad.

"Hey! Monica!" Inez called to her again, gripping her shoulders and shaking her. "What the hell is wrong wit' you, man?"

Tashira could feel her heart pounding in her throat like she was actually about to puke it up.

"I . . . I . . . what ah-happend?" she finally asked.

"Uh . . . well . . ." Dollaz started to speak but looked nervous. "We was . . . finishin' up, and you just started trippin'."

"Finishin' up?" Tashira questioned with furrowed eyebrows.

"Girl, he was bussin' his nut on yo' face and yo' ass got to screamin' like his shot was some hot-ass grits or somethin'," Inez told her, keeping it raw and to the point.

At that moment, Tashira touched her face and felt the sticky globs of cum on her mug.

"Shit!" she panicked. "Block's gonna' kill me!"

"Maaan, that nigga ain't gon' do shit!" Inez shot back.

"Who's Block?" Dollaz questioned.

"My man," Tashira told him.

“No, he ain’t! He just a bitch-ass nigga that steals from ’erybody to live his life!”

“Ahem!” Tashira gave her a look that said, “Really, bitch?”

“Shut up, hoe! I’m a woman! Niggas was put on earth for us to take advantage of! Now get cho’ ass up so we can go! Fucking up my night ’n shit! Dollaz, C-Note . . . we’ll call you another time.”

“Aww, come on, India,” C-Note complained. “We really gon’ let a bad dream ruin a good night?”

“For real, yo,” Dollaz added, looking at Tashira as she was helped up off of her knees.

“I said we’ll get at y’all!” Inez snapped as she hurried to pull up Tashira’s pantyhose, then her dress back down over her ass.

She then took Tashira’s hand and yanked her along, rushing out of the bathroom, not even giving her a chance to wipe her face off.

***

Rushing through the crowded club, Tashira told Inez what had made her freak out. Inez shook her head and continued pulling her towards the exit.

Outside, Tashira pulled her hand out of Inez’s as they got to where Tashira’s pearly-white 2009 Cadillac Escalade sat. Feeling Dollaz’ cum caking on her face, she tried wiping it away with her hands. Inez grabbed her face and licked it all up.

“Happy now?”

“No! Block’s gonna’ find out! I know he is!” Tashira panicked.

“So what! I’ll put that nigga down if he touches you again!”

“Aww, what the fuuuck! Goddammit!” Tashira noticed that her SUV’s front driver’s side tire was flat.

Inez looked and saw it. She cursed as well, pissed that they were stuck.

"Fuck it. Let's go find them Ohio niggas and finish what we started. They finna come up off all that cash and jewelry tonight. On God!"

No sooner than Inez made her declaration, they both heard a horn beep. They looked behind them and a gleaming white Bentley Bentayga rolled up on painted-to-match Forgiato rims.

Behind the wheel was Dollaz, and next to him was C-Note.

"Ladies, what's up? Last chance to finish the night off right," C-Note said out of his window.

"Period! Let's go!" Inez eagerly agreed. "Are you ready, Monica?"

"Yes! Damn, India!"

Inez went to grab the rear passenger's door handle to open the door and get in when the sound of tires screeching halted her. Tashira stood frozen with fear as she saw the maroon-colored Chevrolet Tahoe skid to a stop in front of the Bentley truck. There was no license plate in the front, but she knew exactly whose truck it was.

"Aye, what the fuck?" Dollaz shouted and beeped his horn at the SUV.

Tashira saw the front doors of the Tahoe fly open. From behind the wheel, she saw who she knew was Block, even with the ski mask on, hop out with a Draco and rush C-Note, while who she knew was Cam in a ski mask jumped out of the passenger's seat of Block's whip with another AK-47 pistol and rush Dollaz.

Inez ran to Tashira's side as Block and Cam forced C-Note and Dollaz out of the Bentayga, not giving a fuck that there were people outside the club watching and recording them with smartphones.

"Face down, bitch!" Inez and Tashira heard Cam yell at C-Note, pointing his Draco at the back of his head.

"Aye! Bitch!"

Tashira saw Block looking at her.

"Get cho' ass over here! Now!"

Terrified, she obeyed and hurried to him. He demanded her to take the guy's jewelry and go in his pockets, as Cam did to Inez.

"Aye, my dude. You gon' regret this big time," Tashira heard Dollaz say to Block.

—Wham!—

Block bashed him in the back of his head with his mini-spitter, knocking him out. Cam knocked C-Note out, then ran around the Bentayga and jumped behind the wheel.

"Let's go! Get in my truck!" Block ordered Tashira and Inez.

They again did as told, hopping into his Tahoe. He jumped in, slammed it in drive, and smashed the gas. In the backseat, Inez sat, holding the jewelry she took off of C-Note. Tashira had Dollaz' ice.

I need all this tonight! Fuck these niggas! I am gonna get rich by any means necessary, she thought to herself, then started plotting on how to make it happen; get out of any of them that felt they needed to be in her way.

***

Cynthia's eyes opened up as she felt the bed dip down, then rise up. She turned her head and saw Marcus had gotten up and was making his way to the window, where flashes of lightning came through and heavy rain soaked the glass. He looked out of the window and stayed there. She could tell he was bothered. But despite all that she and Leticia had been through, for some very crazy reason, Marcus brought her so much peace, and she felt safe with him.

Gently, she got up off of the bed without waking her daughter. She padded towards where he stood, staring out of the window at the dreary night.

"Hey?" she called softly to him and placed a hand on his shoulder.

Marcus turned his head and looked at her. He looked surprised that she was right there instead of in the bed where he had left her and Leticia.

"Are you okay?" Cynthia asked him, looking up into his misty gray eyes with concern of her own.

He sighed first, then looked at her. "I'm tired of bein' broke. These past few days have been crazy. My own homies got down on me, and . . ." he paused, shaking his head. "I just wanna' get money. I wanna' get rich, Cyn. I'm dyin' to get rich."

Cynthia nodded in understanding. "You and me both, Marcus. Ever thought about a job, for starters?"

"Workin' for someone ain't really what I want. If I'm on some legit shit, I'm tryna' be the boss."

"I feel that. I believe you can be that, too, but you gotta start from the bottom and work your way up."

Marcus agreed with her. Sighing, he told her how he felt about filling out job applications, going on interviews, and working with or around people that were not like him. He told her he felt like he was basically applying to be a slave.

"I'm a street nigga wit' Lamborghini dreams and beach house wishes. Cocaine, her'on, pills, and guns is my life, Cyn. I just . . . " he again paused, taking a deep breath in an attempt to calm himself down.

Cynthia then wrapped her arm around him and she hugged him. She kept hugging him, feeling how hard and muscular he was.

"I'm here, Marcus," she told him.

"I just can't catch a break. Why am I the one that the world keeps shittin' on?"

"I don't know, Marcus." Cynthia let go of him but held onto his hands. "But . . . if you feel like the world's been doin' that to you, then how about we shit on the world?"

“And how do you think we can do that? You need money to do that, Cyn. I’m broke as hell. My momma’s and my daddy’s money ain’t mine.”

Her initial plan popped into her head as he spoke. But as he did, Cynthia realized that Marcus was what she needed in more ways than one, and she could ride with him like the down-ass chick that she was.

“What if . . . I could help you?” she then asked.

“You have a daughter. I would never allow you to hit licks wit’ me. Leticia needs you.”

Cynthia smiled at how he really cared about her. She let his hands go then and headed to the closet. Going into one of her duffel bags, she sorted through the valuable merchandise that she had taken from Marcello. She paused when she saw the flat case that held the rarest pieces of Mexican history that anyone could get their hands on. Knowing it was the sole reason that Marcello had not just ordered her to be shot dead, Cynthia planned to hold them until she knew what to do with them.

She then took out the last kilo she had and made her way back to Marcus. She lifted it up and put it in his hands.

“I’ve been sellin’ yayo all around Zion for a couple of months. This is my last brick,” she told him. “And I’m giving it to you, Marcus.”

His eyes went wide with shock. He looked at her, then at it.

“You . . . you’re . . . hold up. What?”

“The guy I was dating down in Laredo . . . he was the head of a cartel. I didn’t know anything of that nature about him until he moved me and my daughter in. It was horrible.”

Cynthia told him the rest of the story, doing her best to keep from tearing up. The memories were so painful, though. Her four-year-old daughter had seen *waaay* too much bloodshed and so many other things that most adults don’t even see, except for in horror movies.

"And so, I decided that if I was going to break away from him and take care of my daughter, I needed money. That son of a bitch made money off of me . . ." Cynthia almost choked up at the thoughts of all the things she had to do while in Marcello's dark pit. "So . . . I took from him."

Marcus nodded in understanding. Taking her hand into his, he pulled her close to him. She looked into his eyes. He had her trembling as he gazed down into hers.

"Fuck him and his cartel. Any nigga that has to exploit women and little girls for money deserve to die. I don't care what you did, Cyn. You did what you had to do for you and for Lety. I respect it."

Cynthia nodded. She appreciated his words. But then, a question popped into her mind that had been swimming around in it since she met his mother.

"Marcus?"

"Yeah."

"How old is your mom?"

Marcus almost busted out laughing. He stopped himself before he woke Leticia up.

"Forty-three. Why you ask that?"

"Because! She is fucking badass, man! And she is gorgeous!"

"And she used to be all dressed up to come get me from school when I was a shortie. Niggas got scraped 'erytime they made a comment about my momma's booty."

Cynthia snorted a laugh. "Hey, who doesn't like a beautiful lady with a big butt?"

Marcus tilted his head to the side and flashed a sly grin.

"Oh hell no! I am not into women, Marcus. Don't get me givin' your mom props twisted."

He chuckled. "I don't know, lil' mama. I think I'ma need you to prove it."

"Oh really? You want proof that I'm into men, and only men?"

"Yup."

Cynthia grabbed him by the collar of his T-shirt, yanked him down to her, and she kissed him. Immediately, every thought and feeling that she had about how soft his lips would feel against hers was confirmed.

Blissful tingling sensations tickled her lips as their kiss deepened. His arm wrapped around her waist; her arms went up and around his neck. Their tongues met and started doing a dance that would score all tens if judges were watching. Cynthia felt their temperature rising, like a little fire in the woods becoming a raging forest fire. He had her hot like coals in the firebox of an old locomotive.

She pulled back a second later, somehow. Breathing hard and feeling sweaty, Cynthia couldn't help but smile.

"Believe me now?" she managed to ask, though she couldn't look him in his eyes for nothing.

"Hmmm . . . maybe. I'm kind of hard to convince. Maybe if we went out for dinner, or to a movie. You know?"

"Like . . . a date? You? Mr. Gangster, dates?"

"I ain't no gangsta, I'm Stone to the Bone, and I'm a gentleman, too. So, yeah. But only when it's a woman that is really worth tryin' to get to know better."

Looking up into his eyes now, Cynthia blushed.

"Don't you have a woman?" she then asked with a raised eyebrow.

Marcus sighed. "Honestly, I don't know what I have. A chick that goes through what she did and doesn't want the man she claims as hers to be there for her, I don't see much of a future between them."

Nodding, Cynthia agreed wholeheartedly. She had been taught by her mother that no matter what, a woman or a man that went through a devastating situation—whether because of the outside world or drama between each other—if they couldn't come together and be strong together, or work it out without giving each other the silent treatment, then they were doomed to crash and burn.

"Thank you for being honest with me," Cynthia told him. "Not many guys do that these days."

"I'm not many guys, Cyn."

"I am finding that out every minute that I am around you, Marcus." She started smiling again. "Let's go back to bed. When we wake up, we can put a plan together to pop the coke off, then we'll go from there."

Marcus nodded. Releasing her, he grabbed the brick and put it in the top drawer of his dresser. Following her, they got back into bed, curling up around the sleeping toddler. For a minute, they gazed at each other there, smiling as the soothing sounds of rain pelting the roof and windows created a peaceful symphony.

Within a minute, they were both back in la-la land, eyes closed, with smiles on their faces as they met each other in dreamland.

Chapter 9

Smack!

"Stop fuckin' lyin'!" Block yelled after he smacked the fuck out of Tashira for the third time. "My niggas was in the club! They saw you go in the bathroom wit' that nigga, bitch!"

After making it all the way down to Chicago, out south, Block and Cam had headed to meet one of Cam's homies that would take the stolen Bentley Bentayga off their hands. En route back with stacks of cash for it, Block and Tashira got into it so hard that at a gas station at 55th and Ashland, he had to pull over, yanked her out of his Chevrolet Tahoe, then dragged her into the bathroom to give her a piece of his irate mind.

***

"Ooww! Stop fuckin' hitttin' me, Block!" Tashira screamed.

"Shut up, bitch! You's a hoe-bitch, joe! On the G!"

Tashira cried her eyes out. "Block, I swear! Them niggas lied to you!"

Block grabbed her by the throat and squeezed, teeth gritted, eyes full of hatred.

"They sent me a video of you goin' in the restroom wit' him, bitch! So since you wanna' be a bathroom thot, I'ma make you one!"

Against her will, Block forcefully spun her around and slammed her up against the wall. She cried out in pain as he held her face against the tile, holding his forearm to the back of her neck, using his 260-pound body to hold her 130-pound frame in place. "Block! lemme go! Get off of me!" she screamed.

Ignoring her, Block yanked her dress up over her hips. The second he saw the big hole in her pantyhose that exposed her ass, he saw red and lost his head completely.

"Grimey-ass bitch!" he growled through clenched teeth, then with one hand, worked his pants and boxers down. "I'ma show you, bitch! Yo' ass gon' learn today!"

Block then mercilessly rammed his dick into Tashira's ass as hard as he could. She screamed in pain. He covered her mouth with his hand and relentlessly violated his own woman in the most brutal, cold-hearted, and inhumane way. She cried into his hand, her pleas for help muffled by it.

Knocking on the door came as he pounded her viciously.

"Aye, Block! What is you doin', folks? You heard what Phil said! We gotta get up outta here!" he heard Cam shouting.

"Get cho' ass away from the door, nigga! I'm handlin' business!" Block yelled back.

Feeling his nut coming, Block then snatched his dick out of her ass and spun her to face him. He smacked the shit out of her, forced her down onto her knees, and grabbing her head, he stuffed his dick into her mouth and fucked her face angrily.

***

Tears poured down Tashira's face as ten inches of dick went down her throat. Her own boyfriend had just raped her in a dirty-ass bathroom and was now forcing her to suck his cock right out of her asshole.

She cried, not from pain, but from embarrassment. She knew Cam heard her pleading for help, and she had no clue where Inez was. All of the things she had done for him and this was how he did her?

Tashira suddenly felt a flash of anger hit her as if she got smacked with a hand made of fire. She grew so angry that murder filled her mind. Her blood boiled at how he was really raping her in a horribly filthy, disgusting bathroom, with his guy right outside and Inez, God knows where. There was only one thing she could do now.

—Bam! Bam! Bam!—

“Block! what the fuck is you in there doin’ to her?” yelled Inez just then.

“Bitch! get back in the truck or yo’ ass is next! Aye! Aye! Aaaahhhh! Stoop! Stoop! Let gooooo!”

***

Outside of the bathroom, soaking wet from the torrential downpour, Inez heard Block go from threatening her to suddenly screaming in pain. Cam started pounding on the door, shouting for his homie. Inez stepped back, having no clue what hell was happening to Block, but as his screams got even more high-pitched, she knew he had to be experiencing excruciating pain. Block was a big-ass dude with the pain tolerance of a pit bull.

Inez looked at Cam as he kept on trying the door. Her eyes went to the bulge under the back of his shirt, where his waistline was. In a split second, Inez acted and rushed up behind him. She grabbed the Glock 21 he had tucked and quickly cocked it.

Cam spun around when he felt his pistol get snatched away from him. He saw Inez pointing it at his face.

“You cum-drinkin’ ass bitch! Fuck you think you doin’? Huh? You gon’ shoot me?” he asked, growling through clenched teeth, glaring at her, trying to intimidate her.

Inez's hand shook as his crazed eyes instilled fear in her. Block's pleas for help had suddenly stopped, and all was quiet inside of the bathroom.

"Just because we behind the buildin' don't mean shit, bitch! Shoot me, and yo' ass gon' be hunted by all my niggas!"

The bathroom door flew open just then. Inez's eyes averted to her left and saw Tashira limp out into the pouring rain with her whole face covered in blood.

Cam looked at her and went wide-eyed. He ran to the bathroom and gasped at what he saw. Inez looked in and could see Block lying on the floor, bleeding profusely from where his dick used to be.

Oh my God! She bit his dick off! Inez realized, flabbergasted by Tashira.

Limping towards Inez, Tashira was in tears and in pain, from what Inez could see. Cam ran into the bathroom to help Block.

"Get that bitch, nigga! Get her!" Block yelled at him.

Cam turned and glared at Inez as she looped her arm over Tashira's shoulder. Inez looked his way when she heard Block again shout for Cam to get Tashira.

He charged forward, looking like a bull. Inez gasped, and jumping from under Tashira's arm, she pointed Cam's gun at him.

"Shit!"

—Bocka! Bocka! Bocka! Bocka! Bocka!—

Inez lit him up. The bullets tore through his chest, spinning him around before he hit the ground hard, blood pouring from exit wounds in his back. She ran up on him and put one through the center of his forehead, making sure he would never point a gun at her again.

"Inez! *Block*!" Tashira urged, knowing the gunshots likely had already been called in by people out front and inside.

Inez quickly pointed the Glock towards the bathroom. Block's eyes went wide with fear. Desperate to live, he dove for the door, pushing it shut a millisecond before Inez could fire a shot.

—Bocka! Bocka! Bocka! Bocka!—

She squeezed the trigger and blew at the door. The bullets slammed into it, but its thick steel composition stopped them from getting through.

"Fuck!" Inez screamed angrily.

She ran up to the door and tried opening it, but Block had locked it.

"Inez! We gotta go!" Tashira pleaded.

Knowing time was of the essence, Inez ran to her, took her by the hand, and hurried to Block's Tahoe. People that were at the gas pumps saw the two and the gun in Inez's hand. A few screamed and took cover, fearing bullets coming at them, while others stood where they were, used to shootings in Chiraq and completely numb to danger and death.

Inez got Tashira up into the passenger's seat, then she jumped behind the wheel, slammed it into drive, and smashed the gas pedal, launching the Chevrolet out of the Mobil lot and onto 55th Street, desperate to get the hell out of Chicago before she ended up in Cook County Jail with multiple bodies on her.

"Inez?" Tashira called softly then.

She glanced over at Tashira. Despite blood being caked around her mouth, Tashira was smiling. In her hands, she held the jewelry that they had taken from Dollaz and C-Note.

Inez gasped. "Is the money Cam got for them niggas' Bentley truck in here?"

Tashira turned around and saw a brown paper bag in the backseat. Ignoring the pain she was in, she reached for it and grabbed it. Groaning as she tried to gently sit back on her seat, Tashira opened it and saw rubber-banded stacks of cash in it.

"Bingo!" Tashira squealed, super geeked, then showed Inez.

"Finally! We got money, bitch!" Inez cheered excitedly, passing through another big intersection with signs for Interstate 55 posted on the light poles. "Oooooo, guuurl, we finna check into cash now, joe! Oh God! We gotta sell off this jewelry, and that shit at Block's house! After that, I think we should head south. What chu' think?"

"As long as we're together, I don't care, 'Nez."

"Uh-huh. You wasn't thinkin' like that when you was around Block, hoe."

Inez made it to the on-ramp for the Stevenson Expressway then and turned onto it, heading north.

"Girl, bye. That nigga, like all them niggas, includin' Marcus, was just another lick that couldn't see past the pussy."

Inez gunned it when she crested the top of the ramp.

"I can't believe you actually bit that nigga's dick off, though. That's some cold-blooded shit. What did you do with it?"

Tashira chuckled. "I flushed that nigga's shit. Maaan, I wish yo' ass would've killed him. It's all good, though. Just like we got Marcus, Block can get it, too. I love money. Fuck a nigga."

Inez burst out laughing. "I ain't mad at you, 'Shira. Fuck these niggas, joe, and fuck love. All I want is money."

"Amen, bitch. Let's go get it," Tashira then suggested before turning the music on and blasting GloRilla's "Hollon."

Chapter 10

"Whaaaat? Aww, come on, man! Really, though?"

Marcus shook his head as he saw what ABC Channel 7 News was reporting. The rap chick phenom, GloRilla, had been arrested on felony drug charges.

"For fucking weed? That's some bullshit!" he continued, looking at the photo of her that the news provided. "Damn, she so bad! On the five!"

He then chuckled as the news revealed GloRilla's real name, which was close to her rap name, minus the two L's.

He heard footsteps as he put his black Ralph Lauren Polo shirt on, which had a red horse and rider embroidered on the chest. With his Polo shirt, he had on red Ralph Lauren cargo shorts, Ralph Lauren shoes and black mid-top Air Force 1s on his feet, with red Nike swooshes and red laces. He'd left plenty of clothes at his mother's house when he called himself leaving home to get rich.

Turning around, Marcus saw Cynthia re-enter the bedroom with one of her bags strapped over her shoulder, holding Leticia's hand.

Fresh from showering, Cynthia's hair looked like it was still wet from the mousse she ran through it. She rocked a white short-sleeved top with *Spicy Latina* in army fatigue-colored letters under the low breast line; with it, a short army fatigue-print mini-skirt. Her legs were freshly shaved and oiled. Down on her feet, fresh ankle socks and white mid-top Air Forces.

Cynthia had dressed her daughter in a pink cotton jacket and skirt outfit, with a shirt that had white hearts all over it, and down on her feet were white low-top Air Forces with pink toes and pink swooshes.

The aromas of Cynthia's *Bath & Body Works Sweet Pea* body moisturizer had Marcus' mouth watering. He was stuck in a trance as he gazed at her beautiful Chicana features and her curvy figure. Smiling at him, Cynthia sat her bag down by the dresser. Leticia ran over to Marcus with a giant smile on her angelic face.

Scooping her up in his arms, Marcus looked at Cynthia.

"I love how good you are with her, Marcus It warms my heart," Cynthia replied, her voice breaking as she spoke.

Marcus started smiling then. Her words hit him hard. He realized that he meant something to the little girl and to Cynthia.

Unable to resist any longer, Marcus closed the gap between him and Cynthia, leaned down, and pressed his lips to hers.

Right away, sparks flew. The sensations they both felt turned their kiss into a hungered frenzy. He stuck his tongue in her mouth so it could meet hers for the first time, and it was a harmonious introduction that was as good as someone's first time smoking weed. Amazing! Crazy! Wild!

"Awww!"

Marcus jumped back from Cynthia when he heard his mother. He and Cynthia turned and saw the statuesque belle leaning against the doorway frame, arms crossed over her bosom, with a teasing twisted lip smile on her face.

The statuesque puertorriqueña was dressed like a *"Go Viral"* magazine centerfold in a skin-tight dress with sheer see-through sleeves, an open back, low breast line, and a flared mid-thigh length hem, which allowed for her sexy legs, encased in black diamond-patterned pantyhose, to be on full display.

With her erotically enticing ensemble, Alondra wore black shark-skin leather stiletto boots that went up to just above her knees and had pointed toes with lace-up backs.

Her fiery mane of hair was pulled back into a sophisticated bun. Red lipstick graced her lips; gold jewelry in her ears, around her neck, fingers, and wrists. Gold-framed Versace shades accentuated her incredibly beautiful face.

Wow, Cynthia thought, swearing to herself that Alondra had to be the world’s baddest, sexiest mother.

“Ma, why do you keep dressin’ like that, man?” Marcus asked with a frown.

“Boy, I am grown and been grown since you were bein’ made. And don’t be spinnin’ nothing on me wit’ cho’ kissy-boo-boo-ass,” Alondra teased then laughed, as did Cynthia and Leticia.

“Uh-huh. Whatever. Where you going?” Marcus asked.

“Same place y’all are going. To the car! March!”

***

The Hellcat was gone from the garage. Parked in its place was a red 2019 Audi A8, sitting on 21-inch Mansory rims, blacked out with red accents, wrapped in Pirelli race tires. Knowing how his dad moved, it was no surprise that his O.G. had another whip to replace the shot-up one.

Alondra hit the remote start and fired up the twin-turbo V8 engine, while Marcus hit the button by the door to open the garage. Cynthia got her daughter in the back of the black leather and red-piped interior, strapped her in, and got in next to her.

“Drive.” Alondra handed her son the key fob and headed to the passenger’s side.

Marcus got behind the wheel and glanced in the rearview mirror. Cynthia was looking at him. Their eyes locked, and she smiled with that twinkle in her eyes that made Marcus want to kiss her again and again and again.

“Ay, Dios mio, freaking lover boy! Come on, Marcus, and drive, cabron!” his mother told him, twisting her lips up at him.

Cynthia and Leticia both started laughing.

***

"What?"

"Yup. Found that nigga wit' fo' of 'em in his chest and his brains blown out outside the bathroom. They said there was a lot of blood inside, too, but they only found one nigga."

Marcus listened to his father as his voice came through the speakers. His mother had called Snoop to let him know they were en route, and he started speaking of GloRilla's petty-ass arrest, then about a murder at a gas station that had happened overnight that was just blocks away from Alondra's house.

"That's crazy. And it would be a gas station wit' broke-ass cameras," Alondra laughed as Marcus reached 51st and Damen and turned onto Damen.

"Baby, that's half the ghetto-ass gas stations in Chicago. Them ones all around downtown, though? Yo' ass ain't gettin' away wit' nothin' at one of them. Hold up real quick," Snoop said.

They all heard him holler to someone.

"Aye, man! Take it to the back! Fuuck you got it out hea fo', dummy?"

Alondra chuckled. "You sound like you 'bout to have to knock one of yo' guys out."

"I am. This nigga took $20,000 out the pot and bought a hot Bentley truck from his hoe-ass friend, then he brought it here and parks it in front of my office!" Snoop exclaimed incredulously.

"Wow. Lemme' guess . . . Phil?"

"Yup. Last fuck-up for him."

"We'll be there in a second, baby. Wait for me."

"A'ight."

Alondra ended the call.

"Hot Bentley truck, Ma?" Marcus asked as he came up on 55th.

"Yup. Yo' daddy is a master mechanic, an artist, and a great businessman," she told him.

"Oh. Okay then," he replied, needing no further explanation.

***

As 58th came into view, Marcus saw to his left a massive plot of commercial land with tall steel-plated fencing around it. His mother had him hit a left onto 58th, then halfway up, before getting to Hoyne, she saw the entrance to where she said they were going.

Marcus turned into what was like a parking lot full of cars, pickups, SUVs, tow trucks, box trucks, garbage trucks, dump trucks, and semis. There were multiple service garages and makeshift huts as well, along with their mobile trailer offices.

She told him to go to the right, where a tall garage that had two service and repair bays was along the rear corner of the property. Next to it was another smaller garage, where Marcus saw the white Bentley Bentayga on big rims that matched the truck.

To the left of the two structures, he saw two box trucks, a bigger truck that had a dumpster on the back of it, an old garbage truck, and two semis that were coupled to long car-hauler trailers. He also saw his father's big Hummer pickup next to the garbage truck.

"This is all Dad's, Ma?" he asked, parking behind the Hummer.

"We went half on everything. We just started a . . . a cleaning business, and that's what the box trucks are for. We named it 'Pride Stone Sanitation Inc'."

"Eeee, okay then! Y'all gettin' it like that?"

Alondra didn't answer. The sounds of yelling and cursing took her attention from him to where Marcus saw his father march out and grab a dark-skinned man with long messy dreads up from the ground.

"Hold that thought, baby boy. Gotta stop Papa Pride from killin' ol' boy."

Alondra hurried and jumped out, rushing to stop the furious man. Snoop had the dread hemmed up and damn near ready to break his neck.

"Stay here, Cyn. I gotta help my pops out," Marcus told Cynthia.

"Uh . . . okay," she replied, sounding unsure as she watched through the windshield.

Alondra made it to the intimidating old head; the BG goon had set the younger dread on his feet. Then she saw Marcus run up, ready to help out. It made her smile at how close Marcus was with his mother and father. Family was big in her world. It was just unfortunate for her and her daughter that their family was gone.

***

"You gots to be the dumbest muthafucka in Chicago! How the fuck you think there was anything good to come from takin' pot money and buyin' this hot piece of shit?" Alondra heard Snoop spazz as she ran up.

"Pride, I didn't know, fam! It's a Bentley truck, joe! Who the hell would expect that?"

"What's goin' on, baby?" Alondra asked her dude while glaring at the dread.

Snoop groaned. Frustratedly, he squeezed the bridge of his nose, then looked at his woman.

"Phil here, he handles runnin' VIN numbers of all the vehicles we get under-the-table, know what I mean? He's in charge of decidin' if we can change the VINs, or jailbreak 'em so we can completely erase the manufacturing date and part the muhfucka out. This dumbass nigga bought this Bentayga, then ran its registration when he knows we run 'em first. Guess what we learned about this Bentley truck?" Snoop told her, right as Marcus made it to them.

"What?" Alondra asked, seeing Phil's head and shoulders down.

"It's registered with Lake County Sheriff's Department Violent Crimes Division."

Alondra gasped in shock. "It's a fucking cop car?" Marcus' jaw dropped.

"It's undercover," Phil finally spoke. "Maaan, I'm sayin', joe. Who ever seen a Bentley as an undercover police vehicle? How would I have known?"

Alondra walked up to Phil, stood eye-to-eye with him, then without warning, she cocked back and cracked him dead in his jaw. Marcus then ran up and shoved Phil again, knocking him to the ground. Then he went apeshit on him.

"Bitch-ass nigga! Tryna' get my dad locked up again?"

—Crack! Crack! Crack! Crack! Crack!—

"Okay, okay, calm down, lil' Moe." Snoop pulled his son off of Phil and held him back. "Good lookin' out, though."

"Get cho' ass up, take that fucking hot-ass thing out of here and burn it!" Alondra demanded of Phil.

Bloody and swollen, he hopped up and all but ran to the Bentley truck and hopped in. He started the engine and peeled off, dipping out of the yard like the devil himself was chasing him.

"Dad? You just gon' let that nigga go? You really trust him after he did that?" Marcus asked with a raised eyebrow.

Alondra and Snoop turned and looked at their son. He took a step back and raised his hands, not wanting any problems.

Snoop pulled his phone out of his pocket. "Trust no one, lil' nigga," he stated, then he made a call.

"Your father is very careful at what he does, papi," Alondra added, as Snoop got an answer.

"Aye, man. Tap into Phil's phone and go find him ASAP. Roll 'im up and take him down to the farm. His ass is tired and needs a nap."

He then ended it all like a boss that had spoken and didn't need a reply.

"Hmmm." Alondra bit her bottom lip as she gazed at her man, dressed in dark blue Dickies and Timbs, with his dreads hanging loosely.

"Damn." Snoop looked at his woman and shook his head. "You look so good right now, baby. That's what chu' on?"

"Hey! Your son is here, nasty people!" Marcus chimed in.

"Hush," Alondra told him and went to Snoop, taking his hand in hers. "Dejame hablar contigo, guapo, en tu garaje," she then whispered to Snoop.

"Let's go," the old head eagerly replied back.

Marcus stood where he was, watching his mother pull his father towards the entrance door to the garage, enter, then slam the door shut. He heard the lock engage and shook his head.

Walking back towards the Audi, he got in behind the wheel. He turned and looked toward the back to see Cynthia with a comical grin stretching from ear to ear.

"Don't say it. Please," he begged, embarrassed.

Cynthia busted out laughing then. Marcus looked at Leticia, who was giggling, though she had no actual clue as to what was going on.

"Lety, yo' momma is crazy," he told the toddler.

"Nuh-uh. Don't be mad at me 'cause Momma got a big ol' butt and Daddy can't resist her, Marcus."

Marcus again shook his head, but found the sound of her laughter bringing him great joy.

***

"¡Aayy, paapi! Ooo, shit! Yeah! Oohh! ¡Coño!"

Alondra's back arched up and her toes curled up inside of her high-heeled boots. Leaned back on the couch in Snoop's office with her legs up, pantyhose at the tops of her boots, and her G-string to the side, the still-so-very freaky Puerto Rican's head was being spun around and around as Snoop sucked on her clit like a pussy-sucking animal.

He moaned, loving how good she tasted. She leaked like a broken faucet, and he drank her up, savoring her flavor.

Alondra hooked her arms under her legs to hold them up high. She closed her eyes and reveled in the pleasure her man was giving her.

"Shit, papi! ¡Ayy, Dios mio! ¡Me vengo papi, me vengo!" she cried, announcing that she was cumming.

Snoop kept on sucking on her clit until she exploded seconds later, climaxing all over his face.

Without wasting a minute, he got on his feet. Alondra let her legs down and went for his pants, dropped them and his boxers, freeing his bone-hard length. She slid forward and got down on her knees before him. Taking his cock into her hand, she started kissing it, then licking up and down his shaft, going down to his balls.

"Oohh fuuuck!" he groaned gutturally when she took his nuts into her mouth and sucked on them while he jerked his dick with his left hand.

Alondra pleasured his sack for a minute longer, then gripping his manhood with both hands, she engulfed him and started sucking and jerking him at the same time.

Snoop went bananas. He groaned, cursing loudly, throwing his head back, squeezing his eyes closed as her unbelievable oral skills made his toes curl up in his Timberlands. She went ham on him until he couldn't take it anymore and took his dick from her mouth to put her back on the couch.

He put her legs back up and slid inside of her soaking wet pussy. Alondra moaned out his name as he filled her up. He held her legs for her and started jackhammering her pussy, hitting it hard and fast.

"Oohh! Oohh! Ooohhh! Yes! ¡Ay, Papi! ¡Asi!" she screamed out as his thighs smacked against the bottoms of her ass cheeks so fast that it sounded like someone was clapping.

Alondra came a minute later, crying out at the top of her lungs as he drenched his dick with her sweet juices.

He pulled out of her and she immediately was put on her knees on the couch, facing away from him. Snoop slid into her from behind and as she held onto her ass, he pounded her from the back. Alondra threw it back at him while looking back at him. She gave him her sexiest fuck-face and felt his dick swelling up inside of her.

He started grunting then, strokes getting staggered. The contorted faces he made as her wetness overwhelmed him made her cum once more. She pulled him out of her then and tooted it up higher. Snoop leaned down and licked all between her crack, getting her asshole nice and wet. Then he eased his dick into her ass and started stroking.

She took him like a champ while moaning and crying out his name, begging for him to cum for her. She could tell he was getting closer every minute that passed.

"Fuck! I finna buss', baby! Shit!" he shouted out.

Alondra then pulled his dick out and sat back on the couch. She opened her mouth wide for him. He grabbed her head and put his dick back in her mouth and fucked her face until he reached his nut. Letting her head go, Alondra took his cock into her hands again and stroked while sucking his dick, moaning and groaning, looking up at him like a nasty freak.

Snoop exploded seconds later. She jerked and sucked it all out of him, filling her mouth up with his globby cum. When he was empty and her mouth was full, she spit it all out onto his dick, then like a cat slurping up milk, Alondra slurped it all back up, then she swallowed it.

“God damn, ’Londra! Shit!” Snoop took in a deep breath to refill his lungs with air. “Fuck Folgers, baby! The best part of wakin’ up is you!”

Snoop took her hands and helped the giggling Boricua up onto her feet.

“Ayyy, mi guapo maleante is so sweet!” She got a kiss from him that was like having her cake and getting to eat it. “Te amo, papi.”

“I love yo’ ass, too, baby. Be careful wit’ our son’s future wife and daughter,” he told her as he leaned down to help fix her clothes.

Alondra chuckled. “I will. And you be careful wit’ Cynthia’s future marido and Lety’s future papa.”

“You know I will.” Snoop kissed her again, then smacked her ass as she headed towards the door in front of him, with a bright and cheerful dicked-down-so-good smile on her face.

***

“Hold up, hold up, hold up . . . why is y’all tryna’ separate us?” Marcus asked after Alondra and Snoop emerged from the garage looking like sinful teenagers, before walking back to the Audi and telling him what was up for the day.

“Nigga, she ain’t gon’ nowhere! Knock that shit off and come on!” Snoop ordered. “We got shit to do, and so does yo’ momma. Trust me. We gon’ see them in a few.”

Marcus peeped at his mother trying to hold in her laughter. She was leaning against her car’s driver’s door. Cynthia was now in the front seat, and in the back still was Leticia.

“Marcus, tranquilo, mi amor. You know how I move. Her and Lety’s safety is my priority. Later tonight, we can go out to eat.”

Marcus looked at Cynthia. She smiled shyly at him. Giving him a dainty little wave, she put a smile on his face.

"A'ight, pops. I'm ready."

Snoop handed his son a pair of clean coveralls and told him to put them on while he put the suit on over his clothes. Snoop caught another kiss from his woman, then led her into her car.

She waved bye then pulled off, exiting the yard. Marcus then followed his father to where the old garbage truck sat. He looked at the creepy old brown and black 1986 Mack DM-Model, with a rear-loading garbage compactor on its tandem-axle frame.

"Dad? Why do you have a garbage truck that looks like it came out of a horror movie?" Marcus asked.

Snoop opened the driver's door and climbed up inside. "Can't take the city's garbage out in my Hummer, can I?" he walked back, before starting up the big diesel engine. "Get cho' ass inside, man!"

Marcus got chills up his spine as the monster Mack's engine idled. He headed over to the passenger's side and opened the door, climbing up into the prehistoric interior. He was surprised to see the thing had a stereo system in it.

"So?" Marcus looked at his father, wondering why he wasn't pulling off.

"Gotta build air pressure up in the tanks, or the brakes won't release. Takes a minute or two," Snoop told his youngster as he looked at the dashboard, watching all the gauges that displayed the engine functions that let Snoop know if his truck was working properly.

"You need a CDL for this?" Marcus asked him.

"Yep. Class B, but I got a Class A. You goin' need to get yours for what I got planned for you."

Once the air pressure rose to 125 psi, Snoop was ready to go.

"You got a gun on you, son?" he asked, pushing in the yellow diamond-shaped knob that was in the center of the dashboard to release the parking brakes.

"I'm always strapped. Why would I really need one in a garbage truck?"

Snoop put the automatic transmission into drive and slowly pulled forward.

"In this residual waste business, it gets really dirty, know what I mean? So you gotta keep a good cleaner on you. Don't forget, this is Chicago, not no lil' lame-ass suburbs you were makin' noise in."

Marcus chuckled. "I'm already knowin', pop. You and Ma ain't raised no clown."

Snoop laughed. "I know that's right, joe!"

He turned out of the yard and headed towards Damen, the big Mack engine roaring like a T-Rex was under the hood. Marcus caught goosebumps from how powerful it sounded and how high up he was.

Coming to Damen, Snoop turned onto it, then he turned the music on. Seconds after, Ice Cube's classic gangster hit cut "Hello," featuring Dr. Dre and MC Ren, came on. He turned it all the way up and started rapping with the chorus, shouting, "I started this gangsta shit! and this the muthafuckin' thanks I get? hello?"

Marcus busted out laughing at his father getting into his O.G. mode. Snoop looked over at him with a side-brow, then put his eyes back on the road.

"What's funny, lil' nigga?"

"You, ol' man! Who listens to dude's old ass anymore? If it ain't Lil Durk, EST Gee, Yo Gotti, or Moneybagg Yo, it ain't worth listenin' to, joe. On Stone."

Now Snoop laughed. "I listen to Yo Gotti 'cause he a O.G., but anyone else who won't do shit but pick up a gun if he gets beat up, naaaw, joe. I'm cool, lil' nigga. Now sit cho' ass back and stop tryin' to clown Cube before Mack 10 and WC come get cho' lil' ass."

Marcus laughed, then leaned back in his seat while his father navigated the old trash beast to wherever they were going.

Chapter 11

"Oooo! Yaayuuuh! Wooo! That's what I'm 'talm 'bout! Bbbbrrrraaaahh! Haahaaa!"

Inez and Tashira busted out laughing at the 54-year-old dope fiend as he did the dope-fiend-dance in the living room of his two-bedroom apartment in Zion, right on Galilee and 27th Street. The coal-black old man was going berserk off a hit of crack that he cooked up from one of the bricks Inez discovered in Block's Tahoe. Knowing that Hustle Man was a drug wizard, she called him right away as she dropped Block's SUV in a cut in Evanston, burned it, then caught an Uber to get Tashira's 'Lac from the club. She was geeked that it had not been towed.

Inez used her alluring damsel-in-distress act on a beverage delivery man that had just dropped off the club's alcohol supply, and got him to change Tashira's tire, promising him a 'favor' that she would give him after they hurried to get to the hospital to see their dying mother.

After the man got a spare wheel onto Tashira's Escalade, they dipped to Block's crib and immediately ransacked it.

They found all of the merch, loaded the Escalade up with it, then took it all to Tashira's grandmother's house up in Kenosha, Wisconsin, keeping a brick of coke and one of dope on hand to take to Hustle Man's spot.

***

"Maan, that nigga is high as a kite, joe," Inez laughed, wiping tears from her eyes.

"On God!" laughed Tashira.

Hustle Man stopped dancing a minute later, then took a deep breath. He waddled back to where the ladies sat at his dinner table with one of the five bricks that had come from Percy's pawn shop; three of them had turned out to be cocaine, and obviously, was some *kill bill*. The other two were heroin, deemed by Hustle Man's personal knowledge of drugs to be high-quality.

"A'ight, joe. Mmm! Mmm!" he spoke hoarsely then cleared his throat, wiping sweat from his forehead. "Y'all got some fi'ass cocaine, joe, and I put that on Cicero Insane!" he said, swearing upon his allegiance to the Vicelord Nation that he had been a part of since way before fuel-injected engines came into existence. "I can cook each of 'em up and turn one into two, and make it so good that it'll fry a muhfucka's eyebrows off. What up? Talk to me now, Inez."

Inez nodded. "How much you gon' charge, Hustle Man?"

"A couple of hunnid and an ounce per joint."

"Done," Inez agreed. "When can you get to it?"

"As soon as I got the work, shortie."

"Can you cut dope, too?" chimed in Tashira, as Inez left to go get the other bricks from the Escalade.

"Anything to do wit' drugs, lil' mama, I can do. Cook, cut, enhance, blow up, bubble up, sell. I'm called Hustle Man for a reason."

Tashira nodded, peeping how that dope-head nigga was trying to put on for her.

"A'ight then, Hustle Man. Do what chu' do, joe."

"Aye? I seen you around wit' Block a lot out here. That's yo' nigga or somethin'?" Hustle Man then asked, switching topics.

Subconsciously, Tashira had went towards her bag, where she had a .22 revolver inside that she took from Block's personal cache of weapons.

"Naw. We just cool, but his ass a snitch. Fuck him. That's yo' homie?" she then threw back at him, ready to put a hot one in his eyes if he tried her.

"Hell naw. I'm Vicelord, shortie. I don't fuck wit' folks. I know a lot of niggas that'll put him down if he rattin'," Hustle Man told her, right as Inez came back in with the other kilos in a bag.

"Yeah, he did! Block tricked on a few dudes out in Nogo and down in Chicago. His ass got niggas knocked for dope and murders, joe," she lied, looking at Inez.

Inez, quickly picking it up, started grinning. "And I know the man that has a $5,000 hit on Block's head to blow it off."

"Five grand! Hell, *I'll kill* his ass for that! Set it up! I know where he be, too! I'll throw a Drano bomb in his crib then smoke his ass the second he runs up out of it!"

Inez and Tashira smiled slyly at each other.

***

Cynthia laughed her ass off at Alondra's reminiscing of Marcus' childhood as she pushed the Audi A8 through K-Town. The windows were up, keeping people outside from being able to see them through the limo tints, while the sunroof was open, letting in fresh air and sunlight.

In the back seat, Leticia played a game on Alondra's iPhone, having a ball with Candy Crush.

"Hell yeah, though. Caught his ass so many times tryin' to sneak little tragas in my house, and I embarrassed him every time," Alondra told her.

Cynthia was in tears from laughing so hard. The images of such were hilarious to her. She could only imagine his father when his mother caught him ass-naked, and how the chick he was trying to smash looked.

"He had to have been beyond embarrassed," Cynthia said.

"He was red as a tomato," Alondra confirmed, as she rolled along Roosevelt Road with Keeler up ahead.

Glancing at where she was going, she was just able to catch a glimpse of the guy she had to holla at, standing outside of the old hotel's entrance, smoking a cigarette.

"I wonder what he's doing right now," she heard Cynthia say, just as she reached the parking lot of a laundromat at the corner of Roosevelt and Keeler.

Laughing her ass off, Alondra turned into the lot and backed her car into a spot, facing the building.

"Girl, you got it bad for my son. That's the gray eyes he got and his skin tone."

Cynthia blushed, lost for words.

"Uh-huh. Mark my words. If y'all go there, make sure you can handle other little conejas tryin' to jock him. It happens a lot. Shit, I had to smack a few thirst-buckets up in the past."

Cynthia nodded in understanding, but getting better acquainted with Marcus was what she really wanted. She was a Taurus, well known for stubbornness.

Alondra reached over to her glove box and opened it. Inside, a new Heckler & Koch 9mm with an extended magazine, and an extra one next to it. Cynthia's eyes went wide in surprise, then looked at Alondra.

"Keep that close, and keep the doors locked, engine running."

"Okay? Uh . . . what's going on, Alondra?"

Alondra turned her whole body towards her.

"My man and I started a . . . cleaning . . . business. Sometimes, when people get dirty, we get called to come clean 'em up. But sometimes, the people that call us are even dirtier." She reached down to grab her handbag and opened the door. "I'll be back in a minute."

"Alondra! Wait! If something happens to you while I'm with you, Marcus won't ever forgive me."

Alondra smiled. "Aww! Cynthia, you are truly a sweetheart. How old are you?"

"Thirty."

"Oooo, you' ass rockin' cradles, Cynthia!"
"Wait! No, I . . ."
Alondra laughed her ass off. "Nope! Nope! Uh-huh! Yo' ass is busted! Naw, don't even trip, though. I'm seven years younger than my man. You're seven years older than Marcus. We all grown. Don't deny your feelings, though. Now post up. I'll be back in a few." She turned around and blew Leticia a kiss, then with her handbag, she got out of the car, locking the doors then shut hers.

***

"Mommy? Where's Miss Alondra going?"
Cynthia watched the statuesque Boricua strut like a runway model towards the lot's exit at Roosevelt, then she dipped left and disappeared from her line of sight.
"I don't know, Lety." Cynthia grabbed the 9 millie and stashed it on her side. "But if I have to get out to get her, I promise I will be back for you. Okay?"
"Okay."

***

Flex walked the halls of the old run-down hotel. Like they were trained to do, each of the girls that occupied the many rooms with 'clients' came to the doors and handed off the cash they had collected so far, then they went back to provide the services requested by those that chose to pay for it.
Six-feet, five-inches tall, black as a starless nighttime sky, with a clean-shaven head, a thick Rick Ross-style beard, and gold teeth. He sported a silk Versace button-up with white slacks and Italian leather loafers. The gold chains around his neck were worthy of Mr. T's approval, as was the gold Rolex on his wrist and the gold rings on his fingers. The giant pimp was known around K-Town for having a stable of women—bad bitches that did anything as long as they got paid.

***

Flex went up the stairs to collect from the other twelve girls working the second floor. As he got to the top landing, Flex's Samsung rang.

He pulled it out of his pocket and groaned with frustration when he saw who was calling. He answered, though, very reluctantly.

"What up?"

"You tell me, Flex. We've been waitin' very patiently for you, fam. Time's up," he heard her tell him.

"Time's up? Hold up, hold up, hold up. Number one, I'm a muthafuckin' pimp, shortie, you dig I'm sayin'? Bitches don't tell me shit! This is a man's world! Bitches do as we say, and get the taste slapped out of their mouth when they talk back! Number two, I—"

"Flex?"

"Aww, now yo' ass interruptin' me? Bitch, you got me all the way fucked up! I would slap yo' ass if you was here, bitch!"

"Flex?"

"What the fuck you keep saying my name fo'?"

"You lose, my dude. Hope it was worth it."

The call ended without a word more.

Flex looked at his phone, shook his head, then chuckled.

"Bitch think she a muhfuckin' gangsta 'cause of her dude. Fuck that nigga, too. They both can get it in blood if they want it," he said to himself, then continued on with his round, collecting nearly ten thousand dollars total to add to the last three days of non-stop business transactions of the world's biggest industry.

"Aye, Flex? You good, fam'?" asked Twan, Flex's right-hand man, whom played the role in recruiting young ladies to come to the hotel and fuck for a buck from all over Illinois. Whether they were underage or old as hell, if the pussy got wet and Twan could woo them into the 'biz, he brought them to Flex, who broke them 'in', then put them to work. If they refuse or try to leave, then they come up missing. "I heard you yellin' a second ago. Do you need me to handle someone?"

"Naw, Twan. It's just that bitch Alondra, pesterin' me 'bout some money she thinks I owe her."

"Yeah? What, for scoopin' them two dead hoes up after they overdosed in yo' office?"

"Yup. Bitch thinks I'ma really pay $10,000 each. I'll slap the fuck out that hoe if she ever calls me again wit' that dumb shit. I'ma be in my office. If you need me, knock."

Twan nodded. "Got chu', fam. Be cool. Fuck that bitch and her nigga."

***

Flex stepped into his office and made a beeline to where his floor safe stood behind his desk. He entered the code in the digital display, then opened the door. Inside, stacks of cash in rubber bands and a snub-nose .357 revolver loaded with six slugs.

He took out the collection from his pocket and stuffed it inside the safe. Right as he was about to close it, he heard knocking at the door.

"Aye, Flex!"

He heard Twan's voice call out to him.

"Maan, this nigga needs a hobby," Flex said to himself, heading towards the door.

Before he got to it, he heard a thump sound outside of his door.

"Twan, what the fuck you want, man?"

He didn't hear anything.

"Twan?" he hollered.

Still no answer.

"This nigga gon' make me slap the fuck outta him," Flex growled, then as he opened the door—

Fffffffff!—

"Aagghh shit!"

A freezing cold cloud blew directly into his face, blinding him and nearly giving him instant frostbite. He fell backwards and hit the floor on his back hard, wiping the frost from his frozen face. He just was able to make out red hair and a red dress, with a red fire extinguisher pointed right at him.

***

Alondra stepped over Flex's incapacitated partner and entered their office, holding the fire extinguisher in her hands.

Flex looked up at her and went wide-eyed with shock. She pointed the spout at his face again.

"No—"

Fffffffffffffffffff!

She blasted his ass with the bitter cold fire suppressor for a whole ten seconds. When she let go of the handle, Flex was barely moving.

Hearing movement behind her, Alondra saw her son and his father were entering with two old carpets. Marcus wasted no time in rolling Flex's partner up in the carpet he had. Snoop entered and went to rolling Flex up in his carpet. They both taped around the rolls multiple times, preventing either men from getting free once they regained consciousness.

"Hola, mis amores," Alondra said to the two most important men in her life. "Thanks for the assist."

"No problem, beautiful," Snoop replied, heaving the giant up into his arms to carry him out. "See you in a minute."

They kissed, then Alondra watched them take the two creeps out. Quickly then, she ran towards Flex's safe. Seeing that the safe was still open, she grabbed all of the cash, left the gun, and stuffed the loot in a bag. Before she left, Alondra went to where a lamp stood in the corner. She grabbed it, took the shade top off, and slammed the bulb down onto the carpet, causing a fire to start which immediately began burning the carpet up. Alondra backed towards the door then. Seeing the flames spread every few seconds, soon to consume the entire office, destroying evidence of her being there, Alondra rushed out of the side entrance right as the fire alarm went off, and the girls and customers ran out of the front of the hotel, screaming in fear.

***

"Aye! Aye! What is you doin', man? Aye!"

Marcus ignored the guy that he had wrapped up and continued dragging him behind his father through the alley behind the hotel. Snoop's garbage truck sat idling in the cut, hidden from the eyes of those traveling past the hotel.

As he and his father got to the rear of the garbage truck, they heard the hotel's fire alarm start going off, then screaming and yelling filled the air.

"Come on, Snoop! Please, man! Don't do this!" Marcus heard the giant his pops had muscled out, with the skin on his face cracked and bleeding, begging, and crying like a little bitch.

"Shut cho' bitch-ass up. You disrespected my woman and yo' fake-pimp-ass tried to shiesty us out our money. Suck a dick and die, pussy nigga."

Snoop threw the big man into the back of his trash gobbler, then Marcus followed suit. Going to the control levers, Marcus stood at the rear and watched the hydraulic compactor lowered down. The men screamed in fear, but seconds later, the garbage-crushing slab of steel came down on them and smashed them, delivering death then scraping them up into the garbage-storing compartment.

Snoop grabbed a little water-spraying jug from the side of his truck and sprayed the trails of blood left behind until they were gone.

"Good job, son," Snoop told Marcus, hanging the pump back on the truck. "You learn anything yet?"

Marcus chuckled. "Yeah. You and Ma some crazy muhfuckas, joe. On Stone."

Snoop laughed. "The night is still young, lil' Moe. Come on. We got more trash to pick up, then we gotta go dump it."

Nodding, Marcus hopped back up into his seat. Snoop pulled off and tuned up his ol' school rap music, nodding to the same KRS-One as he cruised to get to the next job.

Chapter 12

Inez and Tashira both grinned as they saw Hustle Man's finished product. The bricks they brought in had been doubled, the quality increased. They were geeked up, beyond excited to have all that merch to themselves.

Hustle Man had already begun making calls to his dope-fiend friends, boasting about that phenomenal product. Some were already en route to buy crack and dope. He had identified the pills as well, discovering that they were OxyContin. He took one himself and had been flying ever since, along with hitting the pipe, puffing on some cooked-up cocaine, and taking a couple of snorts of the cut-up heroin, which he had stretched with lactose and brown sugar.

He was so fucked up that as he walked, he moved like he had no bones. Inez and Tashira saw dollar signs all over the kitchen.

***

Within twenty minutes after Hustle Man had finished putting the product together, thirteen crackheads and twenty heroin addicts had come, all of them with nothing less than forty dollars to spend. Thirty more minutes later, twenty-two more friends had come, buying up more *hard*, more *boy*, and Oxies.

In just under an hour, Inez and Tashira had raked in just over forty-three hundred dollars, and their asses hadn't even so much as left Hustle Man's couch cushions.

***

"We fuck 'round, could sit here and his ass pop everything off in two days, joe," Tashira said as Inez puffed on the lit-up blunt of *Purple Kush* and *Blue Dream* mixed together.

Music bumped from Tashira's phone. Cardi B's "WAP" featuring Megan Thee Stallion flowed through its little but loud speakers.

"Straight up. We gon' need us to connect, though, 'Shira," Inez replied, blowing out a thick cloud of smoke through her nose, then passing Tashira the blunt.

"Yo' ass from Chicago, ain't chu? I know you could find one." Tashira puffed the loud and got even higher. "We need a cartel connect, though. Fuck tha middle-man shit."

Inez nodded. "I'll find one. Sexy bitches always get what they want," she stated. Then, as Hustle Man opened the door to step out and serve another wave of fiends, Inez's attention averted to her homegirl's thick-ass thighs.

In an instant, her mind went from money to hunger. Hunger for *her* —Tashira was a bad bitch, and as much as Inez loved her some dick, she loved her some pussy as well.

After a quick trip to the *Gurnee Mills Mall* for a shopping spree, then to the salon for a little pampering, Inez and Tashira came back to Hustle Man's spot looking like ghetto-fabulous divas.

Tashira, in a white form-fitting long-sleeved closed-collar mini-dress with tiger-striped designs on both sides, white fishnet pantyhose, and suede tiger-striped stiletto boots that went to just above her knees, was making sure that everyone knew that she was a bad bitch. Her hair was now dyed a lighter chestnut brown and was braided to the back in four big braids, with tiny little braids in between. Silver jewelry and a light layer of makeup made her photo-shoot ready, and she wore sweet-smelling perfume.

Inez flaunted her voluptuous hourglass physique in a bright white neck-strapped belly-revealing top and a tight short stretchy white mini-skirt that the six-inch pointed-toe stiletto pumps on her feet matched. She knew how white always made her delicious chocolatey skin tone pop, so Inez wore white as much as she could so she always stood out. Her lips matched her hair, faux pearls were in her ears, and around her neck was a silver rope chain.

***

Inez leaned over Tashira and took the blunt from her. Tashira complained but was silenced by Inez putting a finger to her lips. She puffed the bud a couple more times, then she stopped, taking Tashira's hand and pulling her up.

"Inez, what is you . . ."

Tashira's question was stopped by Inez's lips being pressed to hers. Inez pulled back and licked her lips. Without a word, she stubbed out the blunt, then she pulled Tashira to the bathroom and closed the door.

Right away, Inez attacked like a hungry lioness. She backed Tashira up against the door and tongue-kissed her like a horny teenager that had finally got her hands on the one person that turned her into a sex-craving nympho.

She put her hands on Tashira's sides as Tashira's hands went around and cupped her meaty booty cheeks and squeezed them. Inez's hands traveled down to the hem of Tashira's dress. They both raised each other's skirts up over their hips while never breaking their kiss.

Their moans grew louder, breaths heavier and hotter as their temperatures rose sky-high. Inez felt Tashira's hands leave her ass and loosen her top's strap. Then she pulled it off, tossing it away.

Inez pulled back and let Tashira's hands caress her succulent breasts before cupping one and putting her mouth to her nipples.

"Mmmmm . . . ssshit," she cursed, feeling Tashira's tongue swirl circles around it. "Dammnm, that feel so good."

She leaned her head back and closed her eyes, letting the sensation of bliss take her away. Her pussy leaked like a broken faucet down her inner thighs, clit throbbing, aching, begging for some action.

A minute later, Inez pushed Tashira's head up. She maneuvered her around to the sink, then cupping her ass, she lifted her up and put her on the vanity top.

Tashira started smiling with red-hot desire and anticipation. Inez lifted her legs up and opened them to see that under her fishnets, Tashira did not have on panties nor a thong.

She ripped a hole in the soaking wet crotch, then like an Olympic swimmer, Inez dove down between Tashira's thick thighs and ran her tongue up from her asshole, up her wet swollen pussy lips, putting her lips to her clit right after.

Tashira's back arched from the instant bliss of Inez's mouth on her. She put her hands on her own breasts and massaged them, adding to her pleasure.

Inez slurped up Tashira's juices as she continuously leaked, then parting her, she went back to sucking her clitoris.

"Oooohhhm, Inez! Fuck! Oohh yeeaaasss! Eat this pussy! Eat it all up!"

Inez then slipped a finger inside of Tashira. Continuing to taste her, she began finger-fucking her. Curling her finger slightly, she tickled Tashira's sensitive walls. Tashira cried out Inez's name again, louder this time, as the chocolate drop pleasured her, bringing her closer and closer to her orgasm—

Knock! Knock! Knock!

"What y'all doin' in there?" came Hustle Man's voice.

"N-N-Nothing! G-Go away!" Tashira hollered while Inez continued making her toes curl up.

"Can I watch?" Hustle Man then asked after a five-second pause.

"Hu-Hu-Hustle Man! Go awaaaay! Oooohhhm, fuuuck! I'm 'bout to cuuum!" Tashira moaned out.

Inez went bananas on her; she sucked wildly, swirling her tongue around it simultaneously and adding another finger.

Tashira's back arched up so hard she felt like her spine could snap. She raised her legs up as high as they could go, then put her hands on the sink, bracing herself as her whole body shook like she was sitting on a washing machine on the spin cycle.

Throwing her head back, she screamed out at the top of her lungs, not giving a damn who heard her. She exploded so hard in Inez's face that her legs went numb.

—Bam! Bam! Bam! Bam!—

Tashira groaned, frustrated that Hustle Man was still trying to interrupt.

"Hustle man! Can we have some damn privacy? God damn, nigga!" Inez yelled, wiping her face.

—Baaam! Baaam! Baaam!—

"Oh my God! Fuckin' dope-fiend-ass nigga!" Tashira complained.

Pissed, Inez grabbed her top and hurried to put it back on when more banging on the door came.

"This nigga's tryna' break the door down!" Tashira realized and hopped off the sink quickly, pulling her dress down. "Aye, man, Inez, what the hell wrong wit' cho'—"

—Boom!—

The door was hit hard and flew open. Inez got smacked by it and was sent to the floor.

Tashira screamed, terrified beyond ever before, when she saw Block at the door with a deranged look in his eyes.

He whipped out his Colt .45 from his waistline and put it right at her face, so close that she could smell burnt gunpowder residue.

"Block! Please! Don't do this!" Tashira cried.

“Bitch! You bit my dick off!” he roared, then grabbed her by her throat and slammed her up against the wall across from the sink. “And you flushed it!”

“You raped me, Block!” she screamed back.

“You’s my bitch! how was that rape?”

“’Cause you took it when I wasn’t givin’ it, Block!”

Block’s grip was like a vice around her throat. Tashira felt herself being lifted up off of her feet. She tried to claw his hand to make his grip loosen, but Block was strong as hell and very angry.

“Bitch!” he growled through clenched teeth as he tightened his grip even more. “I take what I want! Nobody tells me no!”

Tashira was losing the battle. She could barely breathe, and she was growing weaker by the second. Her vision began to blur. Block’s face became distorted. She felt her bladder let loose a second later, then came black dots as the oxygen in her brain decreased.

She tried kicking him in his crotch, but there was nothing there. He gritted his teeth and, once again, gripped even tighter, trying to break her windpipe. Her arms got weak, and she could no longer hold them up to use her hands to try freeing herself.

“Told yo’ ass, bitch, you gon’ learn today!” Block growled.

Then . . .

—Smash!—

Through narrowed slits, Tashira saw something white crash into Block’s head and break apart. His body jerked, then his face went slack. His hand loosened from around her throat and she dropped to the floor on her ass, at the same time that Block tipped over like an oak tree that had been axed.

He hit the floor hard, unconscious, eyes closed.

Tashira grabbed at her throat, gasping for air desperately. With her eyes bugged wide as her brain registered that she was still alive, she looked to her left and saw Inez standing less than a foot away, breathing heavily, with a crazed look in her eyes and her fist balled. The porcelain top for the toilet was no longer on top of the water tank, but in pieces all over the floor.

Inez grabbed the gun from the floor by the tub and cocked it. She raised it up and took aim at Block's face. She wrapped her finger around the trigger and got ready to dome him, when Hustle Man crept up to the doorway.

He looked in, saw Block, then the gun.

"Oh shit!" he panicked, then ran.

***

Inez jumped over Block's unconscious body and out into the hall, pointing at Hustle Man's rear as he fled.

—Boc! Boc! Boc! Boc! Boc!—

All five shots hit the dope fiend in his back, putting him down on the floor, screaming for help. Inez ran up on him and blew the side of his face off without any hesitation. His brains sprayed out all over the hardwood floor, painted it crimson.

"Inez!" she heard Tashira holler out from by the bathroom.

She took a step to finish what she was about to do to Block, when suddenly, she heard . . .

"Police department! Don't move!"

Inez gasped and saw a cop in uniform round the corner from the living room to the hall. She immediately fired at him. The cop dove back around the corner, narrowly missing getting his head blown off.

"Come on!" she screamed to Tashira, running into Hustle Man's bedroom.

Tashira hurried behind her and went to grab the duffel bag with the cooked-up and cut-up brick that Hustle Man hadn't started selling off yet. Inez grabbed the bag that had the jewelry from Q, and Percy, and the two ballers from the club.

"Police! Freeze!"

Tashira screamed when she saw the cop leaning into the room at the doorway, pointing his service weapon at Inez. Her scream distracted him just long enough for Inez to turn and fire three times at him.

—Boc! Boc! Boc!—

Two hit him in his face and the third went wild. He flew backwards and hit the floor, out of there.

"Come on, 'Shira! The window!" Inez urged.

She ran to the window that looked out to Hustle Man's backyard and opened it. Jumping out with the bag of jewelry, Inez waited for Tashira to jump out.

Tashira tossed the bag out to her, then she climbed out herself, then they ran towards the Escalade.

"Inez! Block is still alive!" Tashira panicked as they both jumped in with the bags, hearing sirens wailing out from so very close by.

Inez, behind the wheel, started the engine, slammed it into drive, and smashed the gas pedal, peeling off down Galilee. "I know, 'Shira! I couldn't get to him! Hustle Man set us up!" she stated knowingly, pissed that she trusted the dope fiend that was well known and knew everyone. "Fuck," she then screamed, coming up on 33rd Street. "He had all the money, too, man. Dammit."

Tashira cursed angrily as Inez banged a right turn and raced west on 33rd towards Lewis Avenue, putting as much distance as she could between them and Hustle Man's spot.

"Hurry up and get us somewhere so I can get showered. That bitch-ass nigga made me pee on myself."

Inez took a deep breath, then she exhaled. She was beyond heated to have lost all the cash that Hustle Man had made them, and how they had both come so close to losing their freedom, or their lives. But as she reached the intersection of 33rd and Lewis, flying through the green light, she sighed, relieved that they still had something to bounce back off of. But now, she had racked up more bodies, and one of them was a cop.

***

Block regained consciousness when he heard loud pops jolting his eardrums. Opening his eyes, he saw he was laid out on the bathroom floor with a splitting headache.

He sat up and his head started pounding even more, like a gorilla was inside of his skull trying to beat his way out of it. As he remembered how close he had come to killing Tashira for biting his dick off and flushing it down the toilet, then getting hit hard in the back of his head, Block grew furious with rage. He went to get up when he heard footsteps in the hall outside of the bathroom.

Two men appeared as Block tried standing. He immediately recognized one of them as the light-brown-skinned dude that he had forced out of the Bentley Bentayga, while his fallen homie Cam got the dopehead out from behind the wheel the same night he went to get his bitch out of the club, and later on, got his dick bitten off, right before Inez killed Cam.

"What the fuck!" Block then gasped, seeing they both wore badges clipped on the waistlines of their jeans, with Glocks tucked into side holsters.

The light-skinned undercover smirked at him, while the dark-skinned dreadhead stared at him with a venomous glare.

"Whaz' hanin', Block? Allow me to introduce myself. I'm Detective Wilson," the light-skinned cop spoke. "And this angry brotha' is Detective Tobin. Any chance you know where our Bentayga is? It's property of the Lake County Sheriff's Office."

Shocked and speechless, Block gave no reply.

"Okay . . . how about . . . where are India and Monica? Oops! I mean Inez and Tashira?"

Again, Block gave no reply.

"Hmm. You were pretty loud when you and those crazy bitches were car-jackin' us. It's a'ight, though," Wilson told him as Tobin pulled out a pair of handcuffs. “We know how to help you find yo’ voice.”

Block reluctantly turned around and was cuffed, way rougher than necessary. Then as he was turned around, Tobin ran him into the edge of the door, instantly breaking his nose.

He roared in pain and bled heavily.

“Oh, my bad, fam? Did that hurt?” Wilson asked.

“Don’t worry. The health care unit at Lake County Jail is the best in the state, and it's free!”

“But unfortunately,” came Tobin, speaking for the first time as he and his partner escorted Block out of the bathroom, “somebody has to pay for the body of the officer in the bedroom, and the dope fiend you’re about to walk past.”

The second Block was brought around the corner from the hallway, he saw a gang of what looked like gangbangers posted in the living room. Seven men, three women, all in black wearing fitted caps, black bandanas tied around their necks, black hoodies, jeans, black Jordans or Timberlands, with bulletproof vests on, “Sheriff” stitched on all of them in white, semi-automatic service pistols in their hands, none of them wearing radios.

“Block,” Wilson said, “this is our squad. They were all in line to use the Bentley truck for undercover stings, but now it's gone. They’re pissed.”

Block was pushed forward then, right into the circle of killers with badges.

“Take this nigga to our ‘interrogation’ room. We’re gonna see if we can find the other two,” Tobin instructed. “Not too bloody now, y’all hear?”

Block heard someone grunt, then he walked out of the house and was thrown into a black windowless van to be taken to where he was very sure wasn’t a police station.

Chapter 13

Marcus was floored by what his father and his mother did on the side. He'd always known them to be on some G-shit as he was growing up, but doing wet work was a whole different ball game. His father had did time for attempted murder, so he knew his pops had no problem taking a life, and his mother had always been a blood fiend queen. After crushing Flex's body, while he had still been alive, and his associate, Marcus wanted to follow in both of his parents' footprints.

"Warm Embrace" by Twista & The Speedknot Mobstaz bumped as Snoop pushed his Mack truck along Pulaski, coming up on 15th. Marcus nodded, liking the sound of real Chi-Town G-shit coming through the speakers, and as the chorus flowed, he rapped along with it.

At 15th, Snoop made a wide turn onto the one-way. Cruising through the residential area, he approached an alley on his left that was just before Harding. Pulling past it a little, he saw his homeboy's pick-up truck in the alley, with its front end facing away from the street. Snoop stopped, then putting it into reverse, he backed at a 90-degree angle into the alley, stopping just a few feet away from the pick-up's rear end.

"Last for the day, lil' nigga. Let's ride," the O.G. told his son.

Marcus got out of the cab and went to the rear of the garbage truck. Getting out of the pick-up, Marcus saw two big men, with low-faded, neat braids, wearing work clothes and boots. He then noticed the pick-up's bed had a button-down tarp over it.

"Whaz hanin', Pride?" one of the men spoke to Snoop.

"What up, L?" Snoop dapped the man up, then the second guy. "Marcus, these are my guys from back in the day—L and Goon. Y'all, this my son Marcus."

The two ol' head Black gangsters acknowledged Marcus and embraced him, like one of their own.

"Learnin' the bizness, huh, youngsta'?" L asked him.

"Like father, like son," Marcus replied proudly.

"I heard that. Well. Here y'all go."

L and Goon opened the tailgate and each pulled a body bag out that was not empty. Snoop grabbed one and tossed it into the truck, then Marcus followed suit. His father then hit the controls, crushing the bodies inside, then scraping them into the compactor. Marcus grabbed the water pump this time and sprayed away the remnants of blood.

"Aye, Pride," Goon then spoke. "These two were only a part of the problem, you dig I'm sayin'? They had a lot of bricks of that fentanyl shit. They connected wit' a cartel."

"We been givin' it to they asses, though," L chimed in. "Muhfuckas wanna come in our neighborhood and put that shit on our streets, they gon' die."

Snoop nodded in agreement. "I got Polo on it. Told me he zeroed in on a spot in Pilsen. I'm just waitin' on him, know what I mean?"

No sooner than he had finished his sentence, Marcus heard the sound of a crotch rocket's engine very close. On instinct, he put his hand inside his jumpsuit, through the front seat to grab his pistol. Snoop halted him, telling him to be cool.

A second later, a man on a custom-painted Suzuki GSX-R rolled up, wearing a black helmet with a tinted face shield. He had on a black hoodie, and at his right side, Marcus saw he had a handgun in a side holster. It was then that he noticed the dark blue uniform pants, and police-issue boots.

The man flipped his face shield up when he came to a stop next to Snoop. He fist-bumped him, then L and Goon walked up and fist-bumped him. The man said not a word as he went into his pocket and produced a piece of paper. After he handed it to Snoop, the man kicked his bike into gear, then rode off, disappearing as fast as he came.

"Dad? Was that a cop?" Marcus asked with shock.

"Yup. Before you get to thinkin' crazy shit, you need to know how the streets were in our time. We had structure. Our guys were put in many positions—street soldiers, block boys, trap runners, dope men, cash movers, gun keepers—all the way up to investors, lawyers, cops, judges, hell, fire fighters, aldermen and women. We are our own government, because the real government don't give a fuck about us. And what's even sadder is how many of *us* actually care about us? How many white people did you see marchin' for that man up in Minnesota?"

"And how many others were hittin' the Gucci and Louis Vuitton spots?" L threw in. "When we all should've been supportin' a man killed by a dick-head cop for no reason, like all the other Black men and women, from pandemic times up to this day."

"So, we govern ourselves, and those that go against us," Goon came again.

"End up in a landfill," Snoop finished, looking at his son.

Marcus understood whole-heartedly, and he respected it. He agreed—not many folks from the hood cared for the hood. Or else, why would there be so many shootings, stabbings, murders all over the hood, in every hood in the world? Marcus also knew that it wasn't just people from the hood that went against their own kind, but all mankind went against mankind.

"Look at him, Snoop." Goon chuckled as he looked at Marcus. "He ain't had it raw like that a day in his life."

"You ever do time, young buck?" asked L.

"Naw. Don't want to either," Marcus replied.

“Nobody does, but it's part of the game, son,” Snoop said. “All you can do is be smart, be cool, and be tough. Now let's go. We got one last move to make for the night, and this just might be the move you been waitin’ on.”

***

Back up in the truck, Snoop pulled off and immediately made a call. Marcus wasn’t sure who he called, but hearing his pops tell someone *“Action”* at the end of the call, Marcus knew that the night was most definitely far from over.

Then a thought popped into his head. He pulled out his phone and attempted to call Inez.

Her number had been disconnected.

Marcus shook his head, but actually found that he wasn't as broken up about her as he thought he would be, if something ever broke them apart the way street life almost always did a couple.

Cynthia. He wanted to know her. He wanted to learn her. And Leticia—she made him feel important, like he was someone she needed, for her love, affection, and protection.

Then he thought about the kilo of cocaine Cynthia had given to him. What chick did that? She blessed him with a whole brick, just to help him when she had a child to take care of.

Just thinking about her had Marcus so eager to bust it down, bag it up, and pump it out—to show her that he was that nigga that she felt he was. To show her that she made the right choice to trust him. He then questioned to himself, what would he do when it was gone?

Sighing to himself, Marcus pushed it out of his mind. He would figure it out when that time came. For the time being, Marcus knew he had to stay focused. He wasn't sure where they were going, and he didn’t care. What mattered more to Marcus now was soaking up as much of the game that his father was giving him. The way that his mother looked at his father, with that raw, unblemished thug love in her eyes—Marcus would give anything for a chick to look at him like that.

And not just any chick.

He wanted Cynthia to have eyes for him like that.

"You look like you have real hard thoughts over there, son. She's on yo' mind again, huh?" Snoop suddenly asked.

"A lil' bit," Marcus partially admitted.

"Yeah right," Snoop replied, then busted out laughing at his love-struck son. "Ain't even hit it yet, and yo' ass in love!"

Marcus shook his head at his laughing-ass father, then chose to keep quiet. Going toe-to-toe with the ol' head was not a battle he was prepared for until he was at least eighty years old, walking with a cane, and wearing adult diapers.

***

Frankie D's eyes rolled to the back of his head as the brunette gave him some sloppy-ass head on his couch. She slurped and sucked loudly, deep-throating him with ease. Every so often, she took his dick out of her mouth, spit on it, then got right back to sucking again.

She was one of his cocaine clients. Though a cokehead, the white girl was bad, and she had a bag. She pulled up in a new Mercedes-Benz, rocking a skin-tight Fendi dress with heels to go with it, hair looking all Hollywood streetwalker, with some expensive jewelry on. Frankie D invited her right in when she texted him that she was at the door.

She was no Danielle in his eyes, but man, she had his toes curling up so hard in his Dior x Air Jordan 1s that they swore they were going to break off.

***

“God-d-damn!” he stammered, when she gripped him with both of her little hands and jerked him while sucking.

He gritted his teeth, groaning and grunting. He felt this nut coming and quickly stood up, grabbing her head, then fucking her face until he busted his nut in her mouth. She swallowed it all, then looking up at him, she opened her mouth for him to see his cum and giggle.

“You’s a nasty lil’ bitch, Bonnie,” he chuckled, as she swallowed.

“So? Nothin’ wrong with havin’ a healthy sexual appetite,” Bonnie replied, still on her knees.

“But you’re married to yo’ boss’ son.”

“Okay? He’s a square. He doesn’t have a freaky bone in his body, so a bitch gots to do what a bitch gots to do. And you, my friend, are what I need in my life.”

“I dig that, lil’ mama,” the high-ranking Spanish Gangster Disciple said.

Frankie D’s phone rang just then. He helped Bonnie up and told her to crush up some more coke so after he got off the phone, they could get geeked up and fuck each other's brains out. Grabbing his phone, he had to do a double-take when he saw who was calling. Answering it, Frankie stepped away from where his coke-snorting-cum-guzzling snow bunny was crushing up an eight-ball worth of powder on the coffee table.

“I see you remembered my number, huh?” he answered sarcastically, entering the kitchen.

“Boy, bye,” he heard her say after she smacked her lips. “I had to lay low ’cause shit was gettin’ crazy. But come let me in. I’m at yo’ door and my friend needs to use yo’ shower.”

“Hold up, shortie. How you just gon’ pop up at my crib and expect to get in? I ain’t heard shit from you since I got robbed! And it wasn’t Rigo that set me up! My niggas really think that you set me up! You really think it’s safe for you to be within a mile of me, Danielle?”

"Yeah, I do, 'cause I know who robbed you, and I'll put it all out here so you can find him and get his ass. Now quit bumpin' yo' gums and open the door!"

***

Frankie went to open the door, went wide-eyed at the sight of her and her homegirl. Looking at the thick chocolate drop in her tight white and slutty outfit, with her "fuck-me" stiletto pumps on her feet, his dick rocked up like crack cooked by a master street chef.

"Damn! Where y'all comin' from?" he asked.

"Comin' from outside," his breezy sassed, then stepped inside with her friend behind her, carrying a Walmart bag.

***

"Oh, for real?" Inez saw the white girl in the living room, on her knees, snorting coke off of the table. "You got bitches up in here gettin' high 'n shit?"

"It's my crib, my coke, and if you don't stop talkin', it's gon' be my gun in yo' mouth, since you so good at suckin' on hard things."

"Uhm-uh! Nigga, don't talk to her like that!" Tashira snapped, stepping up next to Inez.

Inez looked at the white girl, who was now just looking her way, holding a straw between her fingers.

"I'm guessin' it's you that need the shower," Frankie D said, wrinkling his nose at the smell of urine invading his nostrils. "Bathroom is that way," he pointed.

Tashira smacked her lips. "You gon' be a'ight, uh . . . Danielle?"

"Yup. Frankie was just finna kick that lil' bitch out so he and I can talk."

"Oh, hell no! I am not going anywhere, Frankie! Tell *that* bitch to go!" the white girl shot back at Inez.

Inez went to take off and get her, as was Tashira. Frankie D stepped in front of them and gave them a look that made them reconsider.

"Bonnie, get at me later tonight. Lemme handle this business. I promise when I come scoop you, it'll all be worth it."

Reluctantly, the girl got up with her Fendi bag, and turned her nose up at Inez and Tashira. She marched into the kitchen and left out of the ground-level patio door.

"Thot-ass bitch," Inez grumbled.

"Talk!" Frankie D barked, then shooed Tashira to the bathroom.

"They call him Block, man! Damn! Stop yellin'!"

Frankie D's eyebrows furrowed. "Block? You talkin' bout *GD Block*?"

"Yes! Him! He been stickin' up 'erybody around the way!" Inez told him, just as she heard the shower turn on.

"How do you know this?"

"I was at a party and heard people talkin' about a well-known friend called Hustle Man, and a cop that got killed in Zion, like, an hour or so ago!"

She saw his eyes go wide then.

Got hiiiim! she thought, doing everything she could to keep from smiling and giving herself away.

"*Man*, I just heard about that before shortie came over! Where that nigga at?" Frankie D asked with urgency.

"I don't know. I was told cops ran up in the crib, like, right after. Not sure if he got locked up or not, but you need to get his ass, baby! For real!"

"I'ma handle it. My bad for doubtin' you," he told her, then leaned down and kissed her lips. "You still my bitch?"

Inez laughed. "Of course, boo. But now you gotta make it up to me."

"Tell me how and I will."

Inez went over to the living room and stood by the couch. She looked with a seductive smile and beckoned him with a finger.

He went to her like a trained puppy. Walking right up to her, Frankie D put his arms around her waist and went to kiss her, but she stopped him.

"You need to make that call before this happens."

Frankie D nodded, agreeing. He pulled his phone out from his pocket and started making calls. Inez was actually amazed to see him making boss calls. It turned her on, but she had to keep to her plan and not fall for the dick.

He ended the sixth call and looked at her. "He in the County. I got a chick that works there and she told me he just came in, and had to go through the infirmary from how bad he was beat up. Yo, that nigga ain't got a dick!" Frankie D exclaimed incredulously.

Inez snorted a laugh. "Wow. Like, literally?"

"Yeah, joe! My nigga said dude told the nurses that his bitch bit it off! On the D, if a bitch even thought about puttin' her teeth on me while she suckin' my dick, fam, I'll chop her mouthfuckin' head off!"

"I would hope so," Inez replied, trying so hard not to laugh at how gullible men were when it came to bad bitches. "So, you put yo' people on dude?"

"Yup. As soon as that nigga gets to Gen Pop, no matter what floor, his ass is grass. On Nation, he outta there."

Inez snickered. "What if they put him on the women's floor?"

Frankie D laughed. "Still grass. Now quit askin' all those questions and gimme that pussy, girl."

She pulled the skirt up then, unveiling what he wanted, with no panties nor a thong to get in his way. Turning around, Inez smacked her own ass cheeks. She started making them jiggle, bending over as she did. She heard Frankie D wowing as he grabbed her ankles and started making her ass clap.

Splitting her legs open, Inez looked at him from under herself. He was licking his lips, rubbing his hands, looking like he was all ready to eat.

Inez smiled deviously at him. She then looked past him and saw the last part of her plan sneak right up on him, and . . .

***

Tashira snuck up on Frankie D as Inez’s ass had all of his attention on it. Without even so much as a struggle, she snagged that tiny cable cord around his neck and held on for dear life as he instantly started bucking and kicking like a rodeo bull.

***

Inez pulled her skirt back down and went to help Tashira with the 6’3” tall monster that she had been fucking and scamming for a very long time. He was a heavy in the streets, and a means to an end for her. Now, it was all or nothing.

Tashira held on like a pit bull, using all of her strength to choke him out. He growled and thrashed wildly. Backpedaling, Frankie D rammed Tashira into an exposed brick wall next to the fireplace. She kept holding on, though, refusing to let loose.

Inez ran up on him and head-butted Frankie D in his sternum as hard as she could.

He yelped as the wind was knocked out of him. She got out of the way as he went down like a tree, falling flat on his face.

Tashira growled like a lioness taking down prey much bigger than her. Inez stood by and watched as Frankie D’s foot kicked as Tashira slowly strangled him. Four seconds later, he went completely still.

Pulling hard on the cord once more, Tashira made sure he was dead. Inez helped her up, then wanting to make sure he was up out of there herself, she checked his neck for a pulse, but found none.

"Yup, he gone." She stood there – fresh and clean – wearing a plain black shirt, tight blue jeans, and sneakers. "Good job," she told Tashira. "Now let's get everything he has that's shiny, green, or filled with white powder. Then, off to Chiraq we go."

Tashira nodded. Without any more words being exchanged, the two ransacked Frankie D's spot until they hit the motherlode.

Chapter 14

"Oh yeah! Now that's what the fuck I'm talkin' about, folks! Nation, nigga! Chicago's 'bout to get hit wit' a real cold summer," Easy exclaimed with the excitement of a kid in a candy store.

"On the *A*, folks, we finna get rich as fuck off this one!" Kite rubbed his hands together in anticipation.

Standing next to Kite, Cali was just as geeked with an ear-to-ear grin. He saw nothing but dollar signs sitting on the pallet that had just been unloaded from the bakery's own delivery truck.

Fifty bricks of that grade-A Colombian scama cocaine, fresh up from Sinaloa, Mexico, were hidden in big paper bags of baking flour and sugar. The Ambrose mob, a Latino gang well known around Pilsen, other parts of Chicago, and other cities around Illinois, were ridiculously geeked. It was their biggest shipment yet from the cartel they were connected with. They planned to turn that fifty into a mind-blowing one hundred by adding fentanyl to each brick, like they had been doing for the past few months. They couldn't care less about how many people were dying from their deadly mix. If people valued getting high more than life, then why should they care?

***

Easy and his guys tore the plastic wrap from the goods and removed the baking ingredients, revealing all of the plastic-wrapped kilos of coke and fentanyl.

The main door to the basement opened up just then. The owner of the bakery entered the basement and saw the three most trusted guys in his organization getting to work. He smiled at the sight before him. Between his bakery, which sat right on 18th Street in Chicago's Pilsen neighborhood, right in the heart of a huge Hispanic community, and all of the cocaine he imported from his hometown in Sinaloa, Leon was bringing in tens of millions every three months. His crew was well-fed and loyal, and he had Pilsen on lock, but was seeking to take over way more than just Pilsen. He wanted Humboldt Park, Little Village, the Holy City, K-Town, Crown Town, Moe Town, Cicero, and even downtown. If there was money there, Leon was sending product to it, and didn't care whose toes he stepped on.

***

"Let's get this shit mixed up and outta here," he told the trio. "I'll be upstairs with the wife and my brother getting things ready for the Fiesta Del Sol."

"Eeee, joe, there's finna be so many hoes there!" Cali said, remembering the previous festival that Pilsen held every year.

"Straight up! Aye, let's get this done so we can go get ready!" Easy added.

Leon chuckled and left the basement. Heading back up the stairs, he opened the door at the top of the steps and re-entered the main kitchen area. The smell of meat cooking wafted into his nostrils, making his mouth water.

"Diosa?" he called out to his wife, looking around but not seeing where she had been rolling out dough for pie crust. "Vicente?" he then called out to his older brother.

No answer from any of them. Leon went to his office to check for either of them, but the office was empty. He went to check Vicente's office, but it, too, was empty. Scratching his head, he looked around the kitchen area. All was silent.

As he continued looking around, the aromas became burning smells.

Alarmed, Leon ran over to where the large industrial ovens were. He saw black smoke coming out of one of them. He rushed to it, grabbed an oven mitt, and grabbed the door handle, opening it up.

"Holy shit! Oh my god!" he screamed when he saw both his brother and his wife inside the oven, burning to a crisp.

"Pssst! Aye, fam?" he heard a man say from behind him. "Don't make no sudden movements. Reach for the ceiling and turn around, real slow."

Leon raised his hands up high and slowly about-faced. He saw a young man dressed in black coveralls with a weapon that looked like a shotgun in his hand. Next to him, a stallion of a woman with long, fiery red hair, wearing a tight red dress, pantyhose, and high-heeled boots. She, too, had a weapon that resembled a shotgun, but both of their barrels were way bigger than what he had ever seen before.

"Who are you? What did you do to my wife and my brother?" he demanded, trembling in fear.

Smoke began filling the back area. Leon swore the fire alarm should be going off, but it wasn't.

"I think it's pretty obvious what we did, pendejo," the woman told him, then she pointed her cannon at his stomach and pulled the trigger.

—Foomp!—

"Aaghhhh!" Leon yelped as a beanbag flew out of the barrel and slammed into his gut with the force of a cannonball.

The beanbag hit him so hard that it made him fart and fly backwards to the floor. The next thing he knew, he had been grabbed by his ankles and was being dragged towards the ovens where there was so much smoke that it was hard to see now.

***

Marcus dragged the bakery owner to the oven, despite him trying to kick out of his grip. Alondra popped his ass with another beanbag to his gut, making him curl up into the fetal position.

With an oven mitt, Marcus opened the second oven that was at the highest temperature it could go, while the owner's wife and brother were being charred beyond recognition in the one next to it.

"Wait! Please! Don't do this!" the man begged through the excruciating pain in his gut.

Alondra pointed her beanbag cannon at the man's face then.

"No!"

—Foomp!—

A close-range shot knocked him unconscious with ease.

"All yours, baby boy," Alondra said to her son.

Marcus heaved the man up and tossed him into the oven. Alondra slammed it shut, then Marcus slid a metal bar in between its door handle and the one next to it, preventing it from opening.

They hurried to the basement door then. Yanking it open, Marcus followed his mother down the steps to the basement, where his father had the three Latinos that were about to start mixing the staggering number of kilos with the extremely deadly additive lying face down on the concrete.

"Y'all good?" Snoop asked.

"Yeeessiiiir!" Alondra told him, then took aim at one of the Ambroses' heads and fired her cannon.

—Foomp! Foomp! Foomp! Foomp! Foomp!—

"Oh shit! Eew, shit! Damn, ma!" Marcus gasped as the man's head exploded from the powerful impact each beanbag had on his head.

"Man up, lil' nigga, man up!" Snoop told him, then blew the second man's face in when he attempted to roll out of the way.

The third guy jumped up and tried to run for the door to the loading dock. Marcus ran after him and caught him before he could escape, then flung him back down on the ground.

"Come on, man! Don't do this! Take the coke! Just lemme go!" he begged.

"Nope. You're beat, bitch," Marcus replied, then popped the guy in his face with seven beanbags loaded in his cannon, blowing his top off, blood and brains spraying out all over the floor.

"Okay then, son! Now that's how you handle bidness!" Snoop shouted, proud of his son. "And look at what this shit just got us!"

Marcus looked at all the kilos of cocaine and fentanyl that were stacked up on the table. He went wide-eyed with shock, dumbfounded by the very sight of it.

"Since yo' ass called yo'self leavin' home, dyin' to get rich, you been fuckin' wit' the wrong people, papi," Alondra told him. "Now, you should see. You good now. You're the prince of a king and a queen. Never leave the kingdom unless you are truly ready, and you weren't."

Marcus nodded in understanding.

"Let's pack this shit up and get up outta here. Even though we cut the fire alarm's wiring, that smoke gots to be pourin' up outta the front doors by now, and I know Cynthia and Leticia tired of sittin' in that damn car," Snoop said, looking at Alondra with a raised eyebrow.

"What? She has a kid with her, Bae. Lety can't be seein' this shit, so like you said, let's load up and go. We still all have a dinner date to get to and we all smell like smoke. Vamos!"

***

"Pat-a-cake! Pat-a-cake! Baker's man! Bake me a cake! Pat-a-cake! Pat-a—"

In the back seat of Alondra's car, parked in the alley behind the row of business buildings, Cynthia was playing pat-a-cake with her daughter when she heard sirens wailing out so suddenly. Pausing, she looked out of the windshield and saw Marcus' father's garbage truck shoot out of the recessed loading dock behind the bakery, whipping towards the street and racing away.

Cynthia then saw Alondra running with a big duffel bag. She jumped in, slammed it into drive, and mashed the gas as she pulled the door closed. Cynthia and Leticia were thrown back into the rear seat as the Audi shot forward like a rocket.

Alondra looked back at them. "Oops! My fault, ladies!" she apologized, then turned back around, catching up with Marcus and his pops and following them to get out of Pilsen and take the garbage to its final resting place.

***

Block sat on the medical bed, grinding his teeth angrily. He could hear the nurses still laughing at him, along with the two Lake County Sheriff correctional officers that had escorted him into the infirmary to have his wound tended to.

The beating the cops put on him was worse than all the times he had gotten caught by opps on the street. They fucked him up like they pledged the exact opposite of the motto to *serve and protect*, then brought him to the Lake County Jail, dropping him at the sally port, bloody and swelled up.

He was immediately taken to the medical unit, where he was given care but had no choice but to reveal his lack of manhood. He was examined there thoroughly, by a male nurse of all people. It was infected and looked like he had received one of those "surgeries" that had gone severely wrong.

The male nurse came back with two women, both of them bad as hell. Block saw how they were now clowning him, then telling him they would be right back, they left for the nurses' station and had been laughing and joking ever since.

***

"Don't worry about them, bro. Those pinches putos are as bad as those glorified rent-a-cops."

Block looked over at the Hispanic man that was on another medical bed, a few feet away from him; the guy looked worse than he did. Block could easily tell that whatever cops got the guy had played a role in his swollen face and busted nose.

"Man, they did a number on you, fam. You a'ight?" Block asked him.

"I'll be alright. It's those punk-bitch Zion cops that are gonna be in need of medical attention when I get outta here."

"Wow. Zion did you like that? That's who got me. They did me dirty as fuck, joe. Tryna charge me wit' murderin' a dope fiend and a cop!"

"Did you?"

Block's eyebrows furrowed at the question.

"Sorry. Wrong question. I only asked because I could use fearless soldiers in my squad."

"Yo' squad? What are you? A Latin King, or a Sureño?" Block asked.

He chuckled. "My man, I am way above a street gangbanger, no offense if you are in that world. I represent an organization that cannot be defeated. We're all soldiers."

His words and the suit he had on made Block's mind go to all those cartel movies he had watched. The man was fair-skinned, with a trimmed goatee and what was a slick back of ink-black hair. He looked to be about 5'9" and was slim but athletic. Block put the man in his early to mid-40s.

"Sounds like me and my guys," he told the man. "They call me Block. Nice to meet you, despite the circumstances."

The guy nodded. "My friends call me Araña," he said. "So, amigo, tell me, Block. Are you well-known in Zion?"

"Man, I'm well-known 'erywhere, bro. I'm the nigga 'erybody be tryna see," Block capped, but refused to tell the guy he was just a broke-ass jackboy.

"Oh, okay. You're the man, eh?"

"Yeah, I was doin' it big til' the cops hit me and took 'erything. It's cool, though. I'ma beat all this bullshit, then get up outta here and take over . . . if I can find myself another . . . *in* . . . if you know what I mean?"

Araña chuckled. "I think I'm picking up what you're putting down, bro. You see, I, too, am looking for someone, and I need to find her . . . fast. If you truly are as known as you say you are, then perhaps you could assist me in finding her?"

"Wit' all due respect, bro, I'm a Black man facin' a murder charge on a white cop. If you want my help, you might wanna grab a Snickers."

Araña chuckled. "Your word to me would make that pointless, amigo. You don't know me, so you do not know what I can do. As I said before, I represent an organization that cannot be defeated, and that means even by the law."

Before Block could say anything else, two CO's that were in green tactical squad jumpsuits and shock-proof vests entered. The two Hispanic men looked at Araña, then Block heard one speak Spanish to the man.

"El jefe te quiere, carnal. Vamonos, guey."

Having no clue what was said, Block figured out mostly what was up when the guy got up from his bed with a triumphant smile on his face.

"Block. Keep the faith, my friend. I will see you soon. Be ready," the guy told him.

Following the Emergency Response Team COs, Block watched the man head out. He heard others in the infirmary talking.

"That dude is definitely cartel, bro," one said in a hushed tone.

"Hell yeah. I wonder if he knows El Chapo?" another voiced.

Block sat quietly thinking, *Even if dude is cartel, ain't no way he got enough pull to get me up outta this jam.*

Taking a deep breath, Block exhaled, then laid back and closed his eyes, mentally preparing himself for a very long battle with the judicial system, then catching Tashira and biting something of hers off, if he ever got the chance.

***

As nightfall fell upon them, Marcus and his father arrived at a big waste landfill out in Joliet. Snoop entered the property with Alondra trailing behind him. Taking the long dirt road to the massive refuse burial area, they came upon a group of Black men and women, a few in humongous Caterpillar bulldozers, others standing by a fuel truck.

Snoop pulled his garbage truck over to where the two D10 dozers had scraped a large section up, then backed his truck up to it. Marcus watched as he handled a lever in between their seats; he heard some type of noise that sounded like a machine had just started up. The next thing he knew, the truck shook.

He looked in the mirror and saw the rear of the truck rising upwards.

"Come on, son. Follow me," Snoop told him, opening his door.

He got out and followed his father to the rear of the dump truck, seeing that the hydraulic compactor inside the garbage container had pushed out all of the smashed bodies and the actual garbage in it. Another vehicle rolled up at that second and backed up next to Snoop's Mack.

"Remember dude from earlier? The one that brought that Bentley truck to my business?" asked Snoop, as a tall and skinny man got out of the van and opened the rear doors.

"Yeah! Yeah!" Marcus replied, then watched as the guy grabbed a body bag out of the van and hurled it in with the others.

"Never allow a goofy to jeopardize what you work hard to build, son."

The crew at the fuel truck then doused the pile with gas. Another set it ablaze with a flame-thrower, then after it all burned for a few, the dozers buried it, allowing for it to join the tons of decomposing waste already in the ground.

Marcus' father then dapped the man driving the van up, saluted the others, then got back into his truck. Marcus joined him after lowering the rear-loader back down and disengaging its power source. Snoop pulled off, exiting the landfill with Alondra right behind him, en route to get back to the city.

***

Snoop dropped his garbage truck at the yard, then showed Marcus how to "cleanse" it after such jobs. Afterwards, Marcus hopped into the Audi with his mother, Cynthia, and Leticia, both who were ecstatic to be back with him. Alondra drove to her house, stashed the coke, then after they all showered and changed, they headed back out to meet up with Snoop at a popular restaurant out West.

Just before ten, Marcus, Cynthia, Leticia, and Alondra arrived at MacArthur's, where Snoop was already waiting inside with a table for them. Like a gentleman, Marcus escorted Cynthia and his mother inside, holding Leticia's hand while she walked next to him, bouncing up and down with glee.

Snoop welcomed his woman with a kiss, dapped his son up, then gave warm hugs to Cynthia and Leticia. They all sat and ordered their food and enjoyed the delicious cuisine when it came, delivered by the most professional and friendly waiter.

Golden fried chicken wings, spaghetti, greens, French fries, cake, and soda filled their table in Styrofoam trays. The Southern-style delicacies had them all so stuffed that they could barely move afterwards. Marcus, though, had something on his mind.

"Dad?"

Snoop halted his conversation with Alondra and looked at his son.

"Can I holla at you real quick?"

Nodding, Snoop rose up from his seat and gestured to Marcus to follow him.

***

Cynthia wiped her daughter's face of spaghetti sauce while her eyes were on Marcus exiting the restaurant with his father.

"Daaayuuuum, girl!"

She heard Alondra start laughing. Looking at the Boricua, Cynthia saw that she was rolling in laughter.

"What?" asked Cynthia, looking just as puzzled as Leticia.

"Girl, yo' ass gots it bad for my son! He finna wife yo' pretty ass! Watch!"

There was no way she could hold it in. She tried, but Alondra's refreshingly hilarious personality made her start laughing, which then made Leticia giggle. But the idea of being someone's wife was enough to fill Cynthia's mind with a huge "What If?" especially when it came to Marcus.

***

Leaning against his dark-blue and chrome-trimmed '94 Cadillac Fleetwood, squatting on chrome 22" hundred-spoke wire rims, Snoop listened intently to his son. Marcus had every reason in the world that he should get some of the coke they came up with.

"Marcus," he cut in, stopping his youngster from further explaining. "You really think I'm gon' have you ride wit' me on this and not put chu' all the way in?"

"Sort of," Marcus admitted.

"I should muff yo' ass, lil' nigga. Miss me wit' that fool-talk. Yes. You can get down. We gon' split it; you get half, and me 'n yo' momma get the other half. When's the last time you holla'd at yo' Moe brothas?"

"I haven't talked to them since I went Up North, to be honest."

"And you think they solid?" Snoop questioned.

"No. They Stone to the Bone, pop. Ain't nothing solid about us."

Snoop laughed. "Listen to you, Moe man. I hear you, though. But you know you said the same thing about Block, right?"

Marcus got quiet real fast.

"Yeah, that's what I thought. You betta' think real hard about who you gon' trust, Marcus. It's like I told you at the pit. A muhfucka threatened yo' livelihood, yo' family, you gon' have to put 'em down, joe. No hesitation."

"I understand, pop. But I trust Smack and Rahseed. I really do."

Snoop nodded in understanding. "Then get cho' team on point and put a plan together. Structure 'yoselves and be smart. It's round-about here, son. Real rough."

"I'm already knowin', ol' man," Marcus let him know, then he dapped Snoop up before they both headed back to rejoin the ladies.

***

“Yeah, we’re good. Just trying to stay out of the way,” Cynthia told Carmela.

She had turned her phone back on to check in with her friend. Last time they'd talked, Carmela had been worried about her lying low. Cynthia assured her friend that she was. Then Alondra was at the door, and things had been turned up ever since.

“I’m glad y’all are okay, Cyntie. I miss you both so much.”

“I miss you, too, chica. Maybe you could come up for a visit one day?”

“Hey! That sounds great!” Carmela exclaimed. “I always wanted to visit Chicago. That’s where you are now, right?”

“Yeah. I was in Zion, but—hey! Alondra?”

Cynthia looked at her after Alondra reached over and snatched her phone. Alondra ended the call and powered it off.

“Mami, I don’t know who you were talking to, but do you trust them to be telling them all of that?”

“My friend Carmela is the one that saved my daughter when a cartel killed my family.”

Alondra looked into her eyes and, for a minute, stared deeply into them. Cynthia shifted in her seat, unnerved by the Chicagoan’s gaze. Alondra gave her the phone back and nodded.

“Trust can be the best thing in life you can have, Cynthia, but it can also get you killed. Learn that, live that. ¡Me entiendes?”

Cynthia nodded. “Si.”

Marcus and Snoop returned just then. Sitting down next to Cynthia, she blushed after he planted a kiss on her cheek. Alondra busted out laughing her ass off again, and now Snoop joined in, teasing the two like they were two teenagers in high school dying for each other.

“Ma!” Marcus scolded.

"Ma my ass!" Alondra shot back and continued laughing. Snoop then fished the keys to his 'Lac from his pocket and tossed them to his son.

"Me and yo' momma have . . . plans. Take Cynthia and Lety to Navy Pier, or to Sky Zone. Have some fun, but be safe, baby boy."

Marcus nodded, then looked over at Cynthia. "Wanna go have some fun?"

"Yes!" Leticia shouted, answering for her mother.

Cynthia laughed. "The princess has spoken."

"Let's find some then," Marcus replied, then he stood, took Cynthia's hand to pull her up, then he picked Leticia up into his arms.

"Love you, baby," Alondra said to him as he and the ladies parted ways.

"Love you, too, crazy lady."

***

"Aww! Snoop, our baby boy has a family!" Alondra sighed, adoring how her young son had literally just turned into a grown-ass man before her very eyes.

"Yeah. Looks that way," Snoop replied, then he pulled his girl to him and kissed her until she felt like she was on fire.

"Yup! Mmhm! Time to go, negro! Vamos!" Alondra urged and yanked him up and out the door to get into their car, got to her house, and went apeshit before Marcus and the girls got back from where they were going.

Chapter 15

Out at Sky Zone, a huge indoor entertainment spot with indoor trampolines all around, Cynthia, Leticia, and Marcus had a ball jumping around together. Cynthia hadn't ever had so much fun in her life, and her daughter was having more fun than she had since they had run from Texas. Cynthia felt truly safe with Marcus, and she hadn't once thought about the age difference that did initially bother her.

They spent just over an hour there and were ready to go when Leticia started yawning, tuckered out from a long day.

Putting their shoes back on, Marcus scooped Leticia up and carried her as she began to fall asleep. Cynthia walked alongside Marcus, holding his hand with an ear-to-ear smile on her face.

"Did I tell you how good you look tonight?" Marcus asked Cynthia, as they strolled towards the Caddy.

Cynthia chuckled. He had been telling her all night since she and Leticia had gotten dressed. The Chicana was flaunting a somewhat loose-fitting black top with gold chain designs all around it, a shiny skin-tight black vinyl leather skirt, and on her feet, she rocked shiny gold five-inch heels with pointed toes. Her hair was swept back and pinned by a gold hair clip, big gold hoop earrings in hearts, and a gold choker chain around her neck. She wore glittery gold eyeshadow and mascara, with classic red lipstick on the perky kissers. Her perfume had Marcus' mouth watering every time he had gotten a whiff of her.

He himself was rocking more Ralph Lauren Polo, with Nike Air Forces on his feet, a G-Shock watch, and a silver chain. Obviously, he wasn't balling, and he needed a haircut, but his aura and confident demeanor had Cynthia unable to resist being glued to his hip all evening. His eyes, though, had her over the moon every time he looked at her.

"Um . . . I don't remember," Cynthia played, "maybe you should tell me, just in case you didn't."

Marcus chuckled. "Seriously, Cyn'. You are truly one of the most beautiful women I have ever talked to, much less, hit me wit' a car and then saved my life."

"Ay, Dios mío, you just had to bring that up. Thank you, though, Marcus. And you, *tu eres un hombre muy guapo*."

"Huh?" Marcus' eyebrow rose up.

Cynthia laughed, "I said, you are a very handsome man."

"Oh. Thank you, *bonita*," he replied, knowing how to say that much at least.

Arriving at Snoop's Fleetwood, Marcus carefully got the sleeping toddler inside, buckling her in, then held Cynthia's hand as she got in on the passenger's side.

Marcus closed the door, hopped in behind the wheel, then starting the engine, he put it in drive and pulled off with the sound of Do or Die's "Sex Appeal" bumping from the custom audio system.

Cynthia reached over and took Marcus' hand into hers, holding it close to her. Marcus smiled, feeling like he was that nigga that needed nothing more in life at the moment than the gorgeous Latina next to him and the beautiful little creation in the backseat, sleeping peacefully.

***

Almost fifty minutes later, Marcus parked his father's Caddy in front of his mother's house and cut the engine off. He hopped out and opened the door for Cynthia, helped her out, then he carefully got Leticia out and carried her up to the front door.

Marcus heard Cynthia shriek suddenly, right as he got the door unlocked. Looking back to her, frantically looking around the darkness, he surveyed the area along with her.

"What's wrong?" he asked, not seeing anything out of place.

Cynthia hesitated for a minute before she answered. "I . . . I don't know. I just . . . I swear I saw someone behind us."

Marcus immediately gave Cynthia her daughter and rushed her inside. He ran to the long couch in the living room, grabbed the Draco that his mother kept there, along with a back-up 9mm, giving it to Cynthia.

"Stay here. I'll be back," he told her, and rushed to the door.

"Wait! Marcus!" she panicked.

He opened the door, then closed it behind him, gripping the mini chopper tightly, ready to end whoever had the balls to intrude on his mother's property.

***

Leticia stirred from Cynthia's panicked call to Marcus before he ran out of the house. She laid her daughter down, told her everything was fine, then stood by her side, anxiously waiting for Marcus to come back.

Thankfully, Leticia fell right back to sleep. Cynthia crept to the front windows and looked out. The street, only visible due to the few streetlights illuminating the area, was nearly desolate. Not a soul was outside, and many of the houses' lights were off.

Cynthia didn't see Marcus anywhere. She looked back at her daughter, seeing Leticia curled up. She made a decision at that moment, headed to the door, opened it, and . . .

"Ah!"

She jumped back in fright from the door, but realizing it was Marcus there, her rapidly beating heart started to slow down.

"Nobody's out there," he stepped in and closed the door, looking behind him. "I checked the front, the side, the back, and the alley. Everything's as it was left."

Cynthia nodded, then tried to relax. Marcus pulled her into his arms and held her. She felt so much better after he kissed her forehead and swore to her that he would not let anything happen to her.

"On my momma, Cyn, I got chu', and I got Leticia," he promised once more.

His words, so full of passion and sincerity, made Cynthia nearly melt in his arms. She looked at him, gazing into his eyes, and felt something she hadn't felt in a long time: desire. She felt a hot, fiery longing that coursed through her entire body as if she had touched a live wire and was being charged up. It all then shot to her lower region and caused her panties to turn into a puddle.

Still holding the Beretta in her hand while Marcus held the AK-47 pistol, Cynthia reached up and she kissed his lips. He kissed her back, matching her hunger.

She reached for something to set the gun down and found a table next to them. She placed the pistol on it. He laid the Draco down, then they occupied their hands with each other.

Cynthia parted his lips as her tongue begged to meet hers. They met in a lustful and eager mania of arousal and need. His hands traveled down her sides, down to her plump ass and cupped it, squeezing her cheeks while he tongued her down.

Her panties got even wetter as she felt his hardness against her stomach; anticipation filled her with wanton, craving him like she did certain sweets and food when she was pregnant with her daughter.

Marcus pulled back suddenly, surprising her. She whimpered, damn near ready to cry from how bad she wanted him.

"Let's put Leticia to bed, then we can finish this the right way," he told her.

Her heart, once again, sang out with a glorious tune, all for him and how he truly cared about her child. Ready to get back into the pleasurable fire, she nodded, then Marcus scooped the sleeping angel up from the couch.

Cynthia followed him up the stairs to his bedroom. He laid Leticia down. Cynthia gently took her shoes off, then Marcus tucked her in. He took Cynthia's hand after they made sure Leticia was still in a deep sleep, then led her out, closing the door behind him.

He took her to the upper living area and picked up where he left off. Like hitting the gas pedal on a Tesla, Cynthia was catapulted right back into the blazes of pleasure and yearning.

He worked her shirt off, tossing it away; her gold lace bra came next after he unsnapped it from the back. When he tossed it, Cynthia felt so proud for him to see her mouth-watering 32C cups. She couldn't ever remember feeling so confident about her body with any other man, including her daughter's father, the first time she allowed herself to be revealed. But the way Marcus gazed at them, like he was truly in love, made her feel like if she was standing next to Becky G and Chiquis Rivera in front of a massive crowd, she was the only one that mattered.

She stepped to Marcus before he could make his move. She raised his Polo shirt up and over his head, getting rid of it, then she relieved him of his tank top. The tattooed canvas that was he had her dropping her things. She marveled at the perfection, biting her bottom lip as some of the naughtiest things she could ever think swam through her mind.

Cynthia then went for his pants, unbuttoning them, then unzipping them. Marcus kicked his Air Forces off, then allowed her to pull his pants all the way down. He kicked out of them and left them. Her eyes went to the bulge at the front of his boxer briefs.

She grabbed the elastic band and tugged them down until nine throbbingly hard inches were pointing right at her and Archer taking aim at his target.

Her eyes went wide when she saw Marcus' tool. Her mouth watered as her desire to taste him—all of him—grew.

Cynthia stepped to him, taking his dick into her hand, wrapping it around him close to the base. She felt him tighten up when she gave it a jerk. He gave off a groan that was like a deep rumble, giving her goosebumps. She was ready to rock his world, but right as she was about to drop down to blow his mind, he stopped her.

"I been wantin' to taste this *chocha* all day, beautiful. Allow me the opportunity. Ladies first," he told her.

All too willingly, Cynthia let him pick her up and carry her to the love seat. He sat down and sank down to his knees before her. Tall enough to do so, he kissed her lips, then her cheek, her jaw, and kissed down to her chest and popped her right breast into his mouth.

Cynthia moaned out, gasping, back arching as he swirled his tongue over her nipple. She leaned her head back, eyes closed, but still seeing him and his eyes.

He switched to her left breast and pleasured her nipple. Her heart pounded in her chest when his mouth parted from her nipple and he started kissing his way down her flat stomach. Assisting him, she leaned back and opened her legs for him. He pushed her skirt up, then pulled her panties off, discarding them.

Cynthia saw how he licked his lips at the sight of her womanhood, which she kept shaved bare and fresh.

He leaned down then and planted a soft kiss on her inner thigh. It caused a tingling sensation that made him lick his lips. He kissed her further up, slowly making his way to her wetness. He stuck his tongue out and lapped her juices up, tasting her essence, loving it.

"You taste so good, Cyn," Marcus told her.

Cynthia got so lost in the twinkling of his eyes from the moonlight that shone into them from the windows behind her. Marcus dove down between her thighs and put his lips to her southern lips, French kissing them while simultaneously sucking on them. She moaned the second she felt him on her clitoris, sucking on it lightly, swirling his tongue around it.

"¡Aayy! Mmm, Marcus! ¡Ay, Dios mío!" Cynthia cried as he snacked on her, sending sensations up her spine that made her unable to sit still.

The sounds of his lips smacking as he sucked on her clit, being extra loud and extra slippy with it, and the sheer blissful feeling of his sublime skills brought her to an intense climax just minutes after his first inner-thigh kiss.

She exploded right in his face. She drenched his mug and nearly went limp afterwards; she sighed, feeling so good, like no man had ever achieved before. And he hadn't even hit it yet.

Marcus licked her clean, then raised up. She again attempted to move in to please him, but he again stopped her.

"It's all about you tonight, Cyn. Lemme' make you cum, baby," he told her, speaking in a low tone that gave her goosebumps.

"But I wanna' please you, Marcus," Cynthia told him, dying to knock his socks off.

"You will, but tonight, this is me makin' you happy, and that makes me happy."

He took her hands and pulled her up. He sat down where she had just been. Following his intentions, Cynthia climbed onto his lap, straddling him. She reached under her, gripped his hardness, then she slid down on it, immediately feeling the stretch that his blessed size did to her tight walls.

Cynthia moaned while biting her bottom lip as he filled her up. The blissful nirvana was foreign to her but so very longed for. Movies, TV shows, music, all had in different instances had Cynthia aching to be loved intensely by a man that knew how to do it right. Marcus was he who she had been needing and wanting; she had always thought it would come from an older dude, one who had been there and done that and was ready to make a woman a wife. Cynthia was a classy and down-to-earth type chick that had no problem killing someone that threatened her daughter's life or her own. Since meeting the handsome young gray-eyed champion, Cynthia couldn't make herself stop thinking about him. He had her. All of her. She wanted him. All of him.

And she planned to make that happen until it was official.

***

Cynthia rode Marcus' stiff cock while he suckled her breasts. She climaxed all over him moments later, soaking his lap. He took over, getting up with her wrapped around him. He laid her on her back and continued putting it down, planting his flag, claiming her as his, erasing the memories of the past.

He went deep, stroking her with the most perfect thrust, speeding up gradually until he was pounding her. She wrapped her legs around him and took him like he was her medicine, making her feel so much better than she did without him.

"Marcus! Ooo! God! Oh, God! Yes, baby! You feel so good!" Cynthia cried out.

His grunting and groaning was the reply she needed, that told her he was most definitely loving how she felt.

Cynthia reached another orgasm seconds later and nearly lost feeling in her legs when she came. She could tell he wasn't too far off himself. Wanting him to achieve his ultimate nut, Cynthia got herself repositioned on her hands and knees on the couch.

All too happily, Marcus slid up behind her, so eager to hit from the back with her stilettos still on and her skirt up around her waist.

He smacked her right ass cheek and rubbed on it.

"What chu' waiting for, Marcus?" she asked teasingly, then leaned her face down and tooted her ass for him.

And in an instant, Marcus went from lover man to love man as he slid up in her from the back.

***

"*Sí, jefe*. I'm about to go in now," whispered Mauricio, speaking as quietly as possible but loud enough so that his boss could hear him through the Bluetooth earbuds he had tucked in his ears.

"Remember what I told you," he heard the top dog say. "If you and Emilio do not bring that little whore to me alive, you both will receive the body parts of your wives and children in the mail until there is nothing left! *Entiendes*?"

"Yes sir," Mauricio replied calmly, though he wanted to address the threat with one of his own. "We won't fail. Nobody's here but them, and from the sound of it . . . they don't even realize that we've been following them."

"Good. If it wasn't for the phone, we would be searching for her like a needle in a haystack. Get it done. Now."

"Copy that. One last question, sir," Mauricio requested, as Emilio picked the lock on the backdoor, successfully getting it unlocked.

"What?"

"Araña made it out of the County Jail?" he asked, stepping inside of the dark kitchen behind Emilio and closing the door.

"Yes. Your uncle is free; he will be exiting sometime soon. Now get in there, get that bitch, and bring her to me. I want what she took from me back; it is irreplaceable."

"Understood, sir. Over and out."

Mauricio ended the call, then took the earbuds out of his ears. Looking at Emilio, screwing a silencer tight with the barrels of his 9mm Glock, Mauricio followed suit.

"What do we do about the boy she's with?" Emilio asked, just above a whisper.

"Kill him. He's not needed. You put one right between his eyes, grab her, I grab her kid, we deliver them, then get back to the precinct to clock in. Understood?"

Emilio nodded, then smiled. "I can't wait to see my new trainee. She's so fucking hot, dude. I gotta fuck her tonight."

"We make it through this, you can fuck all the rookies that will give it up to your horny ass, but 'til then . . . focus!" Mauricio urged his partner.

"Copy you. Let's do it," replied Emilio.

With the blueprint of the house's layout in their heads from looking at them on their phones during the planning of their raid, Mauricio and Emilio crept through the kitchen, entering the living room. They stepped lightly towards the stairs then. The faint sound of moaning came from the top of them.

They tried hard to take light steps, but the old wooden stairs creaked under the police-issued boots, but the sound of sex continued despite the noisy stairs.

Putting some pep in their step, the two hired hitters hurried to the top. Still, the moaning and groaning continued. Mauricio used hand motions to communicate. He signaled Emilio to go towards the lover sounds, then with the bedrooms in his view, doors all open with the exception of one, he stepped towards where he was sure the little girl was, while Emilio headed to kill the young dude and get the mother.

***

Emilio approached where the blissful noise was seemingly coming to a finish. He came to the corner where, just around it, the young boy and mother had been pleasing each other, so very unaware of the unfortunate situation they were seconds away from being thrown into.

The promise of a $15,000 payday to snatch the girl and get her to the rendezvous point was so close that Emilio could taste the delicious steak, eggs, and buttery lobster he and his wife would enjoy out in the Virgin Islands, as they had before, after he and Mauricio had successfully accomplished jobs for the Espinoza Cartel boss and other crime bosses.

But the promise of his wife being killed if he failed was the biggest reason for him to not fail.

Taking a deep breath, Emilio prepared to get it done. He went to run around the corner, but as soon as he rounded it . . .

***

Wham. Crack. Crack. Bink—

"Aahh," Cynthia screamed when she heard thumping and looked up to see one figure beating another dark figure.

Marcus cursed and jumped into protector mode, grabbing Cynthia and ushering her behind the couch. Ass naked, he hurried to the shelf filled with magazines, urban and erotic novels, and grabbed the .44 Bulldog that was stashed behind a novel.

He thumbed the hammer back on the loaded revolver and took aim at the two figures. It was then that he heard the unmistakable sound of the Black Gangster, who he was half of in body, soul, and mind.

***

Crack. Crack. Crack. Crack. Crack—

"Bitch-ass nigga," Snoop roared, then pounded the man's face in more than he already had with his brick-hard hands.

The intruder begged him to stop. Snoop hit him one last time and sent him to sleep. Looking up, he saw his son with a look of shock on his face, standing ten feet or so away with one of his mother's guns, ass naked.

"Might wanna get dressed, son," Snoop said, then hopped up to go assist his woman.

***

"It's okay, *mamita*! It's okay!" Alondra finished the bound that she tied around the man's ankles after she had tied his wrists.

The big, heavy old-school paperweight that she had snatched off of the table in Marcus' bedroom worked perfectly in subduing the intruder. He was out like a broken lightbulb the instant she cracked him in his dome with it.

Alondra ran to get Leticia. The toddler was in Marcus' bed, blankets pulled over her. She cried, scared to death. She had first seen Alondra sneak in and squealed with excitement until Alondra sternly shushed her, grabbed the paperweight, and hid at the side of the door. Leticia had no clue why Marcus' mother was hiding until she heard the bedroom's door crack open.

She saw a guy in dark clothes appear as the door opened all the way up. Before Leticia could even scream, she saw Alondra swing as hard as she could and hit the man in his head with the heavy object. He went down like a tree, face-first. Alondra quickly tied him up so he couldn't get away while swearing to her that everything was okay.

***

Alondra scooped the little girl off the bed just as Snoop hurried in.

"You okay?" he asked, looking relieved that Leticia was okay.

"Yeah! We're good! Where's Marcus and Cynthia?"

"Lety!"

They all turned and saw Cynthia with her shirt on, skirt down, barefoot, running into the bedroom with a half-clothed Marcus right behind her, gripping Alondra's .44.

"Mommy!"

Alondra handed Leticia to her mother when she ran up to her. Cynthia, in tears of joy and relief, held her daughter tightly, thanking the Man Above, then thanking Marcus' parents.

"How in the hell did y'all get here to stop them?" Marcus asked then.

Alondra knew it was coming. "She was telling someone a lot about where she was when we were out eating."

"No! No! Hell no! Carmela would never set me up, Alondra! She saved Leticia's life! Why would she do that just to pull something like this?" Cynthia asked.

"Not saying your friend did, but those people—you know, the cartel," Alondra needlessly reminded her. "They are smart and crafty, and on a hunch, I figured since you were trapped inside dude's world, your phone got bugged so that you could be tracked. You told me that before I came to your apartment, you were on your phone. When we were at the restaurant, you were on your phone. I figured someone would come for you, so we followed y'all, and I'm glad we did."

"Where's the phone?" Snoop asked, chiming in now.

"In . . . my handbag." Cynthia nodded her head towards the nightstand where her bag rested upon.

Snoop went to it and got her phone out. It was off. He looked at Alondra. "We need to go. Now."

Alondra nodded.

"Aye. We have a big problem."

They all looked over to where Marcus had just dragged the other man in by his ankles. In his hand, they saw a shiny silver badge in the flap of a leather wallet.

"This says Chicago Police, man. These muhfuckas are cops!"

Snoop made a call that was answered right away.

"I need you at Landra's ASAP, Pride. Bring a broom and a dustpan," Snoop told the person, and ended the call with nothing else said. He looked at his son's mother then. "Take Cynthia and Leticia to my house. Marcus and I will be there in a bit."

"Wait! Please! I don't wanna leave him!" Cynthia spoke, hurrying to Marcus' side.

"Cyn, it's okay. You need to go. Lety does not need to be in this house," Marcus told her, before leaning down and kissing Leticia's forehead, then Cynthia's lips. "I promise. I will be back to you soon."

Alondra kissed her dude on the lips, willing the tears that filled her eyes to not fall. She kissed her son, then ushered Cynthia with Leticia out of the bedroom to get to her car and get them to where it was safe.

***

"She's gonna really need you when you get back to her, son," Snoop said. "If you are not prepared to go all the way for her and Lety, then you need to break away now."

"I am prepared, pop. On Stone, I am," Marcus swore.

Snoop nodded. "Okay then, lil' nigga. Let's get the other dummy tied up and ready to go. They gon' give us some answers, or we gon' make 'em feel so much pain only death gon' make 'em feel better."

Marcus nodded. "Say less, ol' man," he replied, then went to find something to tie the guy up with.

Chapter 16

Tears fell down her face even though she tried to stop them. Her heart was hurting. Her heart had almost been taken from her. She knew if it wasn't for her and the boy's father's quick thinking, they wouldn't have been able to thwart the attempt on Marcus, Cynthia, and Leticia. Though they had been successful, the stakes were now raised. The enemy had entered her home, where she rested her head. They were cops, working for someone that wasn't a cop, to get Cynthia.

Alondra wondered to herself, why? Why was this person being so persistent in trying to get Cynthia? Most, if not all times that a cartel boss had a target, they just sent someone to spray them. Or they go to their families, hacked them to pieces, and made their mark live with that guilt for the rest of their life.

But Cynthia's family was already dead. Was Leticia's father part of the cartel that was after her? Was the boss her father, and hell-bent on getting his daughter back?

No . . . she said Lety's father died. She has something that the guy wants . . . and he won't kill her, at least, until he gets it back. But what does she have?

Alondra's mind went into overdrive on the drive to K-Town. Cynthia sat silently next to her with Leticia on her lap, wrapped up in her arms. She glanced over at the two. Silently, she thanked the Man Above for being there to help her and her son's father stop the two crooked cops. She legitimately really liked Cynthia, and she absolutely adored Leticia.

They both cared deeply for Marcus. She and Snoop saw how Leticia lit up when Marcus was there, no doubt, but now, with Marcus and Cynthia's new . . . unity, Alondra knew that her son was truly into Cynthia as well. He must be, to have sexed her down in her house after Alondra forbade him doing so.

***

Before she even realized it, Alondra had arrived in Snoop's hood. The 1300th block of Karlov Ave was his world, and everyone in it were his soldiers. It was a jungle. Dangerous territory if it wasn't yours to inhabit.

She paused at 13th and Karlov at the stop sign, looking around at the tall stone and brick apartment buildings where life was lived fast and money was made even faster. Rolling on, she shot half a block up the one-way street and then pulled over to her left, parking in front of where a house had once been but now was a vacant lot of plush green grass.

"Come on. Let's get inside," Alondra told Cynthia, speaking softly.

They got out of the car and made their way to the house that was one up from the vacant lot. Traveling up some steps to the front door, Alondra led the two up. She held the key to the Audi to a small mechanism next to the Ring doorbell. The sensor chip embedded in it sent a signal into the signal system and disarmed all the protective measures that Snoop had installed around his 2,100-square-foot digs.

Alondra opened the door and let them in first, then she stepped into her luxurious fortress, closing and locking the door behind her, anxious for her man and her son to walk through that same door very soon.

***

“Please! Come on, man! You don’t wanna’ do this! We’re cops!”

Marcus ground his teeth in anger as the two men begged, cried, and pleaded for mercy. He gripped the Louisville Slugger tightly in his hands, ready to use it and crack something.

Snoop, accompanied by L and Goon and Polo, stood off to the side. They hung back while the two Hispanic men hung upside down by the chains around their ankles, hooked onto the ceiling-mounted sky-hook inside of Snoop’s auto garage. Under them were wide oil pans, meant for catching oil during oil changes, but for the time being, they would be collecting another type of fluid that a system could not work without.

***

“Who sent y’all, and why?” Marcus asked, gearing up to hit a home run.

Neither of the two cops answered.

“Oh, y’all ain’t got no rap?”

—Crack!—

“Aaaaahhhhh!” screamed one of them when the solid wooden bat broke three of his ribs in one hard swing.

—Crack!—

Marcus hit the other man and broke multiple ribs as well.

“Who sent y’all to my momma’s house?” he demanded, winding up again, this time aiming at faces.

“Aye, lil Moe. Hol’ up real quick.”

Marcus looked back and saw Polo, dressed in plainclothes instead of his Chicago Police Department uniform, walking up with a phone in his hand.

“I got into the guy’s phone,” he told Marcus. “Mauricio Galvez. His last call was to a number tracing down to Laredo. I had one of my niggas at the tech department check the number out. Does a Marcello Espinoza sound familiar to you?"

"Yeah! He is the head of the cartel that's after Cynthia! He sent these bitch-ass niggas at her?"

"No evidence stating that, but I did the math. She worked for a brewery owned by the guy after getting here illegally from Mexico with her daughter, then shit had gone down there and she ended up in Illinois. Looks to me that yo' girl been through hell and back. I think she deserves some peace."

"I agree, so I'ma piece these bitch-ass paisas the fuck up!" Marcus declared.

"Aye. Son."

Marcus heard his father call to him. Again turning back, he saw that Snoop was holding a tool mechanics used to inflate stubborn tires. It was yellow and cylindrical-shaped, with a spout jutting out the front that narrows to a flat exit pipe. Marcus was knowledgeable of the handy piece of equipment. Knowledgeable of what it could do to a human.

Abandoning the wooden bat, Marcus went to grab the Cheetah bead seater from his pops. The two cops looked to where he had gone, up to a big, wide, and tall air compressor hooked up along the rear wall.

"Please, man! We weren't gonna hurt her!" one of the cops cried. "We were just gonna take her and her daughter to the man that hired us! I swear!"

Marcus heard the man's pleas for mercy as he hooked an air hose to the Cheetah gun. Ignoring the man, he flipped a switch and began filling the tank with compressed air.

"So you think abductin' a mother and the child is better than hurtin' them?" he heard his pop's 5-0 homie ask.

"N-No . . . We . . . I—"

—Crack!—

Marcus glanced back and saw the cop's nose gushing blood. He swung back and forth like he was on a swing. The other cop burst into tears and pissed his pants.

Marcus filled the Cheetah gun to 225 psi, detached the air hose, and went to the cop that got his nose broken by Polo.

"No! No! Don't! I have a family!"

"Fuck yo' family, bitch!" Marcus growled angrily.

Mercilessly, he rammed the flat tip of the spout into the cop's mouth and pushed the lever to the hatch forwards. In literally less than two seconds, every pound of compressed air shot out with more force than the punch of a seasoned heavyweight boxer.

The powerful burst blew a hole through the back of the base of his head, nearly decapitating him. Everything behind him was slimy and crimson.

"Oh shit . . . damn!" Marcus exclaimed, dumbfounded.

"Now that isn't somethin' you see every day," said Goon, with a chuckle.

"Nope," agreed L.

Marcus looked at his father, and Snoop nodded, approving of his son's show of retribution for Cynthia and Leticia.

"Next," he then told Marcus.

Marcus dropped the Cheetah gun, grabbed the Slugger, and went to finish the job.

"Nooooo!"

—Smack! Smack! Smack! Smack! Smack! Crack!—

Marcus swung his bat and hit the man in his face four times hard before a gruesomely loud crack ricocheted through the garage. Marcus wound up once more, then with every ounce of strength that he could muster, he swung and hit the man's head so hard his neck ripped completely away from his shoulders and flew into the wall behind him, bouncing off of it and landing a few feet away.

Blood sprayed from the torn stump, filling up the oil pan in no time. His body jerked, nerves still alive and jumping from the shock, then seconds after he lost his head, the body died.

"Bitch," Marcus growled, still grasping the bat tightly in his hands.

Snoop walked up at that moment. He placed a hand on his son's shoulder, bringing him up out of the frenzied state that he had gone into on behalf of the two ladies that obviously meant a lot to him.

"Relax. It's over for them, Marcus. Cynthia and Leticia are waitin'."

Marcus nodded.

Polo got the bat from his hand then. L and Goon told Snoop that they would clean up. Dapping his BG homies up, Snoop led Marcus out of the garage to the Caddy, where Cynthia's duffle bags and the cocaine that Alondra stashed at the house sat in the trunk.

The O.G. got behind the wheel, son riding shotgun. Pulling off, Snoop drove in silence all the way to K-Town, arriving at his crib soon after. He parked behind Alondra's car and they both hopped out, greeted by Snoop's clique that consists of Breeds, a few GDs, and some Four Corner Hustler-Vice Lord, all from around the way that grew up with Snoop.

Making sure the ol' head and his son were good, they all stayed posted up, strapped, while the two got the bags out of the trunk.

Alondra was already at the door when Snoop stepped on the top of the steps. She stood aside for them to enter.

Leticia ran right to Marcus the second she saw him; Cynthia was right behind her. Marcus dropped their bags and wrapped them both in his arms, hugging them close to him, feeling like he didn't ever want to let go.

***

Alondra's eyes welled with tears as she watched the two gravitate to her son like they couldn't be, and didn't want to be, without him ever.

She felt Snoop's arm around her waist just then. He pulled her close to him and kissed her cheek. They both watched Marcus grab the bags, then lead Cynthia and her daughter towards the door that led to where his other childhood bedroom was down in the basement.

"Our son is a man, Snoop," Alondra said, with tears of joy falling.

"Finally. He gon' be a'ight, baby. Cyn is a ride-or-die-type chick. They gon' be a'ight."

Alondra yawned while nodding in agreement to both of his replies. "I'm exhausted."

"Let's go to bed. In this house, nobody that ain't supposed to get in, can get in. Not even the police. Tonight we're all safe. We'll worry about tomorrow later," Snoop told her.

They both headed off to Snoop's bedroom, where they initially had plans to spend the evening but had to put it on hold to save their son, Cynthia, and Leticia.

***

Two Weeks Later . . .

Inez and Tashira both screamed out at the tops of their lungs with excitement when the man had revealed the number he was willing to pay for all the merchandise he was going to take off of their hands. At first, they both thought that they were tweaking, but when Rock repeated the number, Inez knew it wasn't a joke.

After a couple of weeks of hiding out, Inez and Tashira were ready to get everything sold for as much cash as they could get. They had all of the coke, dope, and pills that had come from Percy's spot; they had the pricey timepieces, the cash, and the brick that came from Quinton's spot. The goods that they took from Frankie D's spot—which was two flawless white gold and diamond chains, a diamond Rolex Oyster Perpetual, a couple of pairs of diamond earrings, and a book bag filled with cash. They even had the jewelry that they had stripped Dollaz and C-Note of, and it all made them forget about the loss of product and money due to the fiasco at Hustle Man's crib.

***

Out west in Chicago, Inez had contacted a friend of her father's from back in the days when real gangsters and the street code still existed. Rock, an ol' school Mafia Insane Vice Lord from out south, had built his prestigious pawn shop's reputation for having what everyone wanted. All the time he had the goods, and he had the black-market items that only the city's elite were given access to. He was known all around the west for business, but when he was out south, he was one of the many to see if you needed white, brown, green, or guns.

***

"On me! What! Are you for fucking real right now, joe?" Tashira asked with wide eyes and a jaw hanging agape, as was Inez. "For that alone, $15,000?"

The Cartier Tank watch, an 18-karat yellow-gold piece valued at almost eighteen thousand dollars, was just one of the expensive watches that Inez had Marcus snatch from Quinton. The others were Rolexes, Audemars Piguets, a Tiffany & Co. piece, and two Chanel J12s. The Bvlgari necklaces and the Gucci necklaces added to the number that Rock was ready to pay. He was even ready to buy the remainder of the drugs they had and the custom Damascus steel-crafted 1911 semi-auto .45 handgun.

"Yep," Rock nodded with a big grin on his face. "And I'll give you the $20,000 for your Escalade, or if you want, you could swap it. I got a car lot south and a big selection you could choose from. How about a Benz? Since ladies love Mercedes."

“Oh yeah, I’ll take a new Maybach!” Tashira requested.

Rock and Inez laughed.

“Uh . . . not one of those. You about $220,000 short if you tradin’ that ’Lac truck in, but I do have an ’05 S55 AMG for that price. It has the chrome AMG wheels on it and a Lorinser body kit.”

Rock grabbed his iPad and showed them a picture of the big-body Benz. Tashira was instantly sold and nodded, eagerly accepting the trade deal.

“And for you Inez, I have a sporty little SL65 AMG hard-top convertible for you. All red, AMG wheels too, wit’ the twin-turbo V12 under the hood. It’s a big difference from that Lexus you’ve had for so long.”

“Bet. A drop-top is just what a fly bitch like me needs for down in Miami,” Inez replied, geeked about the plans to relocate to the 305 and live like queens.

“One other thing. The jewelry that I checked last, you can have it back. I can’t do nothin’ with it,” Rock told them both.

“What? Why?” asked Inez, knowing he was talking about the chains and watches that she and Tashira had stripped Dollaz and C-Note of outside the club.

“It’s fake. Silver, with rhinestones.”

“What!” Tashira shook her head. “We did all of . . . that . . . for some fake-ass drip? On God, I hope we run into their asses again! I’ma blow ’em both down, joe!”

Inez sucked her teeth. “Maaan, fuck them fake-ass niggas. We still walkin’ away wit’ over half a million, girl.”

Nodding, Tashira agreed that the come-up was life-changing, and the plans they had with a portion of the money would make them even more money.

“True. I mean, you two go down to Miami and open up that hair and nail salon, along with that clothing boutique, you’ll grow yo’ money real quick. South Beach is a shopper’s paradise, and all them ladies down there eagerly look for new places to go and get pampered. I honestly say that today is a day that y’all should be celebratin’.”

"Hell yeah," Inez agreed. "Aye, Rock? Is that liquor store on Pulaski still open? Up by Washington?"

"That place will never close. Lemme' get y'all's check and cash together for y'all; the cars can be delivered here in an hour."

"Cool," said Inez, ready as hell to leave the Midwest in the dust and head for a much sunnier place to build a good life. "We'll post up 'til then, Rock, if it's cool?"

"Yup. Make yourselves at home, ladies," the ol' head offered, then left to get to finishing their business up.

***

"Ooohhh d-d-damn! Shit!" Marcus squeezed his eyes closed and relished in the blissful sensation her warm, wet, and skilled mouth was giving him as he leaned against the bathroom door in his father's garage.

Cynthia, on her knees, pleased Marcus the way she had been wanting to since the first time he gave her great pleasure to make him feel good. The first chance she got to get her hands on him while they had a few minutes, Cynthia rushed him to the bathroom while Marcus' parents were outside with Leticia, having a ball with the four-month-old puppy that Marcus bought. His first purchase with some of the money he made from selling coke, he bought the pup from a registered breeder, then surprised Leticia with him. Afterwards, he got Cynthia another whip, putting it in his name by her request, and he got himself a whip of his own. With the help of his father, Marcus had also been able to get the Cutlass from up in Zion and brought it down to Snoop's shop. The plans they made to hook it up had Marcus super geeked to see it transform from whatever to a show-stopper.

Marcus got his two Moe homies on business and put them on with half a brick each. They both had it gone in twenty-four hours and came right back for more with every cent that Marcus told them he wanted back. They were too geeked when he gave them each another halfie and told them to keep the money from the first flip.

Cynthia had watched Marcus turn into a young boss in the last two weeks. Everything he did, everything he said, had her so gone over him, just like Monica sang about.

***

Cynthia grabbed his rod with both of her hands and started jerking him with a twisting motion while she sucked sloppily and noisily. Marcus cursed over and over again, head spinning around and around while his toes went wild in his Air Jordan 5 Retros.

She released his cock a second later from her mouth. She spit on it, then slurped it up. She opened wide next and let him stuff it back down her throat and fuck her face while his balls slapped her chin repeatedly.

"F-F-Fuuck, Cyn'! I finna b-b-busss!" Marcus announced.

He threw his head back and groaned deeply from his gut. As he felt her sucking even faster, moaning loudly, Marcus pictured her gorgeous face, her fire-engine red lips, the sexy denim mini-dress she had on that fit her body like it was made just for her with white stilettos on her feet, her long luscious hair styled to look wet, and the light layer of makeup that enhanced her natural beauty effortlessly.

Cynthia let him have his way with her the rest of the way. He fucked her face until he reached his nut and exploded in her mouth so hard that his knees nearly gave out.

"Ohh my mothafuckin' God!" he shouted, as she milked him for every single drop of cum.

She emptied him into her mouth, then with a smile, she swallowed it all, finishing it with a kiss on the tip of his dick.

"Did you like that, baby?" Cynthia purred with a seductive smile stretching across her red-hot lips, though she knew that he did.

"I loved it!" Marcus replied, pulling her up from her knees. "You really know how to treat yo' man like a king. On Stone!"

Cynthia smiled at him with admiration in her eyes. "Baby, you are king. You are *my* king, and I am your queen. When a queen really loves her king, she shows it daily with a smile on her face."

Marcus couldn't help but smile at that. "So you love me, huh?"

She pulled his boxers and pants up, then replied, "Love at first sight. Those eyes had me, but when I saw how good you are with Lety, I knew you were who I'd been needing and wanting. So yes, I love you, Marcus."

"And I, Cynthia, love you," he reciprocated, with it all in his eyes.

Knocking on the door brought their moment to an abrupt halt.

"Marcus, come on, man, we gotta make moves!" they both heard Snoop holler.

"Here I come, pop!" Marcus shouted back.

"Maan, that's yo' business, nigga! Just hurry yo' ass up or you finna walk!"

Cynthia busted out laughing at Marcus.

"Aww! It is so sweet! The relationship you have with your mom and your dad!"

"I love 'em to death, Bae. I just wish I could've met yours."

Cynthia sighed. "Yeah. Me, too."

Marcus kissed her lips and gave her a warm hug, then he took her hand and opened the door. He walked hand-in-hand with her past where his Cutlass sat on a hydraulic-powered floor lift, with wheels that actually had air in them, to the exit door.

Stepping out of the garage, they both saw Leticia running around with her full-blooded German Rottweiler pup. Snoop and Alondra stood over Marcus' gleaming black-cherry colored 1996 Chevy Impala SS, parked next to Cynthia's green 2016 GMC Yukon Denali, watching the toddler and her hyperactive pup play. Leticia saw her mother and Marcus come out of the garage right at that minute and ran to them.

"Mommy! Daddy!"

Marcus felt he had the most honor ever. Leticia had started calling him her daddy a few days ago while they were watching a movie; Cynthia was astounded by her daughter's words.

"I love you, daddy!" she had told Marcus while sitting on his lap as he sat next to Cynthia on his bed.

It was then that she knew that Marcus was not just hers, but also Leticia's, and they were his.

***

Leticia ran up to them, trailed by her pup. Marcus scooped Leticia up into his arms and held her up high in the air while the Rottweiler jumped around him excitedly.

"Happy birthday, Baby girl!" Marcus sang out to her, lowering her down and giving her a kiss on her forehead. "How old are you again? Oh! Yeah! You're fifty-two years old today! Yaaay!"

Cynthia laughed; Leticia pouted.

"Nooo, daddy! I'm five!" She held her hand up, showing him five fingers. "See? Five!"

"Oh, okay! Five! My little girl is five years old today! Maaan, you're getting old!"

Leticia giggled when her pup nudged her leg with his wet nose.

"Daddy, Amor says it's his birthday too!" Leticia picked him up into her arms and held him up for Marcus.

"Uh oh, so we need an even bigger cake since we have two birthday babies," he said, patting Amor on his head.

Marcus kissed his woman, then his little lady. Telling them he'll see them later, Cynthia—seeing him wink as a reminder of the special birthday party they all had planned for Leticia at Rainforest Cafe later on—winked back.

He headed towards where his mother and father were. He kissed his mother, hugged her, then was ready to go to work.

"Let's ride," Snoop told him then.

They headed over to Snoop's 2009 International DuraStar box truck, a non-CDL commercial freight-carrying money-maker with a 26-foot-long box on its frame behind the two-man cab.

Snoop got behind the wheel, his son in the passenger's seat. Starting the engine up, Snoop got out his phone and made a call while waiting for the air pressure for the brakes to build up. Marcus watched his woman, daughter, puppy, and mother get into Alondra's mint-green 2013 BMW 750i and head off, pulling out of the yard seconds later.

"We on the way, joe. Be ready," he heard his father say just then.

Marcus glanced at his pops. "What we haulin' today, ol' man?"

"Erythang, youngin'," Snoop replied, then he released the parking brakes, put it in drive, and rolled off to exit the yard and get to their first pickup spot of the day.

Chapter 17

Block turned off the water in the narrow ten-foot-long shower hole in the pod he was being housed in. He was feeling good after a hard workout in the enclosed outdoor rec area that was the size of a big bedroom. It was high up from the ground, as it was the sixth floor of the tall jail facing the southeast. From it, all that was visible was the staff parking lot, but from his cell, he could see out to Lake Michigan and parts of busy downtown Waukegan.

The charges against him had Block's head all over the place. The prosecutor hit him with murder of a police officer, murder of Hustle Man, and possession of controlled substances on a very large scale, guns, and illegal cash. He was facing no less than 200 years in prison with no chance of parole.

Working out was the only thing he could do to keep his mind off of never again being free. It was the hardest pill he had ever had to swallow, especially since he was actually innocent!

***

Getting dried off, Block put on LCJ-issued underwear, a T-shirt, then his county blue pants and his orange sandals. He gathered his dirty clothes and went toward the door, opening it and grabbing the towel that he used to cover the window to keep the creeps from looking in on him like they loved to do, thinking they were slick.

Out in the dayroom, mostly everyone was out of their cells sitting at the tables. Some played spades or poker, some played board games or were watching TV; a few were in the exercise area looking out the window, wishing they were out there.

The C.O., a short Hispanic chick that was rumored to be affiliated with the Maniac Latin Disciples, sat at the officer's desk watching everyone.

Block made his way towards the steps to get to the top tier where his corner cell was. Walking past her, he felt her eyes on him. He looked and indeed saw she was just staring at him.

"You got a problem?" he asked, annoyed by her very presence.

She was a bitch. A super-cop-ass bitch that played favorites to the Latinos, even ones with sex cases.

Officer Martinez chuckled. "Naw. No problem."

Block could easily hear the sarcasm in her voice. He already knew why she was laughing. She was related to the nurse that was in charge of his severely wounded crotch's healing. It was all over the jail that he had no dick, and though nobody said it to his face, he heard all sorts of whispers.

***

He got to his cell and saw that his dope-sick cellmate was laid out on his bunk, sweating his ass off, shaking, and groaning in pain from the heroin withdrawals.

Block shook his head, pissed that he had to be in a cell with a motherfucker like that. Shitting on himself, puking on the floor, pacing back and forth in the middle of the night from insomnia.

Ignoring the white man, Block set his dirty clothes down by his desk and grabbed his deodorant when his door swung open suddenly. He turned and saw three Mexicans at the door; all three of them were Spanish Gangster Disciples. They had been mean-mugging Block ever since they came to the pod a few days prior. He had no clue who they were, but they acted like they knew him, or thought they did.

“Fuck is y’all niggas at my door for?” he growled.

Without a word, all three of them rushed in on him. Block cursed and immediately started defending himself. His celly jumped up and started screaming for the C.O.

—Crack! Crack! Bink! Bink! Wham!—

Block picked up the first man and sent him flying backwards to the floor. The others jumped on him and overpowered Block. One delivered a hard blow to his sternum and knocked the wind out of him, then the other socked him in his jaw, sending him to the floor.

“C.O.! C.O.! Heeelp!” screamed the dope fiend as Block got trashed mercilessly.

The first SGD managed to get back up on his feet and pulled out a sharpened pencil from the waistband of his pants. He went to stab Block when the next thing any of them knew . . .

Pow! Zzzzzzzzzzzzzzzzz!

A loud pop, then loud crackling sounds came. Block managed to look up and saw the one dude drop and shake like he was having a seizure.

“On the ground! Everyone! Now!”

A mob of C.O.s in green ERT suits had arrived and quickly gained control of the situation, while a white-shirt was out on the tier yelling for everyone to “LOCK IT DOWN!” with her Taser in her hand, daring anyone to defy her.

The C.O. let go of the trigger and another quickly cuffed the one man. Four others ran in and cuffed the other two. Block got up and turned to face the wall, hands behind his back, waiting to be cuffed as well to be taken to seg.

“Robinson, you’re not going to seg today, player,” he heard one of the C.O.s say.

Block turned around and looked at the big black man, who was a known Gangster Disciple from what the hood niggas and hood chicks called *The Set*.

"You're packin' up and leavin', bruh."

"Leavin'? To another unit? Again?" Block asked.

"Naw, man. You are free. We told Martinez to tell you to pack up like thirty minutes ago. Yo' charges have been dismissed. You are a free man."

Block's jaw dropped in shock. He was dumbfounded, but then he remembered what the guy he had been in the infirmary with told him.

"Come on, joe. I just told you yo' ass is free, nigga. You should be at the door already!" Officer Crowns told him.

"Sheeeit, let's go! Fuck whatcha' heard!" Block replied and dipped past the turtle suits, rounding the corner, flying down the stairs, and flicking Officer Martinez off, who wore a very salty facial expression as he got to the entrance door to the pod.

The white-shirt and two other C.O.s opened the door and gestured for Block to step out. After an elevator ride down to the first floor, he was taken to booking. All eyes were on him—the "Cop Killer" being freed.

Yeah, punk-ass police! Let a nigga the fuck up outta this mufucka so I can get back to the money. And on the G, wait 'til I catch that hoe-bitch. This time, I'ma shoot her in the face! Then, I'ma catch that bitch Inez and do her diiiirty for killin' my nigga and leavin' me to take the fall for a dead cop and a dead crackhead.

"Sit cho' ass down and wait to be called!" snapped a black chick that mostly worked booking due to how her smart-ass mouth always got her close to getting her shit split whenever she did work on a pod.

"Shut up, bitch, and process me out! I know who yo' baby daddy is and I know where yo' son goes to school! Talk crazy again and they gon' come up missin'!"

The bitch didn't say a word more. She grilled him with a venomous glare, but her lips didn't part again.

"Thought so!" Block went over to the inmate phone that was for calling for a ride and called Nikki. "Aye, come pick me up from the county jail! Right now!"

"Pick you up? What chu' mean 'pick you up,' nigga?" she asked with obvious confusion.

"My charges got dropped! All of 'em! I'm gettin' booked out now! Bring yo' ass, joe!"

"Wooooow! A'ight, fam! I'm on the way!"

Block hung the phone up and took a seat away from the others that were being booked out or in. He looked towards the desk where the sergeant that walked releases out sat and saw the old white man was staring at him with hatred in his eyes.

"Ya' momma, cracka'," Block muttered, then fell back, focusing his mind on getting up out of there, getting revenge, then getting back to the money.

***

Rock groaned gutturally as he ejaculated all in between Inez's ass crack, coating her puckered asshole with hot globs. On her knees on the floor in his office, he had just finished hitting it from the back while she ate Tashira's pussy as she sat on his couch.

He was surprised by their sudden come-on. He had gone to get their cash from his safe and sent the other half into a Bitcoin account. He ordered the two vehicles that were included in the deal, then came back to his office to see that the two were ass-naked, waiting for him with "come here, sexy" smiles on their faces.

***

"Holy shit! Goddamn!" he cursed, spent of breath.

Rock then went wide-eyed when Inez got up, turned around to face him, and bent over. Tashira scooted forward and, without any hesitation, started slurping his cum up out of Inez's ass crack, extra loud and extra sloppy.

"Oh damn!" Rock gasped, wowed by how untimidly freaky the two young girls were. "You two really get down!"

Inez giggled. "Sex should always be hot, dirty, and nasty, and fuck all that one-person-only shit," she told him as Tashira finished cleaning her crack. "If you look good, I'm fuckin' you. Period."

"Period," Tashira co-signed.

"I see. Well, maybe I might find myself in Miami one day and bump into y'all," Rock suggestively said to them.

"Maybe," Inez shrugged. "Are our new whips here yet?"

"Indeed. They're out front. Let's get dressed and head out, shall we?"

***

They all got dressed and made their way out of the pawnshop, stepping out into the sweltering heat of the summer afternoon. Madison was teeming with activity all around, as was Pulaski. As usual, the popular clothing spot, Tops & Bottoms, had a surplus of shoppers inside.

Inez and Tashira squealed with excitement when they saw the two Benzes double-parked on the street with their four-way flashes blinking.

Inez saw the two-door drop-top and jumped for joy. Tashira double-dutch jumped with glee as she laid eyes on her big-body S55 AMG.

Clutching the Gucci duffel bag that was filled with $325,000 in big bills, Tashira ran to her whip and opened the driver's door to see the cappuccino-colored leather interior, while Inez checked her SL's black and red accented leather interior out.

They both hit their gas pedals. Inez got goosebumps when the twin-turbo V12 let out a luxurious scream from the sport exhaust pipes. Tashira's supercharged AMG V8 engine roared with a whine that got her nipples hard.

Rock walked up and told them to let his guys put the license plates on while he finished registering the two vehicles so they would be all legit and could ride without any worries.

"Fuck it. Let's go get a bottle from the liquor store," Inez suggested.

"And we need blunts, too," Tashira reminded her of the two ounces of Purple Haze they got from Rock.

"Rock, we'll be back in a minute. We finna walk to the liquor sto'."

"With all that money on you?" Rock questioned. "This is Chicago, Inez."

"Exactly. Why would we leave cash like that in a car?" Inez replied. "We'll be right back, joe."

***

"I can't believe it, Inez! Like, joe! We really got this money and all the Bitcoins!" Tashira said, needing to hear it once more for it to sink in.

Strolling past *Tops & Bottoms*, the two walked side by side, chopping it up. The amount of money they had was constantly blowing their minds. They couldn't wait to head south and put their plans into action.

"I still can't believe them niggas from the club was sportin' metal chains n' shit, joe," Inez said, shaking her head at the things she and Tashira did, thinking Dollaz and C-Note were some real ballers.

"I can't stand possers," Tashira added.

"Aye, lil' momma, what up, joe?" yelled a guy from a new Escalade cruising past them.

The SUV was sparkling clean, as were the rims, but they could tell it was a rental.

"Not a damn thing, fam! Keep drivin'!" Tashira hollered back.

"Fuck you then, hoe!! Stank-ass bitch!" the guy shouted back, salty as hell.

"Ya' momma, bitch!" Inez screamed, giving him both middle fingers.

He waved her off and kept rolling. Tashira laughed her ass off when the man almost rear-ended another vehicle due to still trying to look at Inez.

"Niggas be too thirsty, man," she stated as they both continued on strolling with the liquor store in sight.

"Fuck these niggas. Wait 'til we get to Miami. I'ma get me a real dude from the Caribbean. A Jamaican that eats pussy on demand, or a Cuban that's gon' suck my toes! Yeaah! Wooo!"

Coming up on the store, people were coming out and more were going in. It was a pretty big liquor store, and though old as hell with old oxidized iron bars on the tall windows, it was one of the best spots to get any type of alcoholic beverage you wanted, including non-alcoholic, blunts, cigarettes, snacks, and even actual food.

In front of the store, Tashira and Inez peeped at a box truck parked there with its rear cargo door rolled up. Inside, boxes with labels of different brands of liquor were stacked on a pallet. Seconds before they got to the store's entrance door, they caught a glimpse of a tall and built brown-skinned man with long dreads infused with grays, displaying his age.

"Eeeeeee, see, now that ol' nigga right thea look like he could use some young new in his life," Inez said to Tashira, as the chocolate-drop eyed the guy with lust.

He climbed up into the back of the truck and disappeared from the line of sight.

"Here you go. Yo' ass gon' catch somethin', you lil' nasty thot," Tashira told her as she opened the door.

Stepping in, she heard Inez say, “Yup! I’ma catch me the realest nigga ever that loves how freaky a bitch like me can get.”

“Might wanna stop suckin’ and fuckin’ every nigga you meet then, until that time.”

—Smack!—

“Ooww!” Tashira screamed and dropped the bag, grabbing her hot ass-cheek after Inez fired it up with an open hand. “You bitch! That hurt!” she shouted, which got everyone inside’s attention.

“I know.” Inez smirked tauntingly at her. “And if I do remember right, you suck just as much dick and fuck as many niggas as I do, hoe.”

Tashira narrowed her eyes at Inez. A few people inside laughed.

“Shut the fuck up,” Tashira replied, picking up the bag, then turned to head down one of the aisles with a large selection of Vodkas, Bacardi, and other brands.

Inez smacked her ass one more time and laughed when Tashira screamed out to her to stop.

“Shut up, bitch. You know you like it!” Inez teased and continued following behind Tashira through the cool air-conditioned store.

Chapter 18

"Marcus . . . I know you're worried about them, but they are fine!" Alondra yelled. "Stop tweakin', nigga, damn!"

"Ma, come on now, I'ma just tryna check on her and Lety," he replied, as he sat in the passenger's seat of his pop's truck, parked in front of a liquor store on Pulaski, close to Washington.

"Ay, Dios mío, Marcus. Dude, you're on Bluetooth speaker mode! Cynthia and Leticia can hear you. Plus, I'm literally pulling up right now, worry wart!"

Looking out of the windshield, Marcus indeed saw the BMW pull up in front of his pop's box truck. He could see Cynthia up front, smiling at him through the windshield. He smiled back at her, happy to see her.

Movement in his right peripheral caught his attention. He glanced to his right and saw a thick-ass chick with dark skin in a tiny skirt entering the liquor store. His eyes went wide when he saw how fat her ass was. It immediately made him think of Inez's juicy booty.

Marcus then peeped the color of her hair. His eyebrows furrowed as the door closed behind her.

"No way," he told himself, opening the door and jumping out. "Ain't no mothafukin' way!"

"Marcus!" his mother hollered as she opened her door to get out of her car.

He ignored her, locked in on the chick. He yanked the door open and stepped inside the cool store, looking for her.

He caught a glimpse of the booty cheeks as she bent the corner and entered an aisle with all sorts of brands of liquor.

Marcus hurried toward the aisle and turned in. He saw the girl walking towards the other end.

Quick-stepping, he got himself even closer to her. Then, as he caught a glimpse of the side of her face, he gasped to himself.

"Inez!" he yelled, then the girl stopped, turned, and looked at him.

***

Oh shit! Oh my God! Inez panicked when she saw none other than Marcus there, a few feet away from her.

"Inez!" he shouted and ran to her, looking like a man that had been searching high and low for his kidnapped wife and finally found her. "What the hell? What are you doin' here? I thought you went to yo' momma's down in Alabama? I been callin' yo' ass, joe! Worried sick about you!"

He doesn't know I set him up? Holy shit!

"Oh . . . um . . . I'm sorry . . . baby . . . I just . . . I couldn't look you in your eyes after—" Inez paused for dramatic effect and managed to make her eyes water up.

Marcus pulled her into his arms.

"I know! That bitch-ass nigga sent the videos to my phone!"

"Oh my God! I'm so sorry, Marcus! I'm sorry!"

"You didn't do nothin' wrong, Inez. On Stone, I'ma kill that nigga! He ain't gettin' away wit' that foul-ass shit!"

"Hey, Inez, you get it?"

Inez cursed inside of her mind when she heard Tashira's voice just then. Marcus eased his grip around her the second he heard it.

Aw shit . . . Goddammit, she thought, right as Marcus turned around and saw her.

***

What the fuck? Marcus thought when he saw Tashira at the beginning of the aisle, holding the handles of a Gucci duffel bag in her left hand and a bottle of Hennessy in her right.

Her eyes went wide with fear when she saw him. The bottle of Hennessy fell from her hand and shattered all over the floor.

"Bitch!" he roared, then, like a bullet fired from a thumper, Marcus charged at her with intent to do great bodily harm.

***

Cynthia saw Marcus rush into the store, seemingly so suddenly. His mother had called him as she opened the door, but he ignored her and entered the store.

"Mommy, I wanna go with Daddy!" Leticia whined from the rear seat while Cynthia tried to see what had him rush into the store.

"I know, baby, me too. Just hold on, okay?"

"Yes."

Cynthia got out and rounded the front of the car, getting onto the sidewalk. She peeped to her right—Alondra, talking to Snoop, who had a stack of boxes on a hand dolly and a clipboard by the rear of the box truck.

"Hey, Alondra? I'm going in really quick to find Marcus," she hollered to the redhead. "Leticia's still in the car."

"I got her, mama. Go ahead," Alondra replied.

Suddenly, Cynthia heard screaming and yelling inside the store. She looked through the window and saw Marcus run up on a chick and hit her so hard in her jaw that she flew backward at least a foot and hit the floor.

“Oh my God! Alondra!” she screamed, then, as Marcus jumped on the chick to beat her face in, Cynthia took off running into the store.

***

“Aaaaaahhhhhhhh! Somebody heeeelp!” screamed Tashira.

—Crack! Crack! Crack! Crack!—

Marcus pounded her face relentlessly, weighing her down with his body.

“You grimey bitch! Shut the fuck up!” he growled.

—Crack! Crack! Crack! Crack!—

“Aye, man! get cho’ ass up off her!” yelled an old man who was standing a few feet back, but nowhere near brave enough to break it up himself.

The others in the store had found spots and were recording the fight on their smartphones to post on social media sites.

Marcus kept on hitting her. Her head repeatedly bounced off the ground with every punch delivered. Tashira cried in pain, screaming for Inez. Marcus had gone mad. Foaming at the mouth, he was stuck in a frenzy and wasn’t coming out of it until she was dead.

***

Cynthia ran inside and hurried toward where Marcus was destroying the girl’s face. Suddenly, another chick came from behind him with a big vodka bottle in her hand.

“Maaarcuuus!” she screamed to warn him.

—Smash!—

The girl slammed the bottle into the back of his head hard. It shattered from the impact. Marcus then fell to the side and did not move.

“Noooo! Baby!”

Cynthia ran toward the girl, charging at her like an angry bull. She balled her fist and, as she got up on her, trying to grab the strap of a duffel bag, Cynthia swung and fired her jaw up as hard as she could.

***

Inez flew sideways into the shelf lined with bottles, knocking it over. Then she fell to the floor. Dazed, she lay splayed out, seeing double of everything.

The girl that had just rocked her was trying to get Marcus up. She cried and pleaded for him to get up, but he wasn't moving. She could see blood pouring from the back of his head, where she had bashed him with the bottle. Tashira was laid out, no telling if she was alive or not.

She struggled but managed to get up. The second she was on her feet, she heard someone else yell Marcus' name.

Inez saw a tall, curvy lady with red hair in a red shirt, black skirt, and black stiletto boots slide to a stop where the Hispanic chick was cradling Marcus, crying her eyes out. She recognized instantly that it was Marcus' wild-ass mother. The woman screamed in panic when she saw the blood coming out of her son's head at an alarming rate.

"Marcus! ¡Mijo!" she cried.

Inez attempted to step away as the two women cried for someone to call an ambulance. It was when she took her third step that Marcus' mother saw her and turned toward her with a venomous glare in her eyes that gave Inez a case of the bubble guts.

***

"¡Puta Sucia!" Alondra screamed when she saw Inez, shouting at her, "Dirty bitch!"

Seeing Tashira on the ground, then Inez in the same vicinity, Alondra put two and two together and went ballistic.

With Snoop outside with Leticia, keeping the toddler safe, and Cynthia trying to wake Marcus up, Alondra was on her own. Everyone else in the store had hidden themselves, tucked away, hiding, fearing gunshots at any moment.

She charged at Inez, who immediately took off running for the back emergency exit.

In her stiletto boots and her skirt, Alondra tried her best to catch Inez, but she snatched two bottles of Bacardi and launched them at her, hitting her with one, while the other went elsewhere.

"Fucking bitch!" Alondra screamed after the bottle hit her forearm when she blocked her face, shattered, and cut her skin up.

Inez made it to the emergency door before Alondra could catch her. She barged out and cut a left, disappearing when the door shut.

"¡Coño!" Alondra cursed, seeing Inez running down the alleyway.

Quickly, she ran back to Cynthia and her son. Marcus' eyes were open now, but he was in bad shape.

"¡Ay, Dios mío! Marcus! Papi!" Alondra cried.

Cynthia had taken her shirt off and was holding it to the back of his head, trying to stop the bleeding.

"Londra. Loondraa."

Alondra heard Snoop shouting for her. She yelled out for anyone to call an ambulance, then ran to the exit door, stepping just outside of the store.

"What the hell's goin' on in there, joe?" Snoop yelled, standing a few feet away from the front of the BMW, looking beyond worried.

Alondra could hear Leticia crying from the car, screaming for her mother and her daddy, along with Amor barking.

"It's Mar—"

—Boc! Boc! Boc! Boc!—

Four gunshots rang out inside the store. The window exploded, shattering out onto the sidewalk. Screaming came from inside as terror ensued.

"Oh my god!" Alondra gasped and took off running again.

"Alondra, wait!" Snoop shouted, but she had no intention of staying outside and hiding when her son and Cynthia were in danger.

***

Holding Marcus in her lap, glad he was alive but still scared for him, Cynthia hadn't noticed that the girl he had laid out had regained consciousness until someone screamed, "Gun!"

She whipped her head around and saw the light-brown-skinned chick with the bag in her left hand and a Glock 9 in her right. The girl, bloody, face swollen, pointed the gun at Marcus with her body shielding him.

Right before she got off a shot, she was tackled by a random shopper and taken to the ground. They both wrestled with the gun, but before the good Samaritan could take it from her, she fired four times, hitting him in his gut. The other three shots went wild, hitting the window at the front of the store, blowing them out.

***

Tashira limped toward the door with the bag of money and the gun in her hands. She was so very glad that she kept at least one of the guns out of all the rest that Inez sold to Rock. She had kept it stashed in the Gucci duffel with her gwop.

Cautiously looking around as she headed to leave the store, Tashira kept her gun up, ready to pop anyone that even looked like they would try to stop her. Everyone inside cowered with fear.

She got to the door just as a tall, red-shredded chick with caramel skin ran in. Tashira instantly recognized Alondra and knew why she was there.

She pointed her Glock at the Boricua and fired but missed as Alondra dove to her left, narrowly missing getting a hot one in her dome.

Hurrying out of the store, Tashira looked back once more to make sure Marcus' mother wasn't coming. She could still hear the chick that was cradling Marcus screaming and crying.

Sirens wailing from not far away sent Tashira into panic mode. She saw a BMW parked nosed up to the box truck in front of the store. Standing in front of it, while everyone else in the area ran for cover or peeled off in their whips, Tashira saw the dreadhead and instantly recognized his strong yet weathered face. She had seen prison photos of him. Marcus kept a few of them around the apartment he and Inez had, and she'd seen them when she and Block slid through.

He was an intimidatingly big-ass nigga, but Tashira had a gun. She raised it and pointed it at him, peeping that the BMW's engine was on and the windows were open, despite the fact that she could hear a child screaming and crying inside. Tashira needed wheels, and she needed them now.

"Move!" she yelled.

"Fuck no! There's a kid in the car!" he told her, as the crying and barking inside grew louder.

—Bocka! Bocka! Bocka! Bocka!—

She hit Snoop twice in his chest, once in the throat, and once in the face.

"Noooo! Snoooop!" Tashira heard screamed out when the big dreadhead hit the ground, bleeding all over the concrete, not moving.

Tashira took a step toward the idling car when she saw Inez round the corner from Pulaski and Washington, looking out of breath and soon to pass out.

"Come oooon!" Tashira screamed to her, limping toward the car.

"Shira! Behind you!" Inez shouted.

Tashira hurried and spun around and saw Alondra coming right at her.

She went to point the gun at her and shoot.

—Click! Click! Click! Click! Click!—

"Oh fuck!" she screamed, then Alondra dove at her.

—Wham!—

***

Inez saw Tashira try to blow Marcus' mother's head off, but the sound of clicking came. She was out of bullets. Tashira screamed in panic, then was tackled by the Puerto Rican, taken to the ground hard.

The redhead maliciously thrashed Tashira, worse than what Marcus did. Inez was frozen at that moment. The woman was going ballistic on Tashira. Marcus' father was laid out, bleeding profusely all over the sidewalk.

A second later, Inez saw the Hispanic chick come out of the store with Marcus' arm over her shoulder. He squinted, obviously light-headed from his head wound.

An ambulance skidded to a stop next to the box truck, and out came two paramedics with their medical bags. Up the street, Inez saw blue flashing lights that were no other ambulance's nor a fire truck's.

The bag of money was on the ground by Marcus' mother. Tashira screamed for Inez to help her. The paramedics tried to break it up. The girl screamed for them to help Marcus.

Cursing, Inez ran for the BMW's driver door. She heard the kid inside screaming for her mommy and her daddy and a puppy barking. Inez grabbed the door handle and hurried to open it, immediately feeling a tiny furball trying to bite her right elbow.

"Noo! Wait! My daughter's in there!" she heard the Hispanic chick scream.

"Inez! Stop!" she then heard Marcus shout.

Ignoring them, Inez jumped into the car, slammed it into reverse, and mashed the gas pedal to the floor.

***

"Leticiiaaaa! Nooooo!" Cynthia screamed, letting Marcus' arm go as the chick peeled off backward in Alondra's car with her daughter inside.

"Lety!" she heard Marcus yell in panic.

Cynthia ran as fast as she could into the street, nearly getting hit by the cop car that was pulling up.

"Leeetyyyyy! Leticiiaaa!" she cried, right as the girl whipped the BMW hard to the right, sliding to a stop in the middle of Pulaski and Washington.

"Stoooooppppp! Pleeeaaase! My daughter is in there!" Cynthia yelled to the girl.

But her pleas fell on deaf ears as the chick slammed it into drive, hit the gas, and shot off, hauling ass up out of there.

Cynthia reached the middle of the intersection and saw the car's rear end swerving wildly around traffic. Seconds later, the car was gone . . . and so was her daughter.

To Be Continued…

Lock Down Publications and Ca$h Presents Assisted Publishing Packages

Due to an increase in the price of services we have increased our prices. The prices below reflect the price increase as of 11/1/24.

BASIC PACKAGE **$699** Editing Cover Design Formatting	**UPGRADED PACKAGE** **$1000** Typing Editing Cover Design Formatting Upload eBooks to Amazon Upload Paperback to Amazon
ADVANCE PACKAGE **$1,400** Typing Editing (line editing/content) Cover Design Formatting Copyright Registration Proofreading Upload eBooks to Amazon Upload Paperback to Amazon	**LDP SUPREME PACKAGE** **$1,700** Typing Editing (line editing/content) Cover Design Formatting Copyright Registration Proofreading Set up Amazon Account Upload eBooks to Amazon Upload Paperback to Amazon Advertise on LDP's Amazon and Facebook Page

***

Other services available upon request.
Additional charges may apply

Lock Down Publications
P.O. Box 944
Stockbridge, GA 30281-9998
Phone: 470 303-9761
Email: lockdownpublications@gmail.com

Submission Guideline

Submit the first three chapters of your completed manuscript to ldpsubmissions@gmail.com. In the subject line add **Your Book's Title**. The manuscript must be in a Word Doc file and sent as an attachment. Document should be in Times New Roman, double spaced, and in size 12 font. Also, provide your synopsis and full contact information. If sending multiple submissions, they must each be in a separate email.

Have a story but no way to send it electronically? You can still submit to LDP/Ca$h Presents. Send in the first three chapters, written or typed, of your completed manuscript to:

LDP: Submissions Dept
P.O. Box 944
Stockbridge, GA 30281-9998

DO NOT send original manuscript. Must be a duplicate. Provide your synopsis and a cover letter containing your full contact information.

Thanks for considering LDP and Ca$h Presents.

NEW RELEASES

BLOODLINE OF A SAVAGE 1-3
THESE VICIOUS STREETS 1-3
RELENTLESS GOON 1-3
BY PRINCE A. TAUHID

THE BUTTERFLY MAFIA 1-3
BY FUMIYA PAYNE

A THUG'S STREET PRINCESS 1&2
BY MEESHA

CITY OF SMOKE 3
BY MOLOTTI

GET IT IN SLUGS 1 &2
BY B. STALL

STANDING ON HER BUSINESS 1&2
BY DG SANTANA

STEPPERS 1,2&3
THE REAL BADDIES OF CHI-RAQ
BY KING RIO

THE LANE 1&2
BY KEN-KEN SPENCE

THUG OF SPADES 1&2
LOVE IN THE TRENCHES 2
CORNER BOYS
BY COREY ROBINSON

TIL DEATH 3
BY ARYANNA

THE BIRTH OF A GANGSTER 4
BY DELMONT PLAYER

PRODUCT OF THE STREETS 1-3
BY DEMOND "MONEY" ANDERSON

NO TIME FOR ERROR
BY KEESE

MONEY HUNGRY DEMONS 1-2
BY TRANAY ADAMS

HUB CITY MENACE 1-3
BY J. WHITE

A THUGGISH PASSION 1&2
LAND OF DA HOOLIGANZ 1-4
KILLAZ ON STANDBY 1&2
BY IRA B.

FO'EVA ROLLIN 1&2
BY ASSA RAYMOND BAKER

THE LEVEL UP 1&3
BY LUXURY KING

Coming Soon from Lock Down Publications/Ca$h Presents

IF YOU CROSS ME ONCE 6
ANGEL V
By Anthony Fields

A THUGS STREET PRINCESS 3
By Meesha

CORNER BOYS 2
By Corey Robinson

THA TAKEOVER
By Keith Chandler

BETRAYAL OF A G 2
By Ray Vinci

SAVAGE FAMILY EMPIRE 1&2
SOULLESS GOON 1,2&3
THE DIRTY SIDE OF MONEY 1,2&3
By Prince

FOR MY ENEMY'S SAKE
AMBITIONS OF A SLIDER
FRESH OFF DA PORCH
By IRA B.

BY THE TRUCKLOAD 1-4
TIPPIN' THE SCALES 1-3
BAD BITCHES WIT GUNZ 3
PROBLEM SOLVED 2
By Christopher "Diesel" Hornezes

Available Now

RESTRAINING ORDER 1 & 2
By **CA$H & Coffee**

LOVE KNOWS NO BOUNDARIES 1-3
By **Coffee**

RAISED AS A GOON I, II, III & IV
BRED BY THE SLUMS I, II, III
BLAST FOR ME I & II
ROTTEN TO THE CORE I II III
A BRONX TALE I, II, III
DUFFLE BAG CARTEL I II III IV V VI
HEARTLESS GOON I II III IV V
A SAVAGE DOPEBOY I II
DRUG LORDS I II III
CUTTHROAT MAFIA I II
KING OF THE TRENCHES
By **Ghost**

LAY IT DOWN I & II
LAST OF A DYING BREED I II
BLOOD STAINS OF A SHOTTA I & II III
By **Jamaica**

LOYAL TO THE GAME I II III
LIFE OF SIN I, II III
By **TJ & Jelissa**

IF LOVING HIM IS WRONG…I & II
LOVE ME EVEN WHEN IT HURTS I II III
By **Jelissa**

PUSH IT TO THE LIMIT
By **Bre' Hayes**

DYIN' TO GET RICH

BLOODY COMMAS I & II
SKI MASK CARTEL I, II & III
KING OF NEW YORK I II, III IV V
RISE TO POWER I II III
COKE KINGS I II III IV V
BORN HEARTLESS I II III IV
KING OF THE TRAP I II
By **T.J. Edwards**

WHEN THE STREETS CLAP BACK I & II III
THE HEART OF A SAVAGE I II III IV
MONEY MAFIA I II
LOYAL TO THE SOIL I II III
By **Jibril Williams**

A DISTINGUISHED THUG STOLE MY HEART I II & III
LOVE SHOULDN'T HURT I II III IV
RENEGADE BOYS 1-4
PAID IN KARMA 1-3
SAVAGE STORMS 1-3
AN UNFORESEEN LOVE 1-3
BABY, I'M WINTERTIME COLD 1-3
A THUG'S STREET PRINCESS 1&2
By **Meesha**

A GANGSTER'S CODE 1-3
A GANGSTER'S SYN 1-3
THE SAVAGE LIFE 1-3
CHAINED TO THE STREETS 1-3
BLOOD ON THE MONEY 1-3
A GANGSTA'S PAIN 1-3
BEAUTIFUL LIES AND UGLY TRUTHS
CHURCH IN THESE STREETS
By **J-Blunt**

CUM FOR ME 1-8
An LDP Erotica Collaboration

BLOOD OF A BOSS 1-5
SHADOWS OF THE GAME
TRAP BASTARD
By **Askari**

THE STREETS BLEED MURDER 1-3
THE HEART OF A GANGSTA 1-3
By **Jerry Jackson**

WHEN A GOOD GIRL GOES BAD
By **Adrienne**

THE COST OF LOYALTY 1-3
By **Kweli**

BRIDE OF A HUSTLA 1-3
THE FETTI GIRLS 1-3
CORRUPTED BY A GANGSTA 1-4
BLINDED BY HIS LOVE
THE PRICE YOU PAY FOR LOVE 1-3
DOPE GIRL MAGIC 1-3
By **Destiny Skai**

A KINGPIN'S AMBITION
A KINGPIN'S AMBITION II
I MURDER FOR THE DOUGH
By **Ambitious**

TRUE SAVAGE 1-7
DOPE BOY MAGIC 1-3
MIDNIGHT CARTEL 1-3
CITY OF KINGZ 1&2
NIGHTMARE ON SILENT AVE
THE PLUG OF LIL MEXICO 1&2
CLASSIC CITY
By **Chris Green**

DYIN' TO GET RICH

A GANGSTER'S REVENGE 1-4
THE BOSS MAN'S DAUGHTERS 1-5
A SAVAGE LOVE 1&2
BAE BELONGS TO ME 1&2
A HUSTLER'S DECEIT 1-3
WHAT BAD BITCHES DO 1-3
SOUL OF A MONSTER 1-3
KILL ZONE
A DOPE BOY'S QUEEN 1-3
TIL DEATH 1-3
IMMA DIE BOUT MINE 1-6
DYING FOR LIKES
By **Aryanna**

A DOPEBOY'S PRAYER
By **Eddie "Wolf" Lee**

THE KING CARTEL 1-3
By **Frank Gresham**

THESE NIGGAS AIN'T LOYAL 1-3
By **Nikki Tee**

GANGSTA SHYT 1-3
By **CATO**

THE ULTIMATE BETRAYAL
By **Phoenix**

BOSS'N UP 1-3
By **Royal Nicole**

I LOVE YOU TO DEATH
By **Destiny J**

I RIDE FOR MY HITTA
I STILL RIDE FOR MY HITTA
By **Misty Holt**

LOVE & CHASIN' PAPER
By **Qay Crockett**

TO DIE IN VAIN
SINS OF A HUSTLA
By **ASAD**

BROOKLYN HUSTLAZ
By **Boogsy Morina**

BROOKLYN ON LOCK 1 & 2
By **Sonovia**

GANGSTA CITY
By **Teddy Duke**

A DRUG KING AND HIS DIAMOND 1-3
A DOPEMAN'S RICHES
HER MAN, MINE'S TOO 1&2
CASH MONEY HO'S
THE WIFEY I USED TO BE 1&2
PRETTY GIRLS DO NASTY THINGS
By **Nicole Goosby**

LIPSTICK KILLAH 1-3
CRIME OF PASSION 1-3
FRIEND OR FOE 1-3
By **Mimi**

TRAPHOUSE KING 1-3
KINGPIN KILLAZ 1-3
STREET KINGS 1&2
PAID IN BLOOD 1&2
CARTEL KILLAZ 1-3
DOPE GODS 1&2
By **Hood Rich**

THE STREETS ARE CALLING
By **Duquie Wilson**

DYIN' TO GET RICH

STEADY MOBBN' 1-3
THE STREETS STAINED MY SOUL 1-3
By **Marcellus Allen**

WHO SHOT YA 1-3
SON OF A DOPE FIEND 1-4
HEAVEN GOT A GHETTO 1&2
SKI MASK MONEY 1&2
By **Renta**

GORILLAZ IN THE BAY 1-4
TEARS OF A GANGSTA 1/&2
3X KRAZY 1&2
STRAIGHT BEAST MODE 1&2
By **DE'KARI**

TRIGGADALE 1-3
MURDA WAS THE CASE 1-3
By **Elijah R. Freeman**

SLAUGHTER GANG 1-3
RUTHLESS HEART 1-3
By **Willie Slaughter**

GOD BLESS THE TRAPPERS 1-3
THESE SCANDALOUS STREETS 1-3
FEAR MY GANGSTA 1-5
THESE STREETS DON'T LOVE NOBODY 1-2
BURY ME A G 1-5
A GANGSTA'S EMPIRE 1-4
THE DOPEMAN'S BODYGAURD 1&2
THE REALEST KILLAZ 1-3
THE LAST OF THE OGS 1-3
By **Tranay Adams**

MARRIED TO A BOSS 1-3
By **Destiny Skai & Chris Green**

KINGZ OF THE GAME 1-7
CRIME BOSS 1-4
By **Playa Ray**

FUK SHYT
By **Blakk Diamond**

DON'T F#CK WITH MY HEART 1&2
By **Linnea**

ADDICTED TO THE DRAMA 1-3
IN THE ARM OF HIS BOSS
By **Jamila**

LOYALTY AIN'T PROMISED 1&2
By **Keith Williams**

YAYO 1-4
A SHOOTER'S AMBITION 1&2
BRED IN THE GAME
By **S. Allen**

TRAP GOD 1-3
RICH $AVAGE 1-3
MONEY IN THE GRAVE 1-3
CARTEL MONEY 1&2
By **Martell Troublesome Bolden**

FOREVER GANGSTA 1&2
GLOCKS ON SATIN SHEETS 1&2
By **Adrian Dulan**

TOE TAGZ 1-4
LEVELS TO THIS SHYT 1&2
IT'S JUST ME AND YOU
By **Ah'Million**

DYIN' TO GET RICH

KINGPIN DREAMS 1-3
RAN OFF ON DA PLUG
By **Paper Boi Rari**

THE STREETS MADE ME 1-3
By **Larry D. Wright**

CONFESSIONS OF A GANGSTA 1-4
CONFESSIONS OF A JACKBOY 1-3
CONFESSIONS OF A HITMAN
CONFESSIONS OF A DOPE BOY
By **Nicholas Lock**

I'M NOTHING WITHOUT HIS LOVE
SINS OF A THUG
TO THE THUG I LOVED BEFORE
A GANGSTA SAVED XMAS
IN A HUSTLER I TRUST
By **Monet Dragun**

QUIET MONEY 1-3
THUG LIFE 1-3
EXTENDED CLIP 1&2
A GANGSTA'S PARADISE
By **Trai'Quan**

CAUGHT UP IN THE LIFE 1-3
THE STREETS NEVER LET GO 1-3
By **Robert Baptiste**

NEW TO THE GAME 1-3
MONEY, MURDER & MEMORIES 1-3
By **Malik D. Rice**

CREAM 2-3
THE STREETS WILL TALK
By **Yolanda Moore**

THE STREETS WILL NEVER CLOSE 1-3
By **K'ajji**

LIFE OF A SAVAGE 1-4
A GANGSTA'S QUR'AN 1-4
MURDA SEASON 1-3
GANGLAND CARTEL 1-3
CHI'RAQ GANGSTAS 1-4
KILLERS ON ELM STREET 1-3
JACK BOYZ N DA BRONX 1-3
A DOPEBOY'S DREAM 1-3
JACK BOYS VS DOPE BOYS 1-3
COKE GIRLZ
COKE BOYS
SOSA GANG 1&2
BRONX SAVAGES
BODYMORE KINGPINS
BLOOD OF A GOON
By **Romell Tukes**

CONCRETE KILLA 1-3
VICIOUS LOYALTY 1-3
BLOODY MONEY BAGS
By **Kingpen**

THE ULTIMATE SACRIFICE 1-6
KHADIFI
IF YOU CROSS ME ONCE 1-3
ANGEL 1-4
IN THE BLINK OF AN EYE
By **Anthony Fields**

THE LIFE OF A HOOD STAR
By **Ca$h & Rashia Wilson**

NIGHTMARES OF A HUSTLA 1-3
BLOOD AND GAMES 1&2
By **King Dream**

DYIN' TO GET RICH

GHOST MOB
By **Stilloan Robinson**

HARD AND RUTHLESS 1&2
MOB TOWN 251
THE BILLIONAIRE BENTLEYS 1-3
REAL G'S MOVE IN SILENCE
By **Von Diesel**

MOB TIES 1-7
SOUL OF A HUSTLER, HEART OF A KILLER 1-3
GORILLAZ IN THE TRENCHES
OOPS CRY TOO 1&2
THE DAUGHTER OF A CARTEL BOSS
By **SayNoMore**

BODYMORE MURDERLAND 1-3
THE BIRTH OF A GANGSTER 1-4
By **Delmont Player**

FOR THE LOVE OF A BOSS 1&2
By **C. D. Blue**

KILLA KOUNTY 1-5
TENDER
By **Khufu**

MOBBED UP 1-4
THE BRICK MAN 1-5
THE COCAINE PRINCESS 1-10
STEPPERS 1-3
SUPER GREMLIN 1-4
A GANGSTA'S SON
By **King Rio**

MONEY GAME 1&2
By **Smoove Dolla**

A GANGSTA'S KARMA 1-5
By **FLAME**

KING OF THE TRENCHES 1-3
By **GHOST & TRANAY ADAMS**

BAD BITCHES WIT GUNZ 1&2
PROBLEM SOLVED
By "Christopher Diesel" Hornezes

QUEEN OF THE ZOO 1&2
By **Black Migo**

GRIMEY WAYS 1-3
BETRAYAL OF A G
By **Ray Vinci**

XMAS WITH AN ATL SHOOTER
By **Ca$h & Destiny Skai**

KING KILLA 1&2
By **Vincent "Vitto" Holloway**

BETRAYAL OF A THUG 1&2
By **Fre$h**

COUNTDOWN OF A KILLA 1&2
SEX, MURDER AND GOD 1&2
GUNS DOWN, BOTTOMS UP 1&2
By Lo-Life

THE MURDER QUEENS 1-7
By **Michael Gallon**

FOR THE LOVE OF BLOOD 1-4
By **Jamel Mitchell**

DYIN' TO GET RICH

HOOD CONSIGLIERE 1&2
NO TIME FOR ERROR
By **Keese**

PROTÉGÉ OF A LEGEND 1,2&3
LOVE IN THE TRENCHES 1&2
By **Corey Robinson**

THE PLUG'S RUTHLESS DAUGHTER 1&2
By **Tony Daniels**

BORN IN THE GRAVE 1-3
CRIME PAYS
By **Self Made Tay**

MOAN IN MY MOUTH
By **XTASY**

TORN BETWEEN A GANGSTER AND A GENTLEMAN
By **J-BLUNT & Miss Kim**

LOYALTY IS EVERYTHING 1-3
CITY OF SMOKE 1-3
By **Molotti**

HERE TODAY GONE TOMORROW 1&2
By **Fly Rock**

WOMEN LIE MEN LIE 1-4
FIFTY SHADES OF SNOW 1-3
STACK BEFORE YOU SPLURGE
GIRLS FALL LIKE DOMINOES
NAÏVE TO THE STREETS
By **ROY MILLIGAN**

PILLOW PRINCESS
By **S. Hawkins**

CHRISTOPHER "DIESEL" HORNEZES

THE BUTTERFLY MAFIA 1-3
SALUTE MY SAVAGERY 1&2
By **Fumiya Payne**

THE LANE 1&2
By Ken-Ken Spence

THE PUSSY TRAP 1-5
By **Nene Capri**

DIRTY DNA
By **Blaque**

SANCTIFIED AND HORNY
by **XTASY**

BOOKS BY LDP'S CEO, CA$H

TRUST IN NO MAN
TRUST IN NO MAN 2
TRUST IN NO MAN 3
BONDED BY BLOOD
SHORTY GOT A THUG
THUGS CRY
THUGS CRY 2
THUGS CRY 3
TRUST NO BITCH
TRUST NO BITCH 2
TRUST NO BITCH 3
TIL MY CASKET DROPS
RESTRAINING ORDER
RESTRAINING ORDER 2
IN LOVE WITH A CONVICT
LIFE OF A HOOD STAR
XMAS WITH AN ATL SHOOTER

www.ingramcontent.com/pod-product-compliance
Lightning Source LLC
LaVergne TN
LVHW020710110826
845149LV00012B/2201